A STEAMPUNK ANTHOLOGY

MECHANIZED MASTERPIECES

A STEAMPUNK ANTHOLOGY

MECHANIZED MASTERPIECES

ANIKA ARRINGTON, ALYSON GRAUER,
AARON AND BELINDA SIKES,
A.F. STEWART, SCOTT WILLIAM TAYLOR,
NEVE TALBOT, M. K. WISEMAN,
AND DAVID W. WILKIN

Xchyler Publishing
Penny Freeman, Editor-in-chief
www.xchylerpublishing.com

1st Edition: April, 2013

Cover and Interior Design by D. Robert Pease, walkingstickbooks.com
Edited by Penny Freeman and Heidi Birch

Published in the United States of America
Xchyler Publishing

TABLE OF CONTENTS

Forward

Combine leather and lace, brass and steel, flywheels, pistons, levers, and springs, mix an industrialized past with a technocratic future, stir well, steam thoroughly, garnish with a dash of panache, and voila! Steampunk.

Whether one defines it as retro-futurism, Victorian and Old West sci-fi, or anachronistic speculative fiction—whether one defines it at all—it pervades the popular culture of literature, television, and cinema. It has spawned unique fashion, art, and musical styles.

With its origins deeply rooted in the literary works of Jules Vern, H. G. Wells, and Mary Shelley, inspired by the vision of Charles Babbage, Nicola Tesla, and Richard Trevithick, the genre draws its life from fantasy, alternative histories, parallel universes, the paranormal, and post-apocalyptic futures. Steampunk *is* revisionism, and what better material to expand upon than literature that bespeaks the universal human condition and has withstood the test of time?

Classics live on because they leave ajar doors of possibility, even as their stories draw to a close. In this anthology, nine talented writers embrace the invitation to explore those allusive realms. Some have chosen works whose tales untold seem to demand the expansion. Others have used a master's world as a springboard into their own.

Whether their taste bends to *Sense and Sensibility* or *Frankenstein*, whether they pine for love with Ebenezer Scrooge or corner dastardly villains with his nephew, Fred, for diehard Steampunkers and the curious novice alike, these Mechanized Masterpieces will entertain and delight. They may even raise a bit of gooseflesh or send shivers up the spine. Steampunk is all of the above.

Tropic of Cancer

NEVE TALBOT

My father went to his grave without a word of praise for me falling from his lips. He never truly knew me. Even so, he knew human nature, and therein lay his genius and my downfall.

My father knew the profundity of the fable "Sun and Wind."

Sun and Wind argued over who wielded more power. They determined to settle the argument with a competition. They spied a traveler walking down the road, wrapped in a cloak. The contest: wrest the man's protection from him.

Wind accepted Sun's invitation for the first go. It blew and loosened the man's wrap. Then, Wind blew harder, forcing the man to struggle to keep his mantle. However, the stronger Wind blew, the fiercer the traveler held to his cloak. At long last, Wind prevailed by blowing his victim from his feet.

Despite Wind's self-satisfaction, Sun took its turn with confidence. It shone upon the wayfarer. The air warmed. The man loosened his grip upon the cloak as he walked. Then, he removed it and slung it over his shoulder.

Thus, my father wrested my dreams from me.

A passionate youth, a lover of all things mechanical, I fancied myself a changer of the world—an inventor—and so earned my father's patrician contempt. I nursed great ambitions but assumed no generosity on his part. I knew the entire Rochester fortune portioned to my elder brother, Rowland.

I desired only two things from my father: the freedom to make my own way in the world without interference from my family, and his ward and niece, Yvette Fairfax, as my bride. My father bequeathed me neither.

My attempts to keep the latter concealed from him failed. My father's actions professed him perfectly sensible of the attachment between Yvette and me. However, he never mentioned it.

Instead, the man sent me into the sun.

As my father's agent, I traveled from London to Spanish Town, Jamaica, in the prototype airship of my own design. My father assured me linking my fortunes with Jonas Mason, a wealthy cane planter, would set me for life. My friend and partner, Professor Heinrich Rottstieger, accompanied me. Afforded little choice, we resolved to make my father's dictates serve our own ends.

All manner of airships abounded at that time, but with Herr Professor's metallurgic discoveries, and my own invention, a sunlight-dynamo power source, our design would revolutionize air travel. In Jamaica, I would conduct further investigations into the energy-retentive powers of crystals.

My sweet Yvette provided the impetus for every scheme. My hopes in her propelled me forward. And, lest my recollections of her fade, the engraved crystal that hung about my neck continuously brushed my skin and thrust her to the forefront of my thoughts.

Not yet one and twenty, I had never before traveled beyond the shores of Great Britain. The trappings of "progress" and "civilization" defined my world: coal, steam, copper, and steel. Creation seemed made up of these things.

However, in every port of call—Lisbon, the Azores, Bermuda—the greater the distance from my homeland, the more alien and strange the world became to my limited experience . . . the stronger Nature clung to that which is rightfully her own: clear skies, blue sea, unpolluted shores. The breath of life.

We had nothing but ease on our journey: fair winds and a furrowing sea, so to speak. In clear skies over deep waters, with the silver of our triple envelopes gleaming in the sun, our image shone back at us. Our configuration, long and sleek—the fins and rudders, the stern propellers and engine houses—created what appeared a strange creature of the deep running beneath us.

We cleared the emerald-green mountains northeast of Kingston on the morning of the fifteenth day. The absence of man-shaped mechanoids patrolling the streets grabbed my attention. Where were those brutal implements of totalitarianism? Those clockwork weapons with head, arms and legs, but no conscience or compassion?

I realized nothing of mechanization had invaded that island—no airships, no dreadnaughts, no rail guns or steam engines. No sub-aquatics patrolling the deep in an illusion of absolute control. No steam-sweepers or horseless carriages chugging and puffing, filling the air with their noise and soot. The light shone pure and clear, the sky as azure as the sea.

Heinrich circled low over Spanish Town. Children raced the *Andromeda* to her landing site. At the broad expanse of lawn before the Mason mansion, they hesitated. When the airship belched our engineers from the hold, and they rappelled down the lines to anchor us to terra firma, the children cheered. The adults who trailed after them seemed only slightly less eager.

Not the least trace of soot smeared the pure faces before me. Likewise, the weary existence and unending toil of the downtrodden in London seemed absent in Jamaica. In this sea of humanity, their black skin a grace of Nature, rather than the curse of industrialization, I could yet see hope.

Did I see poverty? In abundance. The need for reform? Without doubt. But unlike Mother England, I saw happiness in the faces of the poor. I saw dignity; belief in themselves. I felt myself the serpent in the Garden of Eden with my hold full of cargo and my brain full of technological marvels. I wondered what mischief I had wrought in this island paradise simply by bursting onto the consciousness of those people.

Thus, the inescapable paradox of my life lay bared before

me: mechanization had long since become my great passion, but I detested its natural consequences. Young, sincere, and green as new spring, I swore Jamaica would not suffer the fate of England.

As I copiloted the airship in its final descent, a pair of women on the veranda of Mason's home caught my eye. They stood on the balcony; an old crone leaned heavily upon a cane. Her weathered, ebony skin stood in sharp contrast to her hair of brilliant white. Her bright eyes shone sharp and quick. An aura of calm surrounded her.

She stood beside a young lady at the balustrade, a statuesque beauty whose complexion glowed like aged ivory. A gossamer robe provided token coverage of her nubile form. Her jet black hair hung in loose curtains down her back, and along with the folds of her dressing gown, ruffled in the morning breeze.

She appeared intent on the windscreen behind which I sat, which bubbled out from the cockpit of the airship. Eventually, the heckling of the old woman gained her attention. She then glanced at herself, tugged at her wrap, and turned into the house.

As we landed, Yvette's crystal burned with an icy sting against my chest. I failed to understand the significance at that time, but with the chill, I relived the occasion when Yvette presented the gift, as I often did in future days.

❧

We lingered, just we two, in the Andromeda *cockpit. Yvette sat in the captain's chair, fiddling with the knobs arrayed* on the consoles before her. I knelt beside her, drinking in her lovely, grief-stricken face.

"I dread your departure, Edward," she murmured softly. "I fear you will plunge into darkness and never escape. I cannot . . . It must not be so."

"I told Father one year, Yvette. I go to make my fortune—our future. All of this is a means to an end—a bridge to my heart's one desire. Tell me you—"

Her fingers on my lips silenced my tongue. Her looks forbade my speech. She held my gaze, her eyes swimming in tears.

She took my hand and held it. She turned the ring upon my finger. She had woven it of her own silken tresses. It shone like pure gold. "Promise me you will never remove this ring. No matter what else happens. Give me your sacred honor."

I searched her features, unsettled by the desperation which laced her tone. "Never. I promise."

"And yet, it is not enough," she murmured. A look of firm resolve added complexity to the sadness and loss upon her face. Then, warm stone and cold metal settled into my hand. I raised into the air Yvette's prize crystal hanging from a silver chain. The sunlight refracted through the stone and projected upon the bulkhead an image of the Andromeda herself, ablaze in rainbow colors.

"I had it done. A crystal from your workshop could serve, but this stone . . . you need it for protection."

More than a mere line etching, a master craftsman had carved a relief of our airship onto the stone in minute detail.

Deep in the recesses of my mind whispered the certainty that Yvette had employed forces I would never understand to accomplish what, I dared not speculate.

Yvette loosened my collar, clasped the chain about my neck, then tucked the crystal beneath my shirt. Her hand rested upon my bare chest as she whispered her instructions. "It must rest here, next to your heart, touching your skin."

I riveted my eyes on her, willing her to meet my gaze. She busied herself in setting my attire to rights, yet would not look into my face. Her lips whispered some silent invocation I could not hear. Then, she gave her final instructions. "Use this to remember me. A token of my . . . friendship. To keep you afloat. To light your way home."

I took up her hand and held it to my cheek. "I shall never remove it."

Tears again welled in her eyes. "See that you don't."

"Edward! What the devil are you about?" Herr Rottstieger's intrusion brought me to my feet, and one glance at the lady's ducked head caused him to hesitate.

He harrumphed to clear his throat. "Well, then, mein junge. We must weigh anchor tout suite."

Yvette rose and stepped to the hatch. I moved to follow her. "Just as soon as I see Miss Fairfax home."

Yvette wheeled on me. "No, Edward. No. I have Rowland."

"Yvette—"

"Please, Edward," she breathed. "Let us part here as we are, the best of friends."

*My whole being revolted at the notion of such a cold parting.
I would take her in my arms and bespeak my heart. I would
profess my undying devotion, secure her to me. But I knew she
meant to avoid such a scene. I could not discomfit her.*

*"The best of friends," I repeated, forcing a smile. She ex-
tended to me her hand, but I leaned and kissed her cheek.*

*"Remember your promise," she whispered, and then was
gone.*

At Spanish Town, Rochester coin opened the doors of the
colony's finest families. Naturally taciturn and unsocial, I found
answering the demands of society a most onerous duty, but I got
on by degrees. I dare say, I became good at it . . . at least, I gained
confidence. I became, so it was said, the most popular young
blade on the island.

Every now and again, Miss Bertha Mason—for such was the
beauty on the balcony—would flit across the social stage, but
remained otherwise elusive. I scarcely knew her.

Even so, she wormed her way into my consciousness. She
battled with Yvette for my dreams. In them, the breeze which
caressed the nymph's soft skin with silken tresses, which flirted
with her robe and offered teasing, tantalizing glimpses of a
round of breast, a length of thigh, also wafted jasmine around
me. It encircled and enfolded me until I awoke in a sweat, the
scent still palpable in the air.

But then, the crystal would again cool my skin, and the fever which fought to control me receded at its touch. The clouds lifted, my mind cleared, and dreams of Yvette, fresh and clean and pure, would fill my mind. It felt a brisk early morning after a suffocating, sticky, and stultifying tropical night.

My father's plans progressed apace. Within three months, I shared ownership with him and fully managed West End, a cane plantation at Negil, on the westernmost extent of the island. Within six, I had completed the initial phase of our planned rum distillery. Within nine, I had established myself as a member of the West Indies elite. Investors lined up to underwrite our airship manufactory. The sunlight dynamo in both distillery and sugar mill proved an unqualified success.

I wrote to my father and begged Yvette's hand.

At the end of a year, I had done with waiting. My father's silence on the subject and Yvette's failure to write caused me no small amount of concern. I would attend Herr Professor on a three-month publicity tour of the East Coast of the United States, and from there, we would go to London. I would return with my bride.

Twenty hours and counting. I itched to be gone, but last-minute business at the governor's mansion detained me. There, an acid etching illustrating a newspaper article on the notice board caught my attention.

I burst into the offices high in Hanger One and slapped the yellowed clipping onto the desk in front of Herr Rottstieger.

"Look at it! Just look at it! Tacked up with the notices in the lobby like some tawdry bit of gossip!"

Lately, All Souls Church, Langham Place, London: Mister Rowland Fairfax Rochester, son of Rupert R. and the late Camilla Fairfax Rochester of Thornfield Hall, —shire, wed to heiress and society beacon, Miss Yvette Fairfax, daughter of the late Colonel and Mrs. Harrison Fairfax, last of Hyderabad, India. Couple to honeymoon on the Grande Tour before returning to their home on Wimpole Street.

My friend eyed me warily, without a single glance at the paper. I stepped back, undone by the truths I read so plainly on his face.

"You knew." The words stuck in my throat. Herr Professor winced. His eyes fled mine. "By the devil! You knew and you hid it from me!"

He flinched as my palm hit the desk, a tiny jerk of the head as he stared at the floor. I pushed my hands through my hair with both fists to press back the whorl of disjointed thoughts that assaulted me. Tears rushed my eyes. A leaden weight sat on my chest. I could draw no air.

I stepped away from the violence bursting to free itself. My back to the man, I leaned against the windowsill, my outstretched arms pushing hard against it, as if somehow I could hold back the cataclysm. I stared blankly through the glass, wrestling with a gale of sensibilities, resolves, reckless, insane schemes to make her mine, struggling to cease my trembling and stifle a wail of despair-laden rage. A knock at the door at last shattered the silence. Herr Professor rebuffed it. Footsteps scurried down the wooden stairs.

"I didn't hide it, *junge.*" He spoke softly, feeling his way. "You never read the papers."

"You just neglected to tell me, is that it?" I turned to him. He no longer sat, but propped himself against a file cabinet situated against the wall. "How long ago was 'lately.' There is no date here."

"Six months."

I felt kicked in the chest by a mule. Herr Professor surely read my outrage. "I have not known for six months, Edward— only three months, perhaps. It has been six since the day."

Realization of the truth settled over me like an arctic blast. "My father told you . . . That blasted bounder wrote and told you when, exactly." Rottstieger again winced. "And all this time—all this time you have pretended to be my friend—pretended to encourage me, *to share my joy*! You played me for a fool!"

"No, Edward. When you wrote and asked Yvette to be your wife, I knew nothing of the matter. The letter from your father came after you told me what you had done."

"And so for three months, every time you delayed our departure—all of it was a lie to put me off!"

"I delayed because Rochester told me he would write—*they* would write. They would tell you themselves in their own time. In their own way. I kept waiting for that letter, Edward—for

Rowland to do the honorable thing. I had resolved to tell you . . ."

"When? When, exactly, were you planning to extend me that courtesy?"

"Before we got to England."

"But after we left Boston," I spat. "It would not do to spoil your precious tour."

Herr Professor closed his eyes in capitulation. "No. It would not." His pulse throbbed at his throat and he swallowed hard. "I never wanted this to happen, Edward. I never expected it to end like this."

I peered at him. "What are you not telling me?" He heaved a sigh and I felt the last piece of the puzzle drop into place. "You have been in on it all along," I whispered. "You took his part."

"No, Edward. I never took his part. Anything I did, I did for you."

"For *you*, you mean to say!"

"No, *junge*. For you."

"How much? How much did he pay you to get me away from Yvette so Rowland could marry her? How much to properly merge the Fairfax and Rochester fortunes?" He hesitated, tongue-tied, and I slammed my fist on desk. "How much, Heinrich?!"

"The matching funds. If I could get you to Jamaica, he would match whatever other investors gave you—gave the corporation."

"*The matching funds*? His *club dues* are more than his precious matching funds! You should have asked me, Heinrich. I could have got you better."

"You have no idea what it meant to have Rupert Rochester

invest in us. He is respected, known for his perspicacity. His endorsement gave us *gravitas*. That he would not invest in his own son's inventions—it damaged our cause more than you can imagine. But what harm could a trip to Jamaica do, eh? How much good would come of it . . . at least, so it seemed to me."

I snorted, then flopped to a chair and dropped my head into my hands. A storm raged within. I gripped my hair fiercely, clinging to something—anything—to keep from going under.

My friend sat beside me and placed his hand upon my shoulder. "*Mein sohn*," he ventured after a long moment, "no one could see you together and not know she loved you. That day—the day we left—when you were together in the cockpit, with the door locked and Rowland so frantic to get inside . . . I thought you had secured her promise. By my life, I thought you were secretly engaged."

The pall of his words settled over me and I looked up. I could not deny the overwhelming sadness in his eyes, a mere glimmer of the grief my new clarity gave me. "No, Professor . . . No. She would not hear me. She sent me away."

My anger vented, the resentment seeped from me. In the fog of my self-deception, I believed with all my heart she would wait, but the cold, stark truth revealed my folly, and I could not begrudge Herr Rottstieger his own.

I leaned back in my chair and pushed the hair from my face. I heaved a sigh. "What now?"

"What do you want to do?"

"Besides hurl myself from the highest cliff?"

"*Junge* . . ."

"What is there for me now, professor? Everything—*every-thing* I have done has been for her, for our future together. What good are my dreams without her to share them?"

"Edward, without you, I would be nothing but another iron monger, an engineer forging the inventions of other men without enough mettle to build my own. But with you—I became bigger than myself. Like all the men you employ, who now earn a fair wage and can send their children to school instead of into the fields, I flourish because of your dreams. If not for yourself, *junge*, soldier on for these people. They dare to dream because you live yours."

I could not say how deeply his words sunk into my heart then, but they have since become my mantra—more or less. Then, as now, I felt the caveat: I lived the dream I managed to scrape together from the rubble of my castles in the air. But that had to be enough. I had to prove to them all—to my father, the blasted blighter, to Rowland, to Yvette herself—that they had not inflicted the mortal wound to my soul that then bled bitter tears—and bleeds still.

I rose to my feet and moved to collect the scrap of paper, but my hand hesitated over the desk, distracted as I was by an envelope edged in black sitting on the blotter. I glanced at Herr Professor. "Heinrich? Have you lost someone?"

His brow furrowed with concern. "Nein, *junge*. That came for you this morning."

He must have moved a chair behind me, as I did not hit the

floor when my knees buckled. The letter rattled in my hand. The black border hissed, rearing and ready to strike. I forced myself to rip open the envelope and read my brother's smooth hand.

I snorted. "The old buzzard popped off." A bitter, ironic laugh surged through me. "He gives me precisely one hour to curse him to the devil, and then denies me the pleasure of hating him for the rest of his days."

"The man was the picture of health!"

"Apparently, a rogue mechanoid didn't like the cut of Old Man Rochester's jib. He stepped from his carriage and . . . Do you recall, Professor, my outrage over their use as peacekeepers? He derided me for a stupid boy who could not understand such things. What do I know, eh?" I snorted my disgust.

"And Yvette? She is well?"

The name leeched a bit of acid from my soul and my manner softened. "Yvette is in indifferent health. They have taken a house in Athens for a time until . . . until she is safely delivered. Rowland will not leave her, thus requests that I see the solicitors myself."

Herr Rottstieger peered at me. "And you, Edward? You have just lost your father."

I flapped the papers at my friend. "And gained full ownership of the plantation and all of my father's interest in the corporation."

"There. Do you see? He always intended—"

"No, Herr Professor. I will not temper my feelings. *Rowland* had a momentary flash of guilt, not my father. My brother has relinquished the rights, and now fancies he has purchased absolution for his greed and treachery."

Silence descended over the office. I again stepped to the window and gazed at the horizon, where the sky melded with the sea. I felt Herr Professor's eyes upon me . . . the only thing I felt. It seemed as if the loss of Yvette and the loss of my father canceled one another. The tidal wave of grief left nothing in its wake—not even the flotsam and jetsam of the cataclysm. I felt . . . blank.

"So? Now, what will you do?"

I turned and headed for the door. "Today, West End. Tomorrow, the Cubans; then, on to conquer the Yanks. Then, to England to do the dirty work while my precious brother enjoys his spoils."

I had no real business at West End, but I would have gone mad rattling about Spanish Town for the remainder of the day. As my sleek sailboat skirted the island, I found a bit of peace.

The sun lowered in the west as I slipped into the inlet where we harbored the plantation watercraft. I paused at the path to the bungalow, on the cliffs by the lighthouse. The palms rustled above my head. The scent of jasmine and gardenia wafted on the breeze. How many evenings had I sat upon the veranda drinking in that very sight, imagining Yvette at my side, holding my hand, basking in the joy of living?

As so often before, I found myself clutching the crystal she had fastened about my neck what seemed a lifetime ago. I wondered at the number of times I had felt a warm glow from it, encasing my heart, protecting it—protecting me. I recalled how its cool touch reached out and rescued me from what, I knew not. I had come to feel incomplete without it, and yet, in a matter of moments, it became a weight I could no longer shoulder.

I watched the sun sink into the sea, setting the sky ablaze. I yanked off the chain and held the crystal up to the brilliant light. It seemed to sing in the evening air as it splintered the glory of Sol into a million shards of color.

"No, Yvette," I murmured above the hum. "I will never heal with this piece of you piercing my soul." I hurled the crystal out over the Caribbean. It whistled as it flew, and a too-familiar voice wailed in my ears, 'Oh, Edward! No, dearest Edward!' as it shattered the surface of the sea.

The next six months become a blur in my recollections. When I think back to the weeks and months that followed as we meandered our way to England, as I returned alone, it all runs together like a watercolor wash of grays and browns; overlaid by the stinging, acrid, cloying stench of coal oil and enterprise.

Then, once returned to the only home that remained to me, more blur, more muddled, muddied color. It felt a dream. I cannot pinpoint when the insanity overtook me—for only thus can I explain it: a sort of grief-crazed delirium which plunged my soul into a purple haze, gripped my heart, and stole my breath. I can scarcely recall conscious choice, until one day—one revelatory day—the derangement receded.

I came to myself standing in a bedchamber at the bungalow, staring at the woman passed out on the bed. Images of the previous night's activities flashed through my head but otherwise failed to affect me. Instead of fire in my loins, I felt only disgust.

The harsh morning light shone upon her, but I saw no stunning, exotic beauty, no object for sensual obsession. The illusion cleared and revealed a woman who appeared ten years my senior, prematurely aged by debasement and debauchery. Not even the thick mosquito netting surrounding her could soften the scene.

Her face pressed into the bedclothes and drool dribbled from her mouth as she snored. Locks of her hair, tangled and wild, snaked over her face, around her throat and across her pillow. She sprawled across the mattress, the bed-linen knotted about her limbs. The room reeked of unwashed humanity.

Driven by terror of my inescapable future, I fled down the path and flung myself into the sea, hoping it would somehow free me of the stench of my new bride.

I swam until my muscles burned and my eyes smarted; until the pain blurred the image that Bertha Antoinetta Mason— Bertha Mason Rochester—had seared into my brain.

After six weeks of matrimony, I could not explain why I had formed such an alliance. More still, as the weeks progressed, I grew ever more disconcerted with her aggression and unsettling propensities in our marriage bed.

Returning to the house from the lagoon, as I strode around the veranda, the sound of voices coming through the open windows of Bertha's bedchamber arrested my steps.

"I tell you, Josie, the man has the touch. He sets me ablaze."

"Dat leedle toad, madame? Oh, no. How cood he?"

Bertha laughed. "Not all men can be breeding studs, Josie."

"Eben so . . . I would nebbah—"

"You do not understand, my girl. The man is an *engineer*. He makes a science of pleasure. I have never before had such a lover."

"And Meestah Rochestah?"

"Mr. Rochester is a silly little boy, afraid of his own shadow."

"Den, why do ye let dat ape touch ye?"

"Because Rottstieger is not here, wantwit. And Rochester—his physique surpasses Julian's—*all* of Julian. He is not without promise."

"Den, ye muds let me hab Julian. You hab no fuddah use ub him."

"There you are wrong. Should I find *the* perfect man, with *Herr Professor's* technique, Julian's good looks, and Rochester's stamina . . . well. *Then*, you could have my black. But until then, I require all three, especially since Rottstieger has been away for so long."

"But Rochestah—he will find ye out."

"Josie, one simply disappears into the cane fields, and Julian has *such* an appetite by noonday."

"Rochestah—he promise us a house een down—a proper *English* house. Ye must mek heem do eet."

"Patience, my girl. He cannot keep us here forever. After I have trained him up, then you shall have him for a plaything. And then, he shall be so wracked with his silly English guilt, I shall have him wrapped around my finger. He shall have you every night and do whatever I say all day long."

The maid tittered. "Oh, madam. I could nebbah like heem. He be far too oogly."

"Close your eyes, you simple thing. The face is not the business end of a man . . . or an ape for that matter." A chuckle, deep and sensuous. ". . . and betimes one simply *must* have the beast."

I sat at the breakfast table across from the very picture of feminine modesty and conjugal devotion. I could not stand to look at her. Ire coursed through my veins, hot and quick, and I dared not speak. I stared at the fish on my plate.

"You are not eating, my love," my tender bride cooed. "I had thought you swam this morning."

"Indeed."

"Then you must be famished, especially after . . . last night." She eyed me through her long, dark lashes. "You must keep up your strength."

"I told you, *Mrs. Rochester*, I do not care for the whole of the fish. In England, we gut it before we cook it."

"But we are not in England, my darling. Cook knows nothing of such food. We must go there soon, that she may learn—"

"No."

"Fairfax, darling, you promised to take me to England to meet your family. Do I so shame you that you hide me away? I am good enough for your bed but not your friends? It's because my father is in trade, isn't it?" Her voice grew shriller as she spoke, until it spiked through my brain. "You are so much higher than me. You treat me like the dirt beneath your boot."

I simply eyed her. Her face screwed up into a petulant pout. Tears rushed her eyes. Her hands slapped down on the table. The crystal and china jumped. "I want to go to England!"

"When I trust you within five thousand miles of my family, we will go to England, but not a day sooner." My voice sounded cold and flat.

"Trust me? *Trust* me?! You are a monster—a horrid, beastly monster!"

"Better to say an ape."

She started at the words and glanced up at me. I stared at her blandly. She rose and went to the sideboard. She feigned concealing a fit of tears, but I knew it a ploy to add rum to her orange juice. My mind filled with images of my brother sharing his morning with the polar opposite of my angel wife. I jabbed my fork into the fish on my plate.

The tines hit something hard and screeched across the china. The exposed and torn gut glinted in a stray shaft of sunlight. Dumbfounded, I stared at the mess.

Bertha returned to her seat, glass in hand, once again the very image of a model wife. I carefully slit open the fish's gut and spooned out the innards.

"That really is the best part, you know," Bertha instructed, her cheeks pouched with gobbets of her own mackerel. "After the eyeballs, of course."

I scraped away the offal, and there it was: Yvette's pendant, chain and all. It felt as if the sun burst free of heavy clouds the moment I laid eyes on it. A freshening breeze cleared the cobwebs from my mind. I could breathe again. I still tumbled in unforgiving surf, but I thought, perhaps, I could at last get my feet beneath me.

"What is that, my love?"

I blinked, brought back to reality by the face beaming devotion from across the table. I pushed the crystal out of the sunlight with my fork. "Nothing. Just a bit of rock I found in the fish."

Bertha rose, her eye fixed on the stone. "A gift from the sea! A jewel, Fairfax. Let me see it." She reached for the plate, but I withheld it and picked out the stone.

"No, Bertha. It is indeed a gift from the sea and I mean to keep it."

She eyed first me, and then my fist wrapped around the gem. Had she been a cat, her hackles would have stood on end. Her tail would have been a bottle brush. "Give it to me, Fairfax," she hissed. "I must see it. You do not understand the portents!" She lunged for my hand and fought uselessly to wrench open my fist. "Crystals possess great power!"

"I understand more than you ever will, my darling wife. And, just now, you come precious close to rousing my temper. Now SIT DOWN and finish your breakfast."

22

My tone brought her up short. I held her gaze, implacable and threatening. She released my arm and retreated to her seat. Wide-eyed, she stared at me as I slipped the crystal into my breast pocket.

"What is that?" Her voice came low and sinister, and it seemed all the shadows in the room collected about her.

Startled, I followed the direction of her glare to where I had been absently twisting Yvette's ring around my finger. I stared at it, baffled—and not—that I had not jettisoned it with the crystal when she broke my heart. Rather, it felt as if the weightless trifle had become part of my soul, and nearly my flesh.

"It is from her!" Bertha's wrath exploded with the crystal and china as she flew at me from across the table, her claws bared and aiming for my eyes. "That pasty little bitch you mooned over for so long! That whore who cannot bear the sight of your ghastly face!"

I grappled with her as she clawed at me. Despite her size and surprising strength, I quickly pinned her, prone, her head to the floor with one hand, and her wrist to her spine with the other. I bore down my weight into the middle of her back with my knee, her face pressed into the tiles.

"Heed me, woman," I hissed into her ear. She struggled to free herself and clouded the air blue with invectives to make a stevedore blush. I pressed her more firmly into the ground.

"Calm down, Bertha." As I waited, I forced my temper into better control. She exhausted herself in her struggle, but at last, I felt her cede to my greater strength and lie still. I released her and sat upon the floor. Her face purple, gulping down great droughts of air, she pushed herself up onto her haunches, murder glinting in her eyes. Her rage throbbed in her jugular.

"Here we are, wife," I sighed. "You and I, the very picture of blissful domesticity . . . Howsoever we came to this pass, what do we do with ourselves now? A vexing conundrum indeed." She merely glared at me, wild-eyed and feral.

I leaned my elbows on my knees and watched her attempts to regain control. I could not accept the ruin before me as the sum total of my life. I refused to surrender to that fate.

"As my lawful wife, you are duty-bound to obey me. Thus, I will tell you our course of action. You have only to listen and obey."

I rose to my feet, brushed myself off, and stepped away. I prayed for wisdom, guidance—the smallest inspiration to help me salvage something of that farce. I formulated a plan on the fly.

"We will stay on Jamaica. For now, we will stay at West End. Daughter of a common tradesman you may be, but now, there is nothing for it. You are also the wife of a gentleman. Ladies of your station have no truck with the day labor. You will not traipse through the cane fields like a naked pickaninny. Julian and Josie have left our employ. Starting today, I will engage and discharge our domestics. When you—"

"You cannot—"

"You will *not* interrupt me. When you have earned my trust, when I believe you honestly wish a proper marriage—"

"A proper marriage?! You wear that ring and dare—"

"You *will* remain silent!" I paused, waiting for her to clamp her tongue. I must have appeared the devil himself, for she retreated.

"When you conduct yourself as a proper wife should, *and* I trust your intent, we will take a house at Spanish Town. But you will earn it. With your obedience, your manners, your attempts at civility, your adherence to the rules of common decency. Do you understand me?"

"You cannot hold me prisoner here."

"Indeed, I cannot. You are free to do whatsoever you like, go where you wish, but I control your purse strings. You have already made me a cuckold. I will *not* allow it to continue. I *will* govern my wife."

"I have my fortune. I do what I like!"

"No, my sweet one. *I* have your fortune. All thirty thousand pounds of it."

"You cannot—"

"Yes, I can. I will—unless, of course, you choose to return to your father's house. In that case, I will willingly, gladly, dance my way to the solicitor's and sign over every last pence with the divorce decree."

"Never! I am a Rochester!"

"Indeed. Then, I suggest you convince me you can act like one." I walked away but paused at the door. I turned to her. "I received a letter from Heinrich Rottstieger this morning. He wishes us both joy—"

"You *told* him?"

"He writes to inform me he extends his stay in England. Our partners building the engine manufactory find they need him on site. I rather imagine he will stay there indefinitely. He tells me he feels younger—lighter—than he has in more than a year."

She rose to her feet. Blood had smeared across her face. I almost felt a twinge of guilt to see the minor cuts the glass had inflicted—almost.

"I do not divorce you now, Bertha, because I made vows before God and I mean to retain what honor yet remains to me. Blame my silly English conscience. You are my responsibility.

"I am fool enough to suppose that with time and care—and a great deal of determination—we two can nurture this marriage into something akin to love, or at least respect. Perhaps we could even achieve a measure of happiness. Decide now which you will have: keeper and kept or husband and wife."

Her face contorted with bitter derision. "Grunts the ape."

"As you see." I again turned to the door.

"Do not come to me tonight, Fairfax. The thought of your touch revolts me."

"Indeed, madam, you need not fear me scratching at your door." I produced the crystal and tossed it in the air. It flashed brilliance before it landed in my hand. "Shackled together we may be, but I am free."

I left the room. The shriek of rage and shattering china that blasted on the door as I shut it evoked a bitter smile.

Advance nearly five years. In the cloying heat of a sweltering tropical summer, I sat at my desk in a puddle of light, the clatter and roll of my calculations machine and the clock on the wall breaking the silence of night. The hollow sound of footsteps on the wooden stairs did not slow my work, but I looked up when the latch turned and the door swung open. I stared at the nebulous shadow, back-lit by dim bulbs high in the hanger, until it moved into the light.

"So, you finally made it, then."

"Rough passage. I cannot believe you enjoy flying."

"A storm is brewing, isn't it?"

"Even so."

"I cannot believe that as well-traveled as you are, you still have difficulty with it."

"She always preferred the railroad."

"Airships would have been kinder."

"In some ways."

We fell silent. Stared at one another through the darkness. The sound of my chair scraping across the floor made him jump.

"You look like hell."

"And you don't. How is that?"

I shrugged. "Heavy labor. One gets on." I extended my hand, Rowland grasped it, then pulled me into his embrace. I stiffened, but just for a moment. In all my life, he had never demonstrated such affection. I chose not to analyze it and took comfort where I found it—the comfort we both needed, desperately.

"I promised her we would not quarrel," he choked into my shoulder.

27

"And we shall not." I thumped him on the back and released him.

"Fairfax . . ." he stammered. Words would not come. His eyes flitted about, and if they managed to settle on my face, they rose no higher than my chin. The tension in his jaw and pooling tears further emphasized the storm of sensibilities roiling within him. I watched him expectantly, and he produced from his breast pocket a fat packet of letters bound up in a bit of ribbon.

He laid them upon the desktop. My heart leapt to my throat. The entire year of my correspondence to Yvette appeared worn from much perusal but carefully preserved. "I found them," Rowland murmured. "After she— . . . She kept them in her writing desk. I thought . . . I thought you might want them back."

I swallowed hard. "Did you read them?"

Rowland shook his head, almost in a panic. "No. Never. She was so good to me, but I made a wretched husband. She deserved the comfort these letters gave her. I did things . . ."

My head jerked up. "Do not make me your confessor. Let me believe you made her happy. Leave me with my delusions and I shall leave you with yours."

Rowland nodded his agreement, swallowed hard, and blinked back a tear. I deposited the letters in the safe. "If you will wait just a moment, I need to get these papers ready for the packet for London." I nodded toward the window looking into the hanger. "Fancy a tot? Or have you had enough on the trip over?"

Rowland snorted and moved to the étagère. "Light?"

"The lamp's electric—there at the base."

His nightcap forgotten, Rowland flipped the switch like a toddler. "Fancy that. Electricity? Here?"

"I've worked up a magneto—no steam; only a sunlight-dynamo array and wind-power. It will power Spanish Town and Kingston both with the cable run."

Rowland's brow twitched as he processed the idea, then redirected his attention to the range of bottles and carafes on the étagère. "I wish Father would have lived to see this." He held his snifter before the light, and the liquid glowed like molten gold. "The best rum to be had. He would have been proud." He snorted. "He would have been rich . . . *er*."

"'Anything doing is worth doing right.' . . . How *is* Herr Professor?"

"Well . . . Heartbroken. She was light, Fairfax. She was heaven on earth—an angel—a pure angel. Everyone loved her . . . She wanted a child so badly."

I pretended not to hear Rowland's morose self-indulgence. I tried not to blame my brother; I knew firsthand Yvette's determined nature, but three miscarriages in four years exceeded all decency. The fourth time . . .

He should have left her be. He should have loved her enough to deny her. He should have . . . something—not allowed her to die . . . not had a hand in her death.

"Those are sinister-looking things. What the devil are they?"

I looked up. Rowland waved his snifter at the window. Below, a dozen eight-foot behemoths lurked in the dark, ranked along one side of the hanger floor. "My new automatons—an improvement on steam-driven mechanoids. Mine are made of the same material as our airships. I made them to harvest the cane."

"Still working on them, eh?"

"No. I just can't use them. With the unrest in Haiti, it is not wise."

"Why the devil not? It looks like one of those would replace five human workers."

"Ten, actually. But, I refuse to force that many men out of work. Haitians are starving for lack of employment. The oppression there is terrible. The French use their mechanoids to literally crush any uprising. The colonists will be murdered in their beds one day. I will not have it spread here. Until I have other jobs for the men, I will not use the automatons."

"Then what do you mean to do with them?"

"The war is finally over in the States. There is no one left to fight."

"So bad as that?"

"They have had terrible—obscene—loss of life. The Gatling guns, the rail cannon. The airship bombings devastated the cities—tens of thousands of civilians buried in the rubble, burned alive with the incendiaries. Washington was leveled. Richmond, Philadelphia—even New York. What matters now is survival, not who retains control."

"And so?"

"The provisional government is desperate to stave off invasion by the British. They need to recover quickly. We donated this lot to help rebuild the infrastructure. We have others for farms and factories and such. We will not be displacing workers, but providing a desperately needed workforce."

"Not as soldiers?"

"After *Father*?"

Rowland ducked his head, abashed. I moderated my tone. "The Americans have gone off wholesale mechanized murder for the moment . . . We will rebuild the right way, on sunlight dynamos and wind-power, perhaps harness the energy of flowing water, or even tap into the earth's internal furnace. If we could do in the New Alliance what we have done here . . . the possibilities are endless."

"And what of England?"

I snorted. "The Empire upon which the sun never sets? *The* Great Industrial Power? Do you truly think they will listen to anything I have to say? The madness is self-perpetuating. Industry and coal, coal and industry. They are in lock step and nothing will dislodge the men who profit by it."

"Except, perhaps, a devastating war."

"Heaven forbid."

We again fell silent, but I could feel Rowland mulling over more than his kill-devil.

"What is it?" Rowland looked up, startled. "What is it you need to say to me that you will not?"

"It's not my place to say."

"And yet, you have come all this way to say it. In six years, you have not once made the passage, but now, here you are."

"You never returned home. You never came to see us."

"I am shackled to this island."

"No one is that indispensable. You have men enough to deal with the sugar business. Rottstieger runs himself ragged trying to manage things because you insist on living here. You could accomplish so much more from London."

"The business does not shackle me. The matter is more personal. I would rather not discuss it."

"You mean Bertha."

I carefully set down my pen and blotted the ledger, then stuffed everything into the courier pouch. I locked the safe, switched off both lights, and opened the door for my brother.

"You cannot just ignore me, Fairfax."

"What would you have me reply, Rowland? You have said nothing."

"I would have you assure me all is well between you and Bertha. I am concerned for her—for you both."

"*Bertha*, is it?"

"What else would you have me call my sister-in-law?"

"Whom you have never once laid eyes on." I peered at him in the darkness. His face, despite the distant light, revealed more than I cared to understand. "I cannot see how that is any of your concern." I moved down the stairs, then stopped and turned to him. "In point of fact, I have stayed away from London specifically to keep it private, and yet, here you are, *intruding*."

"It *is* my concern when I see you destroying yourself, Fairfax. I scarcely know you any longer."

I snorted at the irony. "You have never known me, *Rochester*.

You, dearest brother, have never gotten past taunting me with that lesser name at school. I have been Fairfax to you since I was eight years old, I have always hated it, and you have never, ever, attempted to leave off. You make me a stranger, so you have no right to advise me."

I tromped down the stairs, but Rowland remained where he stood. "Just tell me why Bertha is so terrified of you."

"And how could you possibly know that?"

"She told me."

"She told you. You have been *corresponding* with *my wife*?"

"She wrote to me pleading for help. You have turned everyone against her—even her own family. She has no one else to turn to. I am her only friend in the world."

"Indeed. And how long, pray, has this tender exchange been taking place?"

Rowland flinched. I huffed my derision and turned away. Rowland came trailing after me as I circled the hanger, securing doors, testing anchor lines. "What are you doing?"

"A storm is coming." I reached the power box and levered-up the handle. The hanger flooded with brilliant light. Rowland winced at the assault, then fairly jumped back at the sight of my automatons looming over him. They looked even more sinister illuminated, I suppose, despite my best efforts to humanize them—or perhaps because of it.

I wheeled on him, my army of mechanical men menacing behind me. "How long, Rowland? How long ago did you begin writing? Before you lost Yvette?"

Rowland swallowed hard. "A year . . . a year before she . . ."

Blazes. He looked even worse with the lights on. I doubted he had slept in the six months since Yvette had gone. The anger dribbled through my fingers. Poor, stupid Rowland. Had he been the picture of health, I would have roundly resented his presumption. As it was . . . poor, thickheaded, warm-hearted Rowland.

I opened the chest panel of the first auto-enhanced mecha-noid. A flip of the appropriate switches and its eyes lit. Another series of twists, pushes, and toggles, and the thing sprang to life and marched toward the door. I ignored it and went to work on the others.

"What are you . . . what are they doing?"

"They secure the compound, put up the storm shutters, clear the decks, batten the hatches. Menial things easily programmed into the crystal board. The men locked down your airship as soon as you disembarked." I shrugged and gestured at the barometer. "A storm comes."

Rowland absorbed himself in the weather station as I contin-ued activating the line of my man-droids. "So, tell me. Of what does my dearest wife accuse me, eh? How have I offended my tender hothouse orchid? That paragon of virtue?"

Rowland turned to me, his shoulders squared. "She says you are no longer the man she married—"

"Indeed. I should hope not."

"—that you have spies watch her every move. She says you keep her imprisoned. You allow her to see no one. You deny her any friends. She has to smuggle out her letters. You have become a tyrant—power-crazed—since . . ."

"Since?"

"Since you . . . animated your metal men with evil spirits." He sounded progressively more sheepish and shamed as the words tumbled from his mouth. I said nothing but waited for him to continue. "She fears for her life, Fairfax. Everything she writes has the ring of truth to it."

"And you have come to rescue her from her terrible fate, of course."

"I came to stop you from doing something rash. You conceal strange doings here. America will fall to this hell-spawned army you amass, and after that—what? England? Europe?"

"And you see my 'fleet' of airships—all six of them—my improvements on other men's mediocrity, my *empire* housed in three hangers and an office, all the makings of world domination."

"And the manufactories in Kingston and Montego Bay? They say you built a city of them."

"Ah. The dreaded sugar mills. The distilleries."

"If that is what they are."

"Do you *hear* yourself, Rowland?" His silent sincerity spoke for him and I mended my tone. "People fear what they cannot understand. Because my manufactories resemble nothing they have ever seen, then they must not be what I claim. Because I choose this unlikely place, they think I have something to conceal."

"Like your drinking and your temper? I never imagined you would beat your wife."

I sighed. He imagined a great deal. "What will it take to convince you of my innocence?"

"Show me what you keep under lock and key—what you allow no one else to see."

"Not tonight, nor tomorrow neither. A storm is coming."

"What has that to do with anything?"

I snorted and wagged my head.

"Let me see her," he amended. "Let me speak with her. Let me see for myself that you treat her as a husband ought."

"That I can do. Has she seen you?"

"Pardon?"

"Does she know what you look like? Would she recognize you?" Blood rushed to Rowland's cheeks and his eyes slid away from mine. "Ah. My brother and my wife have exchanged Daguerreotypes. How touching."

"You never brought her to us."

"So, goodness itself, she introduced herself. One must have family bonding. Let me see it."

He seemed startled that I would expect him to have it on his person but produced it from his breast pocket just the same. I reached for it, but he snatched it back and clutched it to his breast. I glared at him, held out my hand, silently demanding compliance. His hand visibly shook as he forced himself to relinquish it.

I had to free him of its hold on him . . . if I could. I struck a match and set it alight.

"Here now! What are you doing?!" He attempted to wrest it from me, his agitation growing the more the flames licked at the image, but I held it out of his reach. Frantic, he screeched invectives. He reminded me of a little boy attempting to get his toy from a bully. When it burned beyond redemption, I dropped it into a dustbin.

He stared at it while it turned to ash. He visibly shook and clutched his arms about himself. Tears streamed down his face. "Why did you do that, Fairfax? How could you do that? You have no idea what that meant to me."

I put my arm around his shoulder. "Indeed, Rowland. I fear I do."

As the last cinder faded away, he seemed to come round to himself. The color crept back into his cheeks. I yet held him. He eyed me, surprised, then scrubbed the tears from his face. "What—"

"You'll feel better by and by. Perhaps you already do."

He sniffled and swallowed hard, dragged his sleeve across his nose. He laughed anemically and stepped away. He could not raise his gaze to mine.

Distraction seemed in order. I escorted him into the different workshops, explained a project or two, showed him the designs of my new winged airship. With time, his equilibrium seemed restored and I took him into the tack room. I found a likely pair of worn coveralls. Rowland eyed them skeptically as I shoved them at him.

"What for?"

"To properly meet the flower of my existence, my only purpose for living."

"You do little for your case to speak of her with such bitterness."

"I have a case, do I?"

"She means to sue for divorce. She claims your indiscretions have become too difficult to bear. You spurn her bed for housemaids and peasant girls."

"The epitome of feminine delicacy has discussed with my brother our conjugal relationship. Indeed, I am impressed." I slammed down the lever and the lights winked out. As I strode toward the door, Rowland eyed my automatons suspiciously, once again all ranked perfectly against the wall.

My mechanized velocipede hummed as we sped toward town. Rowland kept his shrieks of terror to himself, although he dug his fingers into my shoulders, clinging for dear life behind me. I had no time for niceties. I raced the clock and the storm.

A heavy brume clung to the atmosphere and darkened the night to pitch. At Kingston Bay, ranks of tall sailing ships and steamers cast off from the quays, heading for the better odds of open sea.

On a certain wharf, I pushed open the door to a seedy alehouse tucked between two warehouses. A giant of a man standing behind the bar looked up as we came in, met my eye, and nodded. Dark and ill-lit, I led Rowland to a table in the blackest corner. I ensured he had a clear view of the room as he sat, and the room had a clear view of him.

The barkeep approached. His neck and arms bare, his shirt thin, the muscles of his broad shoulders glinted from the sheen left by the torrid murk. On the right, instead of the bone and sinew of his arm, leather, copper, steel, and Herr Professor's latest experiment with titanium glinted in the firelight against his coal-black skin.

"Evening, Julian."

"Ebenin', Cap'n. Ye be let."

"I came as soon as I could." The man eyed my brother warily. "A friend."

"O' course, Cap'n."

"How are we this evening?"

"Bidness, she booms dees night. Sh'ad tree lines ahready—"

"Three lines of what?" Rowland demanded.

"De cocaine. Be ye daft, mon?"

Rowland continued to stare.

"I believe I told you of my experiments in prostheses for amputees?" I explained. "Julian, brave man, allowed me to test a few theories on him."

Julian flexed his elbow, wrist, and fingers proudly, to the soft whir and snick of gears and pulleys in motion. "'Tis quite dee ting. T'almost makes me glad me gots caught een dee crushah."

"Almost," I agreed. Rowland grimaced.

"Sev me life, dee Cap'n deeds. T'would 'ave bleeded to def 'eef not for 'eem."

Rowland eyed me. "Julian and I are old friends," I explained. "We have much in common." Julian snorted. I turned again to my host. "The usual, Julian, if you would."

"Ahready she done two draughts, Cap'n. As I seh, dee bidness she be breesk. Mighty high flyin' dere be dees night, and da soonah what I geeb 'er takes 'old, the bettah, says I. But, dee physic, she don't seem to 'fect 'er like she done."

I glared off into the darkness. Another burst of bawdy laughter filtered to us. "Do what you think best. As you say, we haven't any time. I mean to be at West End at dawn."

"Travelin' t'night, suh? Be dat wise?"

"Better than tomorrow, mate. You've business there as much as I."

"Yes suh, Cap'n. Ye speak de troof. I sees to eet."

After a moment, Julian returned with two flagons of ale. Rowland eyed it warily. "It's my private stock, mate. Drink up."

"Captain of what?"

I shrugged. "Of my airship? My sailboat? Would you prefer 'Captain of Industry'?"

"You are too full of yourself by half, Fairfax. You cannot control the world."

"You mistake me, Rowland. I find precious little within my control."

The vocal protests from three or four men at the far side of the room drew my brother's attention. Someone had abruptly brought an end to their revelries.

Out of the smoky murk slunk a tall woman as sultry as the

night. Although still shapely, her addictions and my attempts at enforced restraint had stripped her of the Rubenesque qualities that had begun to plague her at the onset of our marriage. Her hair hung loose over her bare shoulders and arms. It ranged thick and wild, the soft curls coiling and uncoiling with each movement, as if alive. It caressed her skin and she encouraged the constant stimulation.

She wore a bustier cut of black leather but nothing beneath. Below the tight-cinched waist, a jewel clung to her navel. The cage-work of whalebone stays ended in half-cups in which she nested her ample breasts, although the faulty covering paid scant lip-service to decency.

Leather short-pants rode on her hips and scarcely covered her loins. The head of a cobra tattoo emanated from the open button of her fly. Its tail escaped the pant-leg to wrap twice around her left thigh. Garters held fishnet stockings in place, and stiletto heels added at least four inches to her statuesque height.

She wore a studded leather collar tight around her throat, and encircled her eyes with charcoal, thick and black. Her full lips pulsed a blood red. She walked like a cat in heat and drew just as devoted a following.

A waft of jasmine preceded her, but as she drew near, less pleasant scents bloomed in the mix. Unwashed and unkempt, what appeared seductive in the gloomy distance grew more repugnant with each advancing step.

I pushed my chair back into the deepest recesses of the

shadows. She focused so intently upon Rowland, I escaped her notice. She never saw me when I checked on her. She spoke truthfully about one thing: I always knew where she was and who she was with. Always.

Rowland nervously looked to me for some sort of direction. I said nothing. He glanced again at the hellcat closing in on him. He swallowed hard. He turned to face me but kept his eye on the woman's advance. His breath came in short starts and stops, and he drummed a tattoo on the table. "You . . . I . . . You promised to introduce me to your wife."

"Indeed, I did."

"Then what do we here? Show me where you have secreted her away."

"Understand me, Rowland. Bertha Mason dwells in a prison of her own device. She chooses the where, when and how. I do my duty. I see to her needs. I do my best to keep her safe."

The vamp reached us, acting as if we strained at the leash to get at her. Every calculated move insinuated sensuality. "You're new here, no?" She caressed the posts of a chair as she turned it around to face her, then straddled it, leading with her hips as she sat.

Rowland rose to his feet. "Perhaps we should go."

Bertha looked to him, and then at the corner where he had directed his comment, but she failed to recognize me. Her smile dripped with confidence and determination in the pause of Rowland's hesitation and my silence. She rose and took him into custody. In her shoes, she towered over him.

"The evening is still young." She pressed him back down

into his seat, then straddled him as she had done the chair. She scraped a long, deadly claw across his jawline. "So pretty," she purred. "You shall be pure pleasure." She kissed him long and hard and deep. Rowland resisted for a full two seconds. He made me proud.

I cleared my throat—heavily . . . several times. Rowland drew breath enough to speak, although the trollop on his lap increased her exertions. "Madam," he gasped. "We . . . have not . . . been . . . introduced."

Bertha chortled and murmured something in his ear. He cursed beneath his breath, but his hands pursued their own pleasures just the same. Bertha's powers of persuasion rarely met with resistance.

Julian appeared at Rowland's shoulder. "For dee ledy, as ye ordeh'd, suh." Bertha looked up enough to throw back the shot of rum, then renewed her assault with gusto. Rowland groaned. Julian eyed me. I jerked my chin and he retreated.

"Great Scott, woman!" Rowland gasped, his voice thick and guttural. Plea for deliverance or compliment on technique? To this day, I could not say. Bertha's hands worked his coveralls feverishly, plunging ever lower in search of the deepest buttons.

"By Jove!" Rowland jumped to his feet. His burden fell unceremoniously to the floor. Hands shaking, disheveled, flushed and breathless, he struggled to strip himself of the coveralls, a task already half-completed. "Fairfax! Who is this catamount—this . . . this Jezebel! . . . And what have you done with your wife?"

Still panting and torrid, Bertha slowly emerged from beneath the table, her eyes narrowed and fierce. She peered into my dark corner. "Fairfax?" Her snarl could raise gooseflesh.

I lit my cigar. "Darling," I said between puffs, "I thank you for greeting my brother so warmly. Allow me to *formally* introduce you. Rowland, you, of course, know my wife."

Bertha rose to her feet, wild and wary. She glanced from me to my brother and back again. He had cast aside the drudge, yet still fumbled with the buttons and buckles of his more gentlemanly attire. Bertha worked with great efficiency when properly motivated. "Rowland?" she breathed. "Rowland Rochester?"

I chuckled. "In the flesh, as you see."

Rowland labored frantically. Each fastener restored increased his agitation. "Fairfax, I know not what game you would be at, but either take me to your wife or I will have you in shackles within the hour!"

Bertha spun on him, transformed. Meek and imploring, her eyes wet and shining, she seemed to shrink with each hesitant step toward him. She visibly trembled. Her voice quavered, thick with tears. "Rowland . . . dearest . . . my only friend—my only hope." She reached for him, but he stepped back, yanking away his hands in disgust.

She wheeled on me, wild-eyed, her face hard and flushed with her downfall. "You tricked me. You knew I wanted him. You brought him here to laugh at me. I hate you, you filthy bastard! Why won't you die?!"

She launched at me, but I moved aside as she flew across the table. Amidst the clatter of wood on stone, Rowland gaped at the darkness into which she had disappeared. The color had drained from his face. He could no longer deny the truth.

A moment of silence, vacillation, then he stepped toward the wreckage. She crept into the light, rose to her knees. Where she secreted the Daguerreotype of Rowland, I can only imagine, but she produced it, grasped in both hands which she raised in supplication. Tears streamed from her charcoaled eyes in black rivers down her face.

"Dearest brother," she implored. "My darling Rowland, have pity. See what he has done to me! See what he forces me to do for him to satisfy his perversions! He makes me his whore because he can! Do not abandon me to such cruelty. For the love of God, have mercy upon me."

She broke down into uncontrollable sobbing and curled in on herself. He rushed to her, fell to his knees, and enfolded her in his embrace. She attempted to push him away, but he would not have it. She hid her face in his neck, clinging to him fiercely. Whether or not Rowland noticed she slipped the picture beneath his waistcoat, I could not say. Suddenly, she fell silent and lax.

Bertha's head lolled back and she began to snore. Julian appeared with a bundle of clothes. "What have you done to her?" Rowland demanded.

I declined to answer. Rowland attempted to repulse me as I assumed custody of her, but with Julian looming over him, he had no choice but to comply. Together, my friend and I managed to cover my wife's nakedness. The simple garb of a peasant best served my purpose.

Julian and I propped her between us and struggled to our feet. "Law, dees womon, she geet hebbiah ebey deh," Julian groaned. "Geet de door, mon," he chided Rowland. "Cannuh ye see we's gots our hands fool?"

Julian manned the engine of the vulcanized rubber dinghy as it skipped across the surface of the choppy waves. Encircled with gas-filled envelops, it resembled an airship more than a watercraft. Three electrified iodine lamps mounted on the prow lit the foam-capped peaks before us. The froth glowed in ominous warning.

Rowland gripped the handles embedded in the sides of the skiff, his eyes wide, his knuckles white, his legs braced against the soft hull. It seemed he scarcely drew breath. He apparently cared little for my invention.

"Once one solves the problem of power, anything is possible."

He glared at me, resentful of the place I had refused him but assumed myself. I reclined against the stern envelope, cradling sleeping Bertha in my arms. I pushed back her damp hair and resituated the slicker to better protect her face from the spray.

"Where are we going?" Rowland spoke at last.

"As I said, to West End."

"Why? Why tonight, at this hour?"

I smirked. "You truly lack imagination, dear brother." He glowered at me and I ceded the point. "The storm comes—"

"A storm would have been here by now."

Julian and I exchanged glances. The skiff made a particularly high leap off the top of a large swell, then landed with a thump in the trough behind it. Rowland nearly flew over the side, then fell into the bottom of the boat, where he chose to remain.

"I go to West End to ensure my people are safe. And, West End is leeward. That has to be something."

He jerked his chin at my wife. "Explain this abomination in your marriage."

"Abomination, indeed," I agreed.

Julian snorted his derision, but Rowland shot him a hateful look and the man retreated.

"My wife is ill. Her addictions of every kind—including copulation—her obsessions have reduced her to a kind of madness."

"Why have you not sued for divorce?"

"One can escape infidelity, but the deranged are neither the guilty nor innocent party. Without somewhere to lay blame, the Law denies me any hope of reprieve, or even relief. I am shackled for the remainder of my days. This compassion you see—dare I say tenderness? I trust anyone would extend as much to a wounded and helpless animal."

Rowland attempted to shake off the logic. "No . . . no. You told *no one* you wed. Only Yvette and I ever knew—and that from some slip of the tongue by Rottstieger."

"Do you suppose I wanted Yvette exposed to this corruption?" I insisted, revealing Bertha's haggard face.

Rowland's anger seemed to rise with mention of his wife. "What have you done to Bertha? What did you give her?"

47

"What I must, as I have done for three years. I keep her as safe as possible without endangering the innocent with her violence."

"The mad belong in asylums."

"Rottstieger combed two continents for an acceptable facility and found none. In such a place, Bertha would become an animal because they would treat her thus. I will condemn no-one to such an existence."

Rowland scowled doom and destruction at me but fell silent, which suited. Shouting over the noise of the engine and the rising storm had grown tedious. Lightning cracked open the scudding clouds and the rain began to fall. I shifted my wife into my brother's arms and began bailing.

The lighter gray of dawn had crept upon us when Julian hurled the dinghy up onto the beach. His concern for his family broke free of his determined calm as soon as he drove the boat aground. He ran ahead. The rain had stopped for the moment, but the wind and sea continued to roar.

I hurried up the path toward the bungalow, torn between the people before me and those trailing behind. Bertha clung helplessly to Rowland, who smothered her with solicitous attention.

The darkening mantle scuttled across the sky. Another cloudburst broke loose, and I surged forward. A sound of pain— a grunt? A cry? Shredded by the growing gale, only the hint of distress reached my ears. As I turned, Bertha flashed past me. Behind me, Rowland had fallen to the ground.

I hurried to him. He held his head but rebuffed my attempts to assist him. His hand came away stained in red. I insisted, applied my handkerchief; dragged him to his feet. Talking into the howling gale proved useless. I compelled him up the trail and into the bungalow.

My people had been diligent: everything secured, the storm shutters in place, the house deserted. Hasty and careless, I tended to Rowland's wounds as much as time would permit.

"Why would she do such a thing?"

"You tell me. What did she say?"

"I do not . . . something about . . . bond-yee? Gree-gree? Akachi making some sort of blood sacrifice . . . How the devil am I to know? It made no sense."

I knew where she had gone and compelled my brother back out-of-doors. "Move, Rowland. The storm comes."

"Are you mad?"

I wanted to smack some sense into that thick head but reminded myself he was Rowland. And English. He could not see how fragile became the bungalow in the face of the cyclonic forces bearing down on us.

We stepped from the lee of the house and the wind and rain slammed into us, nearly knocking us off our feet, saturating us to the skin. I pointed him up the path toward the rising hills.

"Follow the trail!" I shouted. "Do not stop until you get to the caves! Go! Run!"

Rowland turned to confront me. "Where are you going?!"

"After Bertha!"

"Not without me! You will never lay another hand on her!!"

I hadn't the time to argue. He could keep up, or get left behind.

Our way wended through thick rainforest. The wind lashed us with vines and foliage, raising welts and breaking skin. I burst into a small clearing wherein a small shack stood on stilts in a rising torrent. We ducked into the lee of the house to reconnoiter. I knew better than to approach blindly. Bertha had before caught me by surprise. I had the scars to prove it.

Bertha's shrill voice reached me, and I peered through the whipping curtains and into the shack. The room resembled a crow's nest, with all manner of trinkets and baubles, strings of feathers and beads, bones of small animals, all flailing wildly in the wind which buffeted the scanty shelter. The extinguished wicks of candles still smoked—a crucifix hung on the wall above a shrine to the Holy Virgin, surrounded by other symbols I have never seen elsewhere. A human skull sat on a shelf. An iguana blinked at me from beside it. I imagine Rowland looked on with the same mixture of aversion and curiosity I had felt when I first came upon the place.

Bertha argued vehemently with Akachi, the old woman from the balcony the first time I laid eyes on the pair. She brandished an ornate dagger. "You were wrong! Rowland *has* come for me. He is mine. You cannot stop me from leaving the island now!"

"Ye hab an époux, Berta—a good man."

"And I will be rid of him. But nothing I do touches him! Time and again he escapes. You will help me, *mémère*. Fairfax will not *die*! Kill him! Perform the rite! Do it now!"

Akachi wagged her head. "I tol' ye eet weel no' work. Hees *gris gris*, eet be too strong."

"Then give me something stronger!" Bertha appeared purple with rage. "I will be free of him! I will see him dead!"

Akachi's eyes betrayed her grief. "Ye hab crossed the Ioa, *fille*. Ye no respect dee speereets. Dey comb for ye. Be gone weed ye lest ye bring dere fierce angah upon me de sem."

Bertha sneered her hatred at the woman. What light remained seemed to flee. "I *call* this storm, you fool!" she shrieked above the howling wind. "The spirits do my bidding! I will be free of Edward Rochester if I have to destroy this island and everyone on it!"

The shack creaked and shifted on its pylons, knocking Rowland from the post upon which he balanced. I dragged him from the onrush of water and onto high ground. I fumbled for the picture Bertha had planted on him. He fought me savagely. He landed a firm right hook on my jaw. I pushed him down and tried to reach into his waistcoat. He sunk his teeth deep into the side of my hand.

Both of us muddied and slick, I struggled to retain him. On a sudden impulse, I pulled the chain from beneath my shirt and forced it over Rowland's head. He attempted to fight me off, but I prevailed. I slung the crystal talisman around his neck, bloodied as it was.

"From Yvette," I shouted into the gale. "To keep you safe!"

He landed another blow, then scrambled away from me and to his feet just as Bertha fled the shack and into the rainforest. "Get her to the caves!" I shouted as he ran after her. "Hurry!"

The wrenching of wood and iron added to the shriek of the storm. The ground gave way beneath the shack and it listed to its side. I ran inside and found Akachi lying in a heap on the floor, unconscious. With a jolt, half the stilts failed and the structure fell into the stream, knocking me off my feet. I managed to extract the frail old woman from the wreckage just as the flood swept it away.

I lay Akachi onto a pallet deep in the caves. Her friends rushed up to assist her. "Where is Rowland?" I demanded. "Where is Bertha?"

Julian strode forward, two heavy lengths of rope slung over his shoulders like bandoliers. "Dey hab not comb." He expertly knotted the ends together as he spoke. Grabbing two coils myself, we stepped out into the hurricane.

I cannot say what directed my steps. Perhaps I followed that invisible tether that bound me to Yvette's crystal. It felt attached to a rib just beneath my heart. It drew me onward, and I followed the compulsion.

We slipped and slid down the path to the shore, compelled

from behind by the blow. The palms bent to the ground or snapped like twigs. Great shrieks of splintering wood transcended the continuous howl of the tempest. Debris filled the air: bits of plank and net and limbs of trees as thick as my thigh. We navigated a minefield of destruction, and God only knows why we survived.

We came to the bungalow, but I pressed on to the sea, the top of the lighthouse my beacon. The pounding of the surf surmounted the scream of the gale. I rounded the bend and stopped short. Despite my reputation of imperturbability, the sight paralyzed me with fear.

The storm rushed the tide forward. With each crashing wave, the thirty-foot cliffs upon which the lighthouse stood became less significant. In very few moments, the shoreline would vanish beneath the surge.

In the distance, a waterspout—a cyclone spawned by the hurricane—began to rise up from the sea. Another snaked away from it, while a third cyclone swirled its way over the ridge, the bungalow in its path. In the deafening roar, the three seemed bound in a sinuous, serpentine dance about the lighthouse; and there, in the center of it all, perched on the edge of the cliffs, stood Bertha and Rowland, my brother.

The lighthouse door had never required securing. The thick stone walls had defied the tropics for more than one hundred years. It gave us hope. We secured the lines about ourselves to the iron staircase within, then ventured out toward our object.

Bertha had freed herself of her blouse and skirt. She stood shoeless, wearing nothing but wet leather. Her hair flew in great long black snakes, whipping about in the wind. Her contorted face completed the image of Medusa. She raised her hands high above her head and danced in the spray of the surf. She threw back her head and screeched at the heavens, reached toward the cyclones swirling in the near distance, as if she held them in her hands and ruled their motion.

Rowland appeared small and frail beside her, perhaps because she so easily threw off his attempts to control her. Both Julian and I understood. When the woman became so crazed, the most primal forces within her engaged and overcame men stronger than my brother.

In the face of such wind, I could not understand how he remained upon his feet. I motioned to Julian. He jerked his chin in understanding. We pushed off into the gale and pressed for the pair at the ledge.

Absorbed as Bertha was in her maniacal incantations, I managed to avoid her notice as I approached. Rowland leapt upon me, catching me unaware. We both fell hard onto the stone. Rowland raised his fist to pummel me. Julian pulled him off before he could strike.

Rowland fought against Julian. He could not hear reason. Bertha's dance became more berserk. Rain and spray flew into my face with equal measure and clouded my sight. Bertha, wet and slick, slipped from my hands. She seemed intent not on escape, but in completing her insane ritual. I at last managed to grapple my wife, when again, Rowland assaulted me and wrenched her from my grasp.

The inexorable tide surmounted the cliff. With one relentless blast, it knocked us all from our feet, then sucked us toward the ledge as it drew back for the next wave. Bertha screeched and scrambled for some sort of hold. I lunged for her, but came up with naught but a fistful of hair. It was enough.

Secured by my line, I dragged her toward me by her tresses. Her last fall had rendered her unconscious. I preferred the dead weight to a continuous battle. I wrapped the rope about her, then struggled to my feet as the waves pummeled us. I pulled myself up our tether, my wife strapped to my back, until at last we reached the lighthouse. I stumbled over the threshold. We dropped in a heap on the floor.

I dragged Bertha up a few stairs and away from the encroaching water, then plunged again into the storm. I made my way down Julian's taut line. To my great relief, he had managed to secure Rowland. Even so, my brother retained his consciousness and his loss of reason. He fought against all attempts at rescue, and Julian could not get back to his feet.

I returned to the lighthouse. With the next wave, when the line loosened, I looped it around a pylon in the lee of the thick stone, then began to haul.

As quickly as I could, I dragged the line through my makeshift pulley, betimes making great progress, betimes losing ground. I ignored the searing pain in my muscles, my throat, lungs, and eyes, burning with the salt of the sea. My serrated hands stained the rope red.

An eerie, gray-green light glowed beneath roiling black clouds, broken only by blinding bolts of lightning. The sounds of thunder, surf, and wind, like a locomotive bearing down upon me, became so much meaningless din. I concentrated on the growing pile of rope at my feet, and the line that went taut, then lax with each crashing wave.

I felt certain I had all but achieved my task. I wrapped the line about both my hands and leaned all my weight into one mighty heave. With a jerk, the rope cinched around my fingers. It shot straight up in the air, and me with it. I screamed as muscle and tendon ripped from bone. I hung like a kite tethered to the earth by a string. Buffeted in the whirl of wind and water, I thought Rowland's rope would surely sever my fingers. Then, of a sudden, it went lax, and I dropped again into the surf around the lighthouse.

The tide had risen several feet—enough for me to survive the fall. The surge tossed and rolled me along what had once been dry ground. I snatched a scant breath before the opposing force sucked me back. The ground beneath me disappeared. I had been towed beyond the ledge and into open sea.

It seemed everything slowed, then, like a wind-up toy at the last of its spring. I can still recall every thought, every tick of that internal clock, every sensation of that second of time.

I knew my life over. My thoughts flew to Yvette. Perhaps I would soon greet her beyond the veil of death. My soul already reached out to her, grateful—almost eager.

And then I felt the fierce yank of the rope securing me as it reached its extremity. It forced out what air remained in my lungs.

The realization flooded me that I yet could live, were I of a mind. The next instant, ferocious pain bloomed throughout my body as, unable to wrest me free, the enraged sea hurled me against the jagged stone of the cliff-side.

Everything went black.

How I survived, I can only surmise. I came to my senses as I again scraped along the ground in the roaring surf. I grappled the line and pulled myself forward to the door of the lighthouse. The currents swirling around it had brought me again into the leeside.

Agony screamed through me. The clear water rushing over me washed pink, and then red, back into the sea. My right arm hung uselessly at my side. I half-swam, half-crept through the portal in a desperate bid to escape the pummeling of the surf. Safely inside, I attempted to rise, but a white hot, searing pain nigh overwhelmed me, and my legs crumpled beneath me.

I forced myself calm. I pushed back hair and blood and water from my eyes. My line still flailed in the surf. I hauled in first it, then Julian's tether. The ragged and frayed end drew my gorge.

I managed to force the door closed. The hurricane hurled itself impotently against the immutable stone of the lighthouse, its deafening bombardment at once stifled when I sealed the breach.

I leaned back against the door, panting for breath. The water reached to my chest. My mind raced as I groped about for some means to rescue Rowland. However, every attempt to rise resulted in failure. My determination, my denial of the excruciating torment which constantly assaulted me—useless. I could not stand. I could rescue no one. I doubted I had saved myself.

Bertha crouched upon the stairs where I had left her. She shivered uncontrollably. Terror filled her eyes as I dragged myself toward the steps and higher ground. Wild and feral, her arms clamped about herself, she rocked back and forth, keening. Weeping. Muttering incantations beneath her breath.

Not yet midmorning, what little daylight remained faded as the heart of the storm approached. I felt the encroachment of a long, oppressive night ahead.

Sun had surrendered to Wind.

Every night for the past fourteen years, I have relived that storm. Every time I lay my head upon my pillow, darkness enfolds me. Just as in the hurricane, I plunge into the depths of excruciating pain without any hope of relief.

Nightly, as my eyes grow heavy, I curse Yvette for saving my life, and Bertha for not taking it. Alone with my wife as the storm raged, I prayed for death, but death would not come. I prayed for unconsciousness, but that, too, was denied me. Throughout endless hours, my thoughts tormented me as the gale battered the island, as they plague me even still.

I should have saved my brother. Instead, I sacrificed Rowland to the cyclone for a woman debauched, debased, deranged, whose last semblance of sanity the storm stripped away.

That night, my end would have been a simple thing for her to accomplish. None would have questioned or suspected her. I would count it a blessing, relief to my guilt-riddled heart. She had me at her mercy. Wealth and independence sat at her feet, and me helpless to stay her hand. Yet, my insane, spite-filled, murderous wife refrained.

Although it broke his neck, the cyclone failed to wrest Rowland's corpse from Julian's grasp. My people found them lashed together high in a tree, where Julian had snatched his own life from the jaws of death. His mechanical arm had saved him. It never failed, although his natural limbs had done.

I buried Rowland in the cathedral at Spanish Town. He had buttoned Bertha's Daguerreotype beneath his shirt, against his skin. Even Yvette's crystal had not the power to intercede. I obliterated the picture in a crucible fueled by grief, but the purging failed to return Rowland—or Bertha.

After a year of recuperating myself and my ventures, I took Bertha away from the islands, hoping to affect some sort of improvement in her sanity. But, fourteen years with the best care money can buy and her condition only worsens. Only her brother knows I hide her away at Thornfield. None at that house know her as my wife.

Magic is nothing but the execution of knowledge beyond the understanding of the ignorant and superstitious. So I maintained as a youth, and so I always shall. But, I have become convinced that Yvette purchased my life at the cost of our happiness together. Because of it, for fourteen years, every morning I awaken to the warmth of her crystal resting over my heart, and I resolve anew to make good use of the gift she made such a sacrifice to bestow. I do not comprehend the how of it. But then, the sun does not require my understanding for it to shine. It simply does.

Even so, for fourteen years I have waited for . . . something. The other shoe to drop. The rest of the story. Some explanation as to why Yvette would demand this life of me, miserable as I am, shackled to a maniac but otherwise alone, unable to seek the true companionship of a loving wife. Pleasure, I have sought and sometimes found, but never happiness.

Had Yvette, or the Fates, or God, or whomever holds the whip that cracks over my head and now and again lashes my back—had they any mercy, they would free me of this torment, but Bertha remains as hale in body as I do myself. Decades yet will pass before either becomes infirm enough to anticipate the release of death.

My conscience prevents the neglect that would speed either of our demises. And so I plod through life seeking diversion where I can find it—and betimes dissipation when my soul grows weary, and my wits dull.

But I do make use of my talents. I resolved that the hurricane's devastation would not impede our plans to assist the new American Federation, and it did not. That nation thrives, in large measure due to our efforts, and those of men like us.

I have managed to keep Jamaica unpolluted by the mores of industrialization. My message has taken hold of the Caribbean and begins to spread throughout the Western Hemisphere.

To keep pace and the peace, coal and fascism have been forced to loosen their stranglehold on England. Each Rochester estate or venture enriches, rather than exploits the lives of its people. I have made a name for myself. I dare say I have done some good.

And, even in my blackest moods, I always had Yvette's crystal to warm the ice in my heart and light my way through the bitter darkness. At least, I had done. Until this morning.

I awoke with the previous night's dream of the storm vivid in my recollection. I sought the comfort Yvette's crystal always afforded me, but it was gone. In a panic, I tore apart the bed-clothes. I ransacked the room. I had not removed that rock since the day I reclaimed it from Rowland's corpse. I had clutched it in my hand when I succumbed to sleep the night before.

Then, I saw it. It lay on the table at my bedside. Crushed into dust. As I sat there, staring at it, a sharp pain seared my finger. Before my eyes, Yvette's ring dissolved away like paper before a flame.

Some six months gone, I had returned my ward to that de-pository of failure, Thornfield, where I shuffled away the bleak reminders of my unhappy past. Her mother claims me the father, although I have no cause to believe it. Even so, I could not aban-don her daughter as that faithless French soubrette had done.

I had charged the warden of that asylum to hire a governess

for Adele, and duty requires that I inspect the purchase. I have postponed it too long, but returning to Thornfield always weighs heavily upon my spirits. I keep my stops as brief as I can justify, as long as I can bear. I had relied on my medallion to brace me for the task.

Every right choice to my credit I have made with Yvette and her good opinion as my guide. But apparently, it has all been for naught. Good works have profited me nothing, and I have subsisted on her beggarly ration of affection for far too long. She now leaves me to my own devices, with a madwoman strapped to my back and an urchin clinging to my leg, and I will get on as best I may.

She has abandoned me, and no denying it. She withdraws her light. If I stumble into the black abyss, it is by her hand. She demands I battle Hades itself without buckler or shield, and I shall. Or perhaps I shall simply surrender to it, and take my happiness wherever I can find it, no matter the cost to my charred soul.

On the morrow, I am for Thornfield to alone face my fate, and the devil take her for it. The devil take us both.

Styled after Jane Eyre by Charlotte Brontë

Sense and Cyborgs

ANIKA ARRINGTON

No one makes cyborgs like they does in Singapore. That's why we set sail there when the Cap'n lost his leg. We were sailin' round the Horn, see, takin' ships as they come for Her Majesty's Navy. Privateerin' ain't exactly the most honest way for a sailor to make his wage, but least it's legal.

Well, one great Portuguese tub proved too spirited. One minute we had them on the run, pullin' the best of their cargo from the hold, the next, our first mate is screamin' to heaven on high. In all fairness, the cap'n *is* her husband, but the shrill nature of the female voice ain't exactly intimidatin'.

"Harris! Harris! Help me!" she's wailin' and there's all manner of fear in her face and blood on her hands. We gets him to his cabin, and she turns to me like I got to know which way's north now.

"He'll be all right, Dashwood," I tells her. "Just do what ye can for him, and I'll get the crew goin'. Where're we bound?"

"The Orient," she says, without no waitin'. "There's only one man that can do what we need."

The only question be'n would the Cap'n make it, and it's dicey there for a bit. Caught a storm not twelve hours after he regained consciousness, at which point he passed right back out, if you please. The first mate's still screamin', but in the way that meant we ain't moving fast enough for her tastes.

They say it's bad luck havin' a woman aboard, but when Mrs. Margaret Dashwood-Campbell gets in high dudgeon, it's like sailin' under the command of that Greek Athena, Goddess of War and Wisdom, a thing out o' legend.

"Mr. Harris, get that sail into position, or your wrinkled brow will spend the journey to Singapore on the Maiden's head!"

"Aye, Dashwood!" is all you can say, and hop to it.

We all knew she were worried for the cap'n, so we soldiered on, but two days of tossing on the high seas was nearly all we could take. Lucky for us, the storm blew itself out without leaving us becalmed.

Tweren't easy makin' fast sail at half rations for so long. Even havin' the monsoons wid us, there's more than a few unkind things said 'bout the cap'n and his first mate.

"Ain't right sailin' under a woman," says Beakman one day at mess. "It's her bein' on board got the cap'n hurt. Now only God knows where we're sailin' to. I don't like it. I won't stand it much longer."

"Beakman, you are as daft as Harris is old," says Martin—who ain't more than three summer's my junior. "It was Dashwood saved the captain's life, and we're sailin' to Singapore. Everyone knows that."

"So she says, how do we know she ain't sailin' us all to our doom?" Beakman pipes back.

"'Cuz more than one man on this boat can navigate, you great lump," I puts in. "Just cause you gots kelp and not much else 'tween yer ears don't mean the rest of us can't read a star or two. Now quit yer yammerin' 'fore Dashwood finds outs, and decides to clean her knives on yer face."

In the end, we touched the docks in west Singapore, sweet as you please, 'bout an hour before sundown, and not sixteen days after the cap'n was injured.

Singapore is a swarm of bodies bumpin' and jostlin'—a great mix o' peoples wid all different faces. First Mate Dashwood sets us a haulin' them heavy crates of goods down, and in the midst of the bustle she calls Martin, Beakman, Boarhead, and meself aside. I enters the cabin, and there's the captain all laid out in a wooden box. His face beat up and the color of the sail. His leg is missin', just a great wad of bandages. Next to him is a long package wrapped up so's we can't tell what's in it, but mark me if it ain't just the size to be the leg that ain't there.

"He's dead?!" I asks.

"Of course I'm not dead, you water-logged moron!" he sits up, and shouts at me before he winces and drops back down.

"You think we can just move him through the streets, and no one will say a word?" Dashwood says looking me in the eye. "You think Captain "Dagger" Campbell would be allowed to hobble about looking for someone to bolt him up?"

I feel the shame of my stupidity burnin' me neck. "'Course not, ma'am."

"Do I look like a ma'am to you, Harris?!" she hollers. She grabs the nearest object, being a sexton with all the fine etching, and heaves it right for my face. She's a dapper hand with the thrownin' knives she is, but the sexton's a mite big, see?

I catch the sexton, and cut me hand in the process. Ain't nothin' worse than a cut in a man's hand. Makes all work harder, goes to infection faster than anything I know. Well, I suppose the cap'n's leg is awful bad, but my cut hand feels like a stiff price for callin' the first mate "ma'am".

"Sorry Dashwood, just trying to be 'spectful."

"Well, you can *'spect* me by putting the lid on and shouldering my husband off this tub." She gestures at all of us, and we goes to work.

When a man is bein' lifted in the glory after a skirmish or durin' some good drinkin', he'll stay perched up on the shoulders of two men and hardly weigh two stone. But when he's near death like the cap'n, laid out in the wooden box, it took all four of us to bear him aloft. And no light thing it were, neither. The dock swayed 'neath our feet as we left the gangway. Beakman's knees buckled, and the captain nearly hit the drink.

"Move it along, you louts!" Dashwood hollers, and we know there's a man out of a job or worse if the cap'n goes tumblin'.

We follows Dashwood away from the crush of the pier, the

hawkers of the markets, and the patrols. More than once we had to hold up while some group or other went past, the stillness addin' to the cap'n's weight. And I notices that we go straight past the surgeon's street. I see a few walkin' past us there with a bit of work done on an arm or a leg. You see a man with a bandage or a rag holdin' some bit of hisself together, and you knows he's goin' straight for the street of the butcher surgeons. That's where they can patch any hurt.

A man crosses our path, so's we come up short, and you can hear the heavy fall of one foot that's made of something weightier than flesh and bone. Each physic puts his mark on his work. Some you can see, like the lad with the tree of cogs etched in platin' on his arm, but others don't like folk knowin' where their work been done.

That's Dashwood. No one knows why or when or what for, but when her gloves and her sleeves part a bit you can see there's something shinin' where the flesh ought to be. But she don't turn for the street of the medics.

We wanders back alleys and weaves 'tween houses barely standin'. It's darker here, no lamps, and we stumbles more than walks as we carries the cap'n onwards. The smell of opium slithers about here and there. We huffs and gasps as we does our best to keep the cap'n from banging about in his injured state. Finally, Dashwood stops at a door. It's all bamboo and thatch, and there's an elephant with a dirty great cog rising off its back painted in gold. She knocks twice, and the door opens ever so slightly.

"Please tell the admiral that Dashwood begs a favor, and expects a return on her investment." The words is crisp and sharp with the tension only a long history of deeds and words with a person brings.

A moment and then two we wait. I gets twitchy, thinkin' we ain't welcome, and the sweat is drippin' in my eyes. The cut in me hand is burnin' somethin' fierce after all that carryin', and I adjust my hold to take the heft off it. The cap'n moans a bit at the jostle, and Dashwood turns to eye us a bit. I clears my throat when she looks at me.

Finally, the door opens, completely this time, and there stands the tiniest woman I've ever seen. And then I realize she ain't just small, she's too short to be right in the legs, but the dark masks all the details, and blimey if the cap'n ain't heavy as a shark caught in deep waters.

We haul the cap'n inside, but there ain't nowhere to set him, just a rug and a doorway hung with beads, so it's more followin'. The little woman's feet click and clang as she makes her way cross the floor and through the clatter of the beads. Dashwood disappears behind her, and as we move to follow, we hear, "It's stairs, lads. Careful with the cargo as you step down, now."

Stairs it is indeed, and barely room enough for us and the box. We have to lower it 'tween ourselves and go sideways as the floor becomes the ceiling. The tiny clicking woman stops at the bottom, so we stops too, hangin' on the cap'n by our fingertips. It's black here, and I can't see nothin', but I hear more clickin' and clangin' and then the door swings open and I'm blind again for the light spewing forth. Again we follow, and when me eyes clear I'm near dumbfounded.

Tables covered in silk and food and opium is surrounded by lovely, dark-haired girls with shinin' metal arms, their cogged shoulders peeking out of their robes, men with eyes that glow jewel-bright surrounded by brass fixings that move and turn as they watch us go past, and people who almost ain't got enough flesh left to be people at all.

I'd known a man or two as had work done like the captain needed, injury made right or lameness corrected. They walk up and down the piers lookin' for work like any man. And I'd seen a few of those night ladies by the harbors with they ears plated on the outside so they shines in the dark a bit, but I ain't never seen a lady with silver eyelids clicking open and closed, nor a man with not but metal from his waist up 'fore. Right unnervin' it is.

We follows Dashwood and our miniature hostess through another beaded doorway and then down a hall lit with kerosene lamps. The laughter from the room echoes behind us and bounces ahead of us down the corridor. The click-clang, click-clang, click-clang of those tiny feet fills the passage, but I still can't see her for the crate on me shoulder and Dashwood in front blockin' the view.

We comes to another great door. This one has the cogged elephant on it, too. The smallish lady's arm reaches up, pulls the elephant's nose, and the cogs in the elephant's back whirl and the door opens.

"Come in, Margaret! Come, come, come!" says a most English voice. "I understand you have something for me."

"You know me, Admiral," she says, and suddenly sounds nothin' like our first mate. She sounds like the girlish thing that said, "I do," to the cap'n all them years back. "I never ask a favor empty-handed."

He comes waddling over like some young fop, with spectacles on his face that make him look like a great fish. She allows this short, round little man in a white coat to kiss her hand, and I near drop the cap'n at such ladylike behavior. The other lads groan, and Dashwood remembers we been heftin' him all through town.

"On the table there, lads," she says, and we stumble and drops the cap'n a little harder than we mean. This earns an eye from Dashwood the likes of which could kill a man, and I sees the mettle that makes her the first-mate in her face again. We'll be pullin' barnacles off the sides of the ship, and no mistake.

"Well, let's see, let's see, then!" says the admiral, and he comes bustlin' over. He tosses the lid off like a feather, and I'm wonderin' how many gears he's got on his own self under the coat and the simperin'. The captain moans and tries to sit up, but the admiral just pushes him back, cluckin' like a mother hen. Then he notices the wrapped leg and gasps like a babe at Christmas. He unwraps the bindings at the bloody end and starts inspectin' and pokin' about.

"I think I could reattach it, but the toes would have to be replaced," he says, and I believe he could do it.

"No, no, Admiral. We aren't here to make the best of a bad job. The leg is the gift. He needs full hardware," Dashwood insists.

The admiral gets this simpery little smile on his face, like that's just what he wants to be hearin'. He just chortles a bit and goes wanderin' off to these tables of metal bits and instruments, and starts rummagin' about.

"I'll need two days to get him outfitted properly, and the brass won't come cheap," the admiral looks up to see Dashwood's reaction. He's a man been cheated before and no mistake.

"I'll pay you half now, half on safe delivery." she assures him.

"Splendid!" the admiral gestures her over so they can haggle the price. I feel for him now. No one gets the best of Dashwood, 'cept maybe the cap'n from time to time.

The lads and I are starin' 'round the room, lookin' at the hooks and chains coverin' the walls, and some of 'em ain't empty. Arms and legs lookin' like they ain't fit to be part of any person are danglin' all around the workshop. The skull of a man, long lost to this world, half bone, half plated metal is smilin' forever from a shelf above the admiral's head. And all over the workshop I'm seeing that cogged-up elephant markin' the admiral's work.

I realize now the cap'n's off me shoulders I might get a look at that wee lady, but she ain't nowhere to be seen. And I notice that great metal door is closed behind us, and I shivers a bit to be held up in such a place.

"That'll do just fine," I hear the admiral pronounce, and I wonder what kind of deal could make him so happy.

71

"Come on, lads," says Dashwood, and she leads the way back up to the street. As we go, I don't see the tiny lady nowhere, but there was plenty of others to watch us as we went. When we're finally breathin' air that don't smell like kerosene and opium, she hands us each ten pound.

"Captain Campbell will need strong shoulders to get him back to the ship, so don't be too drunk when you meet back here to fetch him," she says, stern as that storm that blew us here. "You heard the admiral: two days to get him set right, so be here at dawn in two days' time."

"What about the rest of our pay?" demands Beakman.

"How do you think I know you'll come back here? You'll get your pay when my husband is safely aboard his ship again." And there ain't no arguin' with that.

'Tain't hard to find a pub in Singapore. The wine's different, but beer's beer the world 'round. I was guzzling a good portion of my wages with the lads when one of those shiny girls comes walking in the door. Everyone in the place is givin' her a 'preciative eye, and in behind her walks the biggest fella I ever seen outside a boxin' circle. Folks stop lookin', and more than a few realize they have other places they ought to be.

He has a massive piece of metal where his left arm should be and a huge collar of brass round his neck. His left cheek is a brass plate as well, the skin around it puffed and puckered like a quilt, all pieced together. And there, smack in the center of his face plate is the admiral's cogged elephant, its trunk held high, like it's trumpetin' a warning. He might have been there in the admiral's salon, and sittin' among the rest of 'em. Too many bolted and plated for him to stand out there, but standin' here like Goliath in that doorway, can't help but see him.

The lady walks to the bar, and whispers to the barkeep who nods emphatically and goes about his business. I've got a mind to head back for the ship and see how the other lads made out with the cargo, but that big fella is still standin' at the door lookin' like no one is leavin' without his say so.

The shiny lady walks up to our parcel with a bottle of wine and cups enough for the table, but I knows better than to touch libations from strange women with fingers what clink against the glass of the bottle like that.

"You are Dashwood's men?" she asks as she sits herself down. Her accent makes the words sound like fish goin' back and forth in a pool o' water, quick, then slow.

The lads and I just nod and try not to look as nervous as the big guy makes us. I shoot another glance his way and the lady sees where my attention is.

"He is here to protect me, not to harm you," she assures us. "I am Whipsnake."

"Whipsnake?" Martin says, chucklin' like a fool.

She brings her arms up and flexes them twice. Each of her silver, pointed nails begins to grow to nearly four inches and then is followed by a tether of silver cord. Ten lethally-tipped whips hang from her hands, and her statement 'bout needin' the big fella's protection is seemin' less likely.

"He names us as we are built," she says. "I do not even remember what my first name was, but then, I was very small when he bought me. He will do the same to each of you. That is why I am here."

She flexes her wrists again, and the cords work slowly back into place, and I can see the slither of them just beneath the flesh of her arms and the silk of her sleeves.

We're watchin' her, so it takes a minute for the five of us to get hold of what she's sayin'. When it strikes me, my eyes must open to the size of the moon rising out of the water.

"Captain wouldn't let that happen," insists Martin.

"Perhaps not," Beakman says, "but Dashwood might, if it meant the captain gets what he needs."

Whipsnake just nods.

We sits there stunned at the revelation that we's been sold like barrels of cargo.

"What'll he do wid us?" Beakman asks, the only one of us with the courage, or maybe he just wants more reasons for belly-achin' like he do.

"He will drug you, so you do not feel or struggle. Then he will decide which pieces of you should go. Sometimes," she hesitates, "sometimes he just takes what he needs for what he calls ex-per-ee-ments. He did not become as proficient at what he does by going to a physician's school. Here in Singapore, they call him the Elephant Butcher."

The lads and I just looks at each other, and shake our heads.

"No one would go to him, unless they owed him something. Dashwood is not all she appears to be," Whipsnake says, and she's lookin' right at me like she's tryin' to say somethin' more than she's sayin'. I won't lie, I were thinkin' of the metal beneath her gloves and wonderin' how she knows the admiral so familiar-like. But the whole thing churns in me stomach. Something about the look in Whipsnake's eyes ain't right.

"Why you tellin' us this?" I asks.

"There are many that are owned by him that wish to be free. If you keep your freedom, perhaps you will remember it was because you were warned, and come back to help us," she says.

"Why would you need a couple of salt-crusted sailors when you got a big feller like him?" asks Martin. He tips his baldin', red head to the giant still standin' at the door.

"The admiral is not all he appears to be, either, and some of his creations prefer their new life of metal to what they had before." She glances around a little nervous-like, and lowers her voice. "Also, we have no way of leaving Singapore. But you have access to a ship, yes?"

A tiny gasp, just a wisp o' noise comes from behind the big fella. I look but I don't see nothin' at first.

"Whipsnake!" The voice carries all the authority of a sea cap'n, but it came from that tiny woman who had let us in at the admiral's. Now that I sees her properly I can tell that she was small, maybe five feet, even if she where whole. But her legs had been replaced with nothin' but brass seagull's feet, pokin' out from beneath her silk shirt.

She stands there, expectantly. Finally, Whipsnake rises and bows to us, but she don't look at the wee little lady. She goes out the back, givin' the barkeep a look to melt tar. The big feller just flexes his chest at us, and follows Whipsnake out the back.

When I looks back to see her again that wee lady is gone. Such a smalland broken thing as she is to move so fast. I hardly knows what to make of any of it.

The lads is all silent.

"I still say the captain wouldn't do us so wrong." Martin breaks into our ponderin'.

"He'll have a mutiny on his hands when the others find out," says Beakman, takin' another swig.

"Well, it weren't the cap'n who made the choice to pay off the admiral in men's hides," I reminds them. "Look, I ain't sayin' I think she done what that Snake says. But if it's true, I say we finds Dashwood and make her account for what she done."

"Don't feel right takin' on a woman," mumbles Martin.

"What ain't right is her tossin' us to that elephant!" Beakman's roarin' a bit now, and Martin moves his pint out the way. "Harris is right. I say she comes to account to us before she gets the chance to pay off the a'miral." Beakman stands and stumbles backwards over his chair, landin' in a heap on the floor. It's testament to how low we is that we doesn't even laugh.

Well, it would have been all well and good to go about confrontin' Dashwood for what she'd done, but we couldn't find her. The lads at the ship is horrified by the prospect that any one o' them could've been on the list to go, and they're preparin' to make off with the ship before we convinced 'em that there's folks what we owed some help. They agreed to wait until dawn of the day after next. We leaves Beakman behind to see it done, which don't sit well with me. Not that much 'bout this sits well with me. My gut is tellin' me to be wary, and me hand is still smartin' from catchin' that sexton. Nothin' worse than a cut in a man's hand, you know.

We each scoured the city lookin' for any sign of Dashwood, but Singapore goes darker at night than one might 'spect. I decides to go lookin' down the surgeon's street, seein' as it's one of the few places still movin' this hour. No church bells tollin' the hours here, but the stars will tell any sailor worth the salt in his beard that it's half past one.

The smell of the surgeon's street runs to meet you 'fore you ever set foot on the rushes that soak up the blood in the gutters. It's the scent of a thousand cauterized wounds, the smith that forges the bits replacin' what's gone, and all the wee beasties that feed off the spoils.

The door of every surgeon has his mark; the admiral ain't the only one that advertises his wares, see? There's the Three-Legged Dog, the Silver Lion with a wrench for a tail, the Smiling Clock Face, and a dozen others. Each has a specialty. I once knew a bloke who had an eye fitted at the Clock Face. I takes my time, pacin' along like I'm lookin' at the doors, but I'm listenin'. If there's music in the physics' street, Dashwood will be there.

I'm listenin' to the sound of metal feet crushin' the reeds in the street. I'm listenin' to the squeak and grind of fittin's being put in place and the groans that go along with 'em. And then I'm listenin' to the unmistakable sound of a pianoforte. It's out of tune, like it's been pulled from the drink, and like as not it was once, but there ain't no one in all Asia who knows that tune so well as Margaret Dashwood.

The tune takes me out of the surgeon's street, and into a part o' town a respectable bloke might be found. I walk 'long the street to the place where the music's playin', and it's a parlor. All fancy teas and lace napkins and Heaven knows what else the English gentry need when they lands in a place.

Such a fine establishment wouldn't let an old codger like me peer through the windows, so I heads round back. The door is open and all manner of men and women too poor to go in are gathered 'round listenin'.

I manage a look into the room, and the lanterns are lightin' the yeller mass of tangles that only belongs to the first mate, Dashwood, the rag doll of the sea. And she's sittin' there singin' in the most melancholy way, but in all the ten years I've sailed with her, she only sung this way twice.

She were very happy then, and I can't fathom as she would be in such a mood after sendin' four men to their deaths. And I never once in those years of sailin' thought she would turn on a man who sailed under the flag of Cap'n Dagger Campbell. Cap'n couldn't love a thing so cold as to send a man to be torn apart for nothin' more than being member of a good man's crew.

She turns just a little, and the light changes. It glows in her mess o' hair, and drops off her shirt sleeves like sea spray. If she can look like an angel, sing like a siren, and steer a twenty-man crew to port, she can't be the heartless wretch that Snake said she was.

I works my way through to the door and into the room, and I'm about to interrupt when three burly blokes, all metaled-up, come burstin' in the front o' the shop. I sees the Elephant stamped on 'em, right enough, so I slips behind a bamboo screen 'fore they sees me. The crowd at the door scatters, and them blokes start clearin' out the rest, but Dashwood keeps on playin'. I find a tear in the fabric of my hidin' place, and peer out into the room.

Dashwood finishes her song, and just looks at the mates standin' there, but I see her hand restin' on them throwin' knives in her belt. She's lookin' around, markin' the ways out and places to take cover, and sure enough, she looks right at me. She holds out a finger, down low by the seat o' her chair, signalin' me to stay put and keep quiet. Well, I ain't plannin' to jump out and yell 'surprise,' now, is I?

Once the room is clear, in walks that wee, little lady from the admiral's.

Dashwood rises with all the grace of the fine-born thing she is, and goes to kneel before that tiniest creature. She bows her head, placin' her hands together, and says somethin' real quiet-like.

79

I can see that small lady now, in the light of the lanterns, with her seagull feet of polished brass. I'm lookin' for her mark, but I don't see the elephant anywhere on her. Her faced is brown and wrinkled like my own grizzled mug, but there's a kindness in 'er eye that only comes from livin' with those you love, and servin' 'em well.

It's what every sailor dreams o' comin' home to, and most never possess. I can just see her pourin' the admiral's tea each day, in gratitude for givin' her back her feet. Who's gonna mind leavin' bird tracks all they life, long as they can leave tracks at all?

"You may tell your man to come out from his hiding place," the wee lady says, and there's that tone again tells you she ain't askin'.

Dashwood nods and I do like she asks, waitin' to see if I'm about to be dragged back to the Elephant's door to pay Dashwood's debts.

"Harris, don't stand there dithering like a beggar on the stoop." Dashwood waves me over, and I does my best to put each foot in front o' the other 'til I'm standin' just behind her.

"Harris, this is Li Dao Ming. She is a great friend of the captain's." The gesture of her hand is smoother than a well-sanded keel.

I bows to Li Dao Ming, and she grows three feet. I blink a few times, makin' sure it ain't the drink come up on me slow-like, but there she stands, nearly a head above me. Her legs are what's done it, extended 'til she's eye-to-eye with the tallest of her lads.

"Your captain is a good man," she says lookin' me straight in the face. "I hope he has good men sailing with him." I know she reckernizes me from the tap room. She just looks at me like she's waitin' for an answer.

I swallows. "When a cap'n 'spects his crew, then his men is always wid him," says I.

"And does Captain Campbell respect his crew?" Li Dao Ming asks me, still starin' right through the soul o' me.

"Dashwood would have to answer that, ma'am." I'm treadin' the waters now, I know. One of Li Dao Ming's boys flexes his mechanical arms, and I swallow, though I don't mean to.

"What are you talking about, Harris?" Dashwood asks. She stands up, lookin' me in the face with that same intensity.

"Whipsnake found me and the lads in the pub, and she said—"

"Whipsnake!" Dashwood shouts. "That harpy is back in town?" She looks to Li Dao Ming, who only nods. "Harris, whatever she told you is a lie. She has been after the captain since he sailed out of Jakarta without her. Her life changed because of him, and she never forgave him."

"No offense, Dashwood," I insist, "but I remember Jakarta. She weren't never there." That Indonesian job 'bout eight years back were a nasty bit of business, and we barely left with what we came for, but there weren't no ladies involved. Dashwood always stayed with the ship when we was on the job, 'cept in this here mad bit o' circumstance, o' course. Cap'n not wantin' to risk her gettin' pinched, see? And there's no one else he trusts better to see that the ship stayed put and were ready to sail.

"Yes, she was. And so was I," Li Dao Ming says. "In a little shelter by the side of the road was a lame woman and her child. Captain Campbell paused long enough to—"

"—throw a handful of coins to 'em." I says in wonder. Sure enough, I remember now, 'cause I was runnin' like the devil hisself was behind me, and I nearly run straight into the cap'n's back when he stopped. Thought he was mad to waste a cut on a street wretch. Seems I weren't so wrong.

"I took my little girl and the money to a man who was rumored to repair the lame. He refused my money, but accepted my service, insisting that I use the gold to buy my girl an apprenticeship. I sent her away to my home in China, to a woman who knew how to weave." Li Dao Ming bows her head and her eyelids are flutterin' fierce. "But she never arrived in my village."

"She was kidnapped by a group of mercenaries who used her for her body," Dashwood says. "They made her choose between death or training so she could serve their band. It was with the mercenaries that she ran into the captain again, and knew him for who he was. It didn't go well."

Dashwood sniffs in a way that tells me she don't want to talk about what transpired 'tween the Snake and the cap'n, but a trained seductress and assassin—well, you can guess.

"When she returned to me six years later, she had become a weapon. Made of metal and twice as cold," Li Dao Ming says. "She blamed me and the admiral for sending her away. Blamed the coins that had fallen as if from the sky, and the man who rejected her." She looks at Dashwood. "She will not stop until she takes her revenge."

I huffs out a sigh of relief. I was certain our Dashwood wouldn't do something so wicked as send a good man to die when he'd been loyal more years than an old sea dog can count.

"Where is she?" Dashwood asks.

"I do not know, but she will not come back out in the open now that I have seen her," Li Dao Ming says. "She will stay out of sight until she means to strike."

"She didn't say nothin' 'bout strikin'," I says. "Just that if the lads and I could fight our way to freedom, we ought to feel 'bliged to return to help the others. Get them out of Singapore on the ship."

"That'll all just be extra chaos," Dashwood says. "A distraction from what she means to do. You see now that there's no one in the admiral's retinue that needs saving. They love him. He saved them. He takes the cases no one else will, when the work is too much or the price is too high."

"So he ain't the Elephant Butcher, then?" I asks.

"Well, I wouldn't say that," Dashwood admits. "The title of admiral isn't honorary, and you don't get that by stitching wounds, do you?"

I s'pose you never know a man, even when you see his handiwork. No one sees how the clock does the tickin', 'cept the man that made it.

≈≋≈

"No one leaves this ship without the express permission of the captain or myself!" Dashwood bellows from the helm. "Do so and you run the risk of being left behind. That may appeal to some of you, as you may not wish to be captained by a man that doesn't walk on two feet anymore. If so, go now and Godspeed to you. The rest of you will get this ship fit to sail on whatever tide we may have need."

Dashwood insisted on sortin' out the crew herself, though I volunteered to go on me own.

"They'll need to hear it from me," she says. "No man wants a firm hand more than one who's heard a mutinous rumor."

The ship's never this busy at night, men crawlin' all over the riggin', loadin' crates and barrels from the docks, and scrubbin' down anything weren't movin'. There's no sign of Beakman, though. I know'd it was bad idea leavin' that limp bit o' seaweed with the crew. No tellin' what he's got hisself up to, daft thing that he is.

"Martin, Harris, you're with me," Dashwood says over her shoulder as she goes walkin' down the gangplank.

I'm just coming down behind her when me right wrist gets yanked across me, turnin' me all about. I'm flying right off the gangplank, and I knows it's bad 'cuz I can't feel nothing in me arm at all as I'm droppin'. I lands in the drink, right in me face. I'm kickin' and flailin', but I gets me head above the water. There's this pain racin' up me arm, the salt searin' the wound. I reach towards the dock. I try to grab the pilin', spittin' and splutterin' from the water and the pain. But I can't grab, 'cuz I got no hand to grab with no more. The pain makes sense now. I got no right hand. I pull the stump of what was me whole right arm in close to my chest, and I'm kickin' and scramblin' with my left hand tryin' to clear the surface proper, trying to get hold of anything to pull meself up.

Martin's the one pulls me out. I hear Dashwood shoutin' like a fury, but her words make no sense over the pain in my hand. I take a breath, but it comes out a choke and then a scream and then her angel face is there in front of me.

"Is it bad Harris?" She reaches out her hand and I put out my stump. She holds it for a moment without no fear in her eyes. "It's a clean cut. The Snake's work to be sure. She could have taken your life, Harris. That makes you lucky, but she will pay for taking your hand." She looks right in me eyes, makin' sure I understand her. I just nods. "Good, now up you get."

She and Martin haul me up, and I sway like it's me first day 'board ship. "Hold him steady as we go, Martin. We've got to get to the admiral before her."

It's all a jumble from there. Lights and shadows and how my hand were screamin' 'bout not bein' there no more. We run longer than I thought it should take. I catches my boots on the cobbles and in the mud and in the reeds chokin' the gutters. Me arm always shoutin' at me to stop.

Finally, we gets to the door, and that elephant with the dirty great cog stickin' out its back is the most welcome sight. But Dashwood is screamin' again. And realize it ain't just my vision that's flickerin' with the pain. This alley were like black pitch when I carried the cap'n that first night. Now I can see that elephant on the door like noonday sun. And it's all 'cuz the roof of the hut is ablaze.

"Michael! Michael!" Dashwood never sounded more a woman than in her heartbreak. Martin drops me to the ground and pulls her back. She would have gone straight through that door if she thought she could save him.

I don't know how long she screams or how long I sits there feeling every heartbeat in fingers that's gone. The heat don't help the pain, it blows into all the bloody, open spaces. I looks down the alley behind us, back into the dark we came from, and she's standin' there. Taller than I remember, with wickedness in every shinin' whip.

"Dashwood, she's here," is all I says. It's all that seems 'portant. She's here to kill us for a life full of bitterness that started in Jakarta with a deed o' kindness. Maybe it's the pain in me voice, maybe Dashwood was 'specting her to be here, but Dashwood stops her wailin'. Her silence is bigger than the screamin'. Even the flames go quiet, 'fraid of what comes next.

That Snake moves first, though, runnin' at Dashwood, wavin' those shinin' whips into a frenzy no eye could follow. And a howl builds in her that beats against Dashwood's silence, but Dashwood don't move. Martin and I is lookin' to and fro, waitin' for her to do somethin', and watchin' the Snake comin' on like a thing out of a wee child's nightmare.

Martin decides since he's got two legs that he ought to use them, and runs off. I never pegged Martin a coward. It's near as frightenin' as the scene before me eyes, to see him turn tail.

The barbs of the whips reach the Dashwood before I can do

nothin', barely able to stand, and swoonin'as I do. They rips into her face and her shirt sleeves, makin' a ringin' clang as they do. Bits of cloth and Dashwood's fine yeller hair go flyin' away from her. She's bleedin' all over, but she don't move. No man I ever knew could stand before such pain and not move.

Then that Snake's neck is in her reach. One moment those whips are a blur and a fury and the next they lays limp at her side, and there stands Dashwood holdin' her foe by the throat with a strength that defies reason. The Snake is chokin' and strugglin', her weapons in the way now so she can't get hold of the hand that's crushin' the life from her. Dashwood's face is shimmerin' in the firelight, all covered in trails of blood.

I know'd a man from the Ivory Coast, once, could crush a snake in his bare hands. But that were just a plain old snake, and he were a sailor in the prime of his days. He would laugh when he done it. There ain't no laughter in that alley.

Dashwood ain't the angel from the parlor beyond the surgeon's street. She's cold and there's a rage in her eyes, more quellin' than all the waves of the great deep.

"Margaret, stop!" comes a cry from a voice I never thought to hear again. The cap'n walks with another man supportin' him, lurchin' about as he goes. He comes to his wife and places a hand on her arm. "Margaret, that's enough," and he says it tender-like, so's I'm almost embarrassed to hear it.

"Michael?" She blinks, and looks at his face like she's seein' him for the first time. "Michael?!"

"Put her down," he says, like he's talkin' to a child. Dashwood just drops Whipsnake in a heap at her feet and, believe me or not, that witch is still alive. She's gaspin' and coughin' like the typhus got her, but she's alive.

Li Dao Ming comes toddlin' up in her shortest height and lifts the Snake's head, cradled in her hands. She starts whisperin' in her foreign tongue so I don't know what she's sayin', but a mother's love sounds the same the world 'round. The Snake opens her eyes and just says, "Ma. Ma," like she's swallowed the coals of the fire she set in the admiral's home.

I can't stand the sight of that wretch what took my hand no more, but I can't quite look at the cap'n neither as he's all wrapped 'round Dashwood. So I just sits there holdin' me arm 'til Martin comes runnin' back.

"Fat lot of good you were!" I holler in his face. He just waves me and me breath away, 'cuz behind him is comin' the admiral. He bumbles over, tskin' and tuttin' like me own mother.

"Oh, this won't do, won't do one bit," he says, pokin' about in the tenderest bits. I bite my tongue as every inch of my bein' is cryin' out. "Well, I know just the thing. Hoist him up, my good man, and come along with me."

Martin helps me up amidst all manner of groanin', and we wanders off into the dark of the Singapore streets. It don't seem like it could be right, but it sounds like the admiral's whistlin'.

❧

The admiral tells me it won't hurt none and that's so, but I don't know nothin' else neither for two days. And when I can open my eyes again, my throat achin' for water, there's the sweetest face I ever seen starin' back at me.

"Decided to rejoin the living then," Dashwood says, and she hands me a cup, that sainted lady.

I gulp and sputter 'til it's empty, and I sees all the little places in her face that been stitched back up since the Snake tore 'em apart. There's even a bit o' silver in the top of her left ear.

"Where is we?" I asks, not wantin' to see the damage done in the light o' day just yet.

"Only a fool in my line of work doesn't have a second abode," chimes the admiral from across the room. "A second abode and a back door or two."

He minces over to stare into my face. He pokes and prods a bit 'til he's satisfied I'm as livin' as he can get me. "Most everyone got out, I think. Though, there are a few I haven't heard from yet. They may have gone into hiding, or Whipsnake may have caught them as they ran." A shadow passes over his face. "Of course, it did help that most everyone wasn't there when she sent it up in flames."

"What's she got against your lot?" I asks.

"Oh, a good number of them are victims of her training and days as a mercenary," he says, all matter-of-fact. "Whipsnake is not the only one who blames me for the path she was made to tread. I did what I could to make it right."

I looks about as he rambles, and it's all bamboo and thatch, with the sunlight seepin' through. Could be a good place for a rest were it not for me hand. I realize I'm layin' on a table so I tries to sit up, but I'm seein' all the stars a sailor ever sailed by, and gives it up.

Once me head clears, I decides that I had best get it over with. I looks down at me hand. It's a prettier thing now than it were in the flesh. Polished and hinged and strong as the steel it's forged from, and there, on the back, the cogged elephant is raisin' its trunk in triumph. I flex a time or two to test it, and it's the pain of the night I lost it and the fire shootin' through it all over again. I must moan somethin' terrible, 'cuz Dashwood just laughs.

"Easy there, Harris," says Cap'n, comin' up behind her. "It takes time before you can go sprinting off. At least, the admiral keeps insisting that's so." He ain't too steady on that new leg of his yet, neither. He has a stick 'stead of a man to prop him up, but you can see he's gonna be strong on it, come all the wrath of Poseidon.

"You're lucky that Martin fellow came running to find us, you know," says the admiral, liftin' my new hand, one finger at a time, admirin' each piece as he moves it. "I had enough time to do some of my very best work, I think."

"How did Martin know where's to find you, then?" I asks, to keep from hollerin' again.

"Oh, he didn't. He was just running towards the surgeon's street to find someone to patch up whoever was left," Cap'n says. "We got to the ship, crew told us you had gone to the admiral, so we made our way back. Ran into him just before he made his destination."

"Did we ever find where Beakman got hisself to?" I asks.

"Dead," says Dashwood, like she ain't too sorry 'bout it at all. "They found his body yesterday in a gutter behind that pub you were in. He must have gone to warn Whipsnake that the crew wasn't going to cooperate, and she never gave him the chance. Must have thought he was the one that told me she was here."

It's a miserable end, and no mistake, but his mutinous heart made it for him.

"And I just need you to try flexing the fingers again, please," says the admiral, and I can barely stand to do it, but each shinin' finger obeys my command. My pain makes me think of why I'm lying in a hut, dirtier than the admiral's first. My pain makes me angry, now.

"What happened to the Snake?" I asks.

Dashwood looks away, but the fury is still in her eyes. Cap'n pulls her close a moment.

"Li Dao Ming took her away that night," she says. "Maybe to nurse her, maybe to bury her. No one has seen either of them since."

It'd be just like a snake to slither to its burrow. Then again, when last I seen that witch, she weren't breathin' too well. It don't satisfy my loss—not yet—but if she's livin', we'll see her again. I may be a tired old sea dog, but I flex them fingers again, and think of what a hand of steel can do to a snake.

Styled after *Sense and Sensibility by Jane Austen*

Micawber and Copperfield

and the Great Diamond Heist of 1879

DAVID W. WILKIN

Helm, make your heading one-hundred-ten degrees. Blast it, man! I want to head *into* the wind! Another gust like the last and we'll be torn from the sky!" Commander Wilkins Micawber III shouted.

"Aye, sir!"

"Who's on the ailerons?" he asked. Sub-Lieutenant Bates had been, but Wilkins saw him injured, thrown heavily to the deck when the last hard gust hit. The young man had been helped below to the surgeon, and so another of his officers must have taken the man's place. There was always redundancy in the Royal Dirigible Corps.

Weller, the tall and broad boatswain, shouted over the howling winds, "The new middie, sir. Mr. Copperfield."

Wilkins turned but could not see that young man, just finishing his boyhood. He shouted, "I want a full fifteen degrees axis of climb, Mr. Copperfield, if you please! We must get above this blow!" There was a limit to the level to which they could rise. Too much, and the incline would be too steep for men to handle the ship.

Wilkins had been in storms before, and heavy winds, but none like this. A storm like this was a first for most of the crew of the *Golden Mary*. To those in the air, a wind storm was just as dangerous as to those still in the sea service. Men died in such conditions.

The *Golden Mary* was wracked again, moving yards to port as another gust hit them. If he could get the prow pointed dead on, he would slice into it. Yet, no wind blew straight. If he could get above it, then he might find respite.

A sharp pain coursed against his cheek. He used his left hand, for his right clutched at a rope, to feel his face. Wet. He saw the end of a halyard snaking around.

"Airman, catch that line!" Wilkins could not afford the time to wrangle it himself. A loose rope in the wind would go every way but to the person trying to get it. Wilkins would lose his concentration commanding the airship if he went for it himself.

The line would be dealt with. Wilkins saw from his vantage point on the quarterdeck one of the sailors trying to get forward without a rope attached. "Weller, that man! He must have a line." They were over eight hundred feet above the rolling veldt. Were the airman to be blown over the side, he would plummet to his death.

A matter of time only. Time to get out of the blow. Time

before a man made a mistake and got himself killed. Wilkins reviewed in his mind: could he do anything else? Should he have tried to dodge below the winds, releasing air from the balloons? Would that have been faster, safer?

And then, some few minutes later, he could feel the ship below him. A moment before, it had yanked about every time they encountered a gust. Finally, it began to rock. Still with a few yanks this way, or then the opposite way. But it was steadier.

"Mr. Gay, I think we are out of it," Wilkins said to the first lieutenant.

"Aye, Captain, it appears so."

"We'll give it a few hundred feet of elevation more, shall we, and then we can secure." Wilkins took a deep breath, then looked for his handkerchief to wipe the sweat from his forehead. His hand shook a little, but the action of doing something steadied him. Touching the handkerchief to his cheek, which still stung from the rope that had struck him, he looked at the white cloth and found that it was smeared with blood. He pressed the handkerchief back to his face to staunch the bleeding.

An hour later, he, Lieutenant Gay, and the Master, Mr. Bunsby, looked at the charts. The ship had been blown off course, and they would have to calculate a new solution. Did they have the coal? Was the ship sound, for it had taken a beating in that wind. They must reach the border between the Transvaal and Natal. Wilkins had not told his officers the complete reason for their mission yet, but if he could believe the admiral and Mr. Rhodes, the actions of the *Golden Mary* could prevent a war.

Wilkins remembered the previous day. It had been late in the day—the time he liked best—when not only the new midshipman had arrived, but Wilkins had been commanded to report to the admiral for orders. The water below the hull lapped gently against the pier. The dirigible docked at the quay while a more permanent landing field was built for the squadron.

Scanning the docks, he saw a young officer in his duty station blues, probably sweating and staining his collar, marching towards the ship. If not stiffly, certainly with a purpose. A stevedore followed and handled the young man's dunnage.

Wilkins was not much older than the officer, who had been in the Navy just long enough to have gotten himself out here from England. He would learn. That was what a midshipman did: learn.

"Permission to come aboard?" the young man asked. He mounted the scaffolding that led to the gantry. It weaved and bobbed as the air played hell with sails and balloon bag.

Wilkins smiled. The admiral had said the midshipman was no good for sea service. The only day the middie hadn't been sick on the transit from Plymouth had been when the steamship had found calm seas; hence a transfer to the most junior of services, Her Majesties' Royal Dirigible Corps.

A service not even a dozen years old, which occupied just three rooms in the Admiralty for offices, and with only a tad more than two thousand men to their roster. The entire fleet was comprised of six corvettes and twelve sloops. Still, aside from the Air Balloon Corps of the Confederate States of America, the most powerful Dirigible Corps in the skies.

"Aye, permission granted," Wilkins heard the duty officer, Sub-lieutenant Dawkins, say.

The young man must have saluted, and then marched to him.

"Commander Micawber, sir. Presenting Midshipman Copperfield, sir," Dawkins said. Dawkins was a good lad and had advanced from the ranks.

"Midshipman Daniel Copperfield reporting, sir!" A thin young man, no extra weight upon him, and perhaps an inch or so shorter than himself, Wilkins observed. Copperfield, aside from those sweat stains, presented rather well.

Wilkins smiled and thought how he had wanted the young man for his crew.

Saying to the midshipman, "What's this? A Copperfield? Really? Thank you, Dawkins. That will be all. You may stand at ease, Copperfield." Wilkins knew the boy's background. He had been well informed by the admiral, and other sources.

Midshipman Copperfield said, "Sir, yes, sir."

"Enough of all that sirring, Copperfield. We are a lot less formal here in the junior junior service." Wilkins smiled. "I expect you'll learn soon enough. Trouble on the sea, I understand? Well, I expect that of a Copperfield, seeing as your family has some history with the sea and great tragedy."

The young man seemed to struggle to grasp his meaning. Surely, Copperfield had to know of the bond. The admiral acted delighted when Wilkins had volunteered to take the midshipman, but surprised to find him so keen about it.

Wilkins took Copperfield to the railing and pointed towards

the city. Cape Town was growing by leaps and bounds each day, he thought. "Mr. Copperfield, I have three words for you."

He was eager, "Yes, sir? What are they, sir?"

"Barkis is willing!"

There was a blank look on Copperfield's face.

"Surely your family knows of the significance of such an oath?" Wilkins said.

"Sir, the words Barkis had said to propose marriage to Peggotty, the nurse? I thought that was just a legend."

"A legend? Indeed, sir, it is a legend. One that I think binds our families closer than any others. You surely do not think that it is coincidence that you are on the *Golden Mary*? It has to be the hand of Barkis, once again, true in all things."

Copperfield shook his head. Wilkins knew he had to explain, and, as the rest of the crew stood at a respectful distance, did so.

He signaled to Dawkins. "Do you know much of our service, Copperfield? No? Then I shall explain. When President Davis in the last year of the American Civil War approved the design of what they call balloons, dirigibles were born. Fearing the CSA's defeat, two of the designers, Texans, didn't want to live in the Union. They made their way to Australia. In fact, they made their way to Port Middlebay, where we Micawbers make our home. Still, Copperfield, you do not see the connection?" He had a lost look etched on his features.

Wilkins sighed. "My father is Wilkins Micawber II, who has been Lord Mayor of Port Middlebay three times, and owns a great part of the dirigible plant that manufactures the very ship we stand upon! It was thus natural that I, as a lad, helped to build these vessels, take service in them, and now, command one. I am the third of the name in our family. My own grandfather, president of the Bank of Port Middlebay and Magistrate, was once the greatest of friends of your grandfather, David Copperfield. Is that not known by you?"

Copperfield looked about surreptitiously. "Sir, I was instructed, as a lowly midshipman, that perhaps it was best not to make this known. Others might think that you were showing favoritism towards me. The Midshipman's Berth, as I have learned, is one of politics and pain."

Wilkins thought the young man sincere. He chose to believe a Copperfield would be the epitome of honesty and integrity.

"Quite right. I shall not treat you in any way special, but that our grandfathers were good friends, I believe they would be pleased that we serve together," Wilkins said.

They had ascended a hundred feet into the air. The motion was steady, as there were only very light winds, at the moment. The helmsman had angled the planes of the short wings to ensure that the rise had been smooth. The *Golden Mary* remained tethered to the dock. The line had played out gently. Every new midshipman and crewman was always put to the test with this maneuver.

In the sky, they contested against gale-force winds, as one did at sea. But the force of the waves tearing one in other directions was lacking. For the most part, the wind came at the ship from one direction at a time. No contest between Wind and Wave in an attempt to destroy a dirigible; at least none that Wilkins had found, as yet.

"Can you see Government House from here? I have been summoned there for tea, and so cannot spend such time as I would normally with a new officer. You and I have even more to talk of, our two families being known to one another. Patronage is still rife in the senior service, and of course, we are a shadow of them, as well. Though in the RDC, you will find that you have a greater opportunity to make a name for yourself, even if your father is the man responsible for building the fleet." Wilkins smiled.

Copperfield turned to look at the city, just noticing that they were suspended in the air. As with all new crew, Copperfield may never have ascended before his posting to the *Golden Mary*.

"Sir, you did not order the ship leave its moorings," Copperfield observed.

"I prearranged the order. What can you tell me of our present status?"

Wilkins put Copperfield, as a midshipman, to the test. In many circumstances, the technical management of the ship would fall into the man's charge. The lieutenants and sub-lieutenants were expected to know far more, but a midshipman would stand watch as they maneuvered through the air. And do so at night. Sub-lieutenants notoriously handed over their duty stations to the young gentlemen officers so that they could pursue their own sleep.

For the next fifteen minutes, Copperfield, without showing

any signs that he did not have his air-legs, recited all that he had observed. What weight of sail they carried. The air displacement of the balloon envelope, with its six triple-encased inner balloons, two only a quarter inflated to give them such lift. The steam engine, filling the bags, required just one stoker in the engine room.

The ship flew exactly one hundred and seven feet above sea level, per the altimeter. The propellers idled; they were not making way. Half the mid-watch was on deck, the rest dispersed about the ship. Aside from certain warrant officers, the crew distributed between three watches. Each watch served four hours, and then had eight hours off. One of the double periods off, the crew slept. Often, when observing their 'day,' the crew would attend to duties the ship required.

"Very good, Mr. Copperfield. Mr. Bates, if you please, we shall descend," Wilkins called to another of the officers on deck. Moments later, the ship lay along the dock once more. "Now, I am to Government House. Mr. Weller, I believe you have secured transportation?"

Weller had been with him since he had been a sub-lieutenant in Australia, and there was no man more reliable. He was the ship's boatswain as well. None of the men would cross the imposing bo'sun. Weller stood three inches taller than him, and half again broader in the shoulders. The man was a giant. Wilkins thought himself fortunate to have a good relationship with him.

He turned to encompass all the officers on the bridge in his briefing, "And gentlemen, when I return, I believe the addition of our new midshipman calls for a batch of punch from my grandfather's recipe." All his officers liked that indulgence. All of them.

෴

Upon his return from Government House, Wilkins retired to his quarters to change hurriedly. Then he came forward, the captain's quarters always in the stern of the ship, a tradition from the sea-going ships of the fleet. The bridge stood at the prow, an arse-over-tit design if ever there was one, but he had gotten used to it long ago. He did agree that visibility was much improved when charting one's course from the front of the airship rather than from the rear.

The watch officers gathered so that he could issue orders and brief them on parts of what he had learned—but only a part. Not all of it.

During inclement weather, this new class of ship had metal posts that were placed about the deck, then walls fitted to them, and a roof, so that the bridge became enclosed. As it was warm, summer in the Southern Hemisphere, the walls were in stowage, whilst the sun's hot rays were kept from their heads by the balloon bag.

"Gentlemen, we leave for Pretoria at speed! All leaves cancelled and the complement to be gathered for making sail before dusk. I wish to be up and underway no later than sixteen hundred." Wilkins knew his officers were surprised by the orders. Sunset was but a few short hours away.

"We can still dine at eighteen hundred as planned. I am in need of your company and a round of punch to settle my nerves from our orders. Which I shall reveal in due course.

"Mr. Gay, I believe these constitute sufficient orders to keep you busy this little while?" When they gathered, once underway, Wilkins would tell them of his meeting with the admiral, as well as Mr. Cecil Rhodes.

Gay had the watch. "Aye aye, sir. If you please, there are not many hours for us to raise steam for launching at sixteen hundred. I shall attend to the matters of preparing for departure at once. Mr. Copperfield, and Mr. Wemmick, please attend. We will have to conduct a muster of the crew . . ."

Wilkins turned his attention to Jack Dawkins, the ablest of his sub-lieutenants in navigation. He, Dawkins, and the Master, Mick Bunsby, went to plot their new course.

Even should the winds blow against them somewhat, with a good compass and altitude, one could make transit with minute adjustments to their destination. Pretoria: a location that was readily marked on their charts. The biggest worry was stopping for coal at Kimberley.

"We will have to make our way to the depot at Beaufort West," Wilkins said. The depot, only built within the last six months, they had flown their way to it once before.

"The railway still has not reached it, but it is near the middle of any sprint to Kimberley. We should reach it late in the day tomorrow, the winds holding steady," Bunsby said.

Wilkins nodded to this. "True, but one can never count on

the winds to do what they should. That is the first leg; then to Kimberley. And there, we will have to watch the men extra carefully."

Dawkins grinned. The sub-lieutenant commanded the detail that brought the crew back from liberty when they last ventured to Kimberley. There were more than forty thousand inhabitants in that mining town, which meant it was a big town. A city. One filled with vices that miners and airmen each found tempting— and had partaken of, for it took three days to restore the crew to order previously.

Fortunately, the ladies who enticed the crew to frolic while on leave at Cape Town charged rates that were more conducive to the money the airmen had in their pockets. Wilkins knew such ladies of pleasure in Kimberley could cost twenty-five pounds for an evening's entertainment—a significant cost for a captain's wages, and far beyond the means of the men.

And yet, because he had given the airmen leave, they loved him the more for it. Even when he sent Dawkins and a detail to get all to return to the ship, they loved him for it.

Australia's gold rush of the forties and fifties prepared Wilkins for what happened to men who hoped to strike it rich. He told his crew that more ended in poverty than in wealth. The truest way to riches was to sell shovels and stakes to miners. Sell them for claims and what money the miners had. Soon enough, he reflected, storekeepers could be holders of claims like Mr. Rhodes and other magnates.

Three airmen had been forcibly brought back to the ship,

having tried their best to jump. Two weeks in the brig reminded them that the RDC was not a hardship. Working the *Golden Mary*, even when three thousand feet in the air, was rewarding.

When the officers, except for Sub-lieutenant. Bates, who had the watch, assembled in his stateroom in the aft of the ship, Wilkins stood to welcome young Copperfield amongst them. The *Golden Mary* had room for only four junior officers. He had made room for Copperfield when he learned of his predicament. He could do no more. Copperfield, if true to the many legends Micawber had heard about Copperfields, would either fly or fall on his own.

"Gentlemen, before we have our toasts and you shall try this excellent punch I have blended, I will impart to you the details of our mission. As my grandfather always says, remember our family motto. '*Nil Desperandum*! Never despair!'"

Wilkins then explained how the admiral had sent him to meet with the legendary Mr. Rhodes. Then, he told his officers of the theft of the diamonds from Natal, to be retrieved as quickly as they could, ensuring the Army remain above the fray. They would get the diamonds back without the Boers complaining the British violated their sovereignty, although the annexation of the Transvaal meant there was no sovereignty to violate. The Boers seemed to have a different interpretation of what Sir Theophilus Shepstone had done when he had annexed the country.

"The admiral believes that our ability to travel swiftly provides opportunity to recover the diamonds and return before anyone suspects that they are missing." Wilkins did not add that success would forestall the Transvaal's eruption into war. And failure would lead to the very opposite.

When finished, Sub-lieutenant Dawkins stood to be noticed. "Sir, if I may, before the junior officer proposes the loyalty toast . . ." Dawkins looked to young Copperfield, for it would be his duty, his commission as midshipman most recently advanced, "I would offer us all another of your famous sayings."

"Of course, yes, of course. Nothing we old men like hearing better than ourselves quoted back. Shows you young sots really respect us and all." Dawkins was just a few years younger. The Master, Bunsby, easily twice their age, snorted, restraining a bark of laughter. On the bridge, he no doubt would have indulged in it.

Dawkins raised his glass. "Then, 'Welcome poverty! Welcome misery, welcome houselessness, welcome hunger, rags, tempest, and beggary! Mutual confidence will sustain us to the end!' I have always interpreted this to mean that if we rely upon each other when called to do so in service to Her Majesty, all will turn out for the best."

Wilkins hoped his young gentlemen understood that to be so. His grandfather had kept the Bank of Port Middlebay solvent during the crash of '73 with such attention. "Quite right. Quite right. You will have to give the young man credit, Mr. Bunsby, that he knows a little something."

"Bah, I shall give him that he knows little!" Bunsby reached for his drink, then stopped and looked determinedly at young Copperfield.

"Of course," Wilkins noted, "Mr. Copperfield, it is your duty to begin. Mr. Chairman," who was Dawkins, as well, "you must conduct things. The loyalty toast."

Copperfield got his nod from Dawkins and stood. "Captain, Mr. Chairman, gentlemen, I give you, Her Majesty, Queen Victoria. Long may she reign!"

The rest of the gentlemen pushed back their seats to stand, and followed Wilkins' arm as he raised his own glass and uttered the same words. While he only took a sip, Bunsby, as was his wont, along with Dr. Sawyer, knocked back the entire glass. It was to be a long night, and both men, the Commander knew, would have heavy heads the following day.

Captain Micawber acted indulgently to Daniel Copperfield and the other midshipmen since they had left Cape Town. They were two days out, and—all things being equal—things proceeded well despite the blow.

However, at Kimberley, the Captain had said he was going to offer leave. The men knew they were going to face the Boers, and likely combat, something that they had trained for, but had not actually had to do yet.

"Is that Kimberley, sir?" Daniel asked Captain Micawber.

"It is. It is, indeed. We shall coal up overnight and then be gone at dawn."

"But, sir, we can fly quite easily at night. Isn't that a strength of the RDC?"

"Instead of slaving away and taking two hours to top the bins, we shall spend the night and allow the crew to entertain themselves. They will have four hours in each watch to do so. The punishment, should they be tardy, is well understood."

Daniel nodded. The cat of nine tails was long gone, but they still whipped an airman for desertion. Being a second late returning from leave could bring a sentence of ten lashes. Midshipmen still were made to kiss the gunner's daughter.

The captain explained part of command meant knowing when to be strict, and when to appease the crew. Even with leave, the ship had time to intercept the Boer thieves before they found safety in the Transvaal.

The *Golden Mary* could reach Pretoria with what coal they had, but might not fly much farther. Captain Micawber reminded Daniel that Pretoria was in the hands of the Empire just then. If things became volatile, they might not be able to get more coal there.

The *Golden Mary* had spent two hours at Beaufort West tipping up the coal bins into the lowest stowage. Daniel had overseen that last part in the hold, even scooping several shovelfuls, showing the men that he was capable of exertion. The coal came down a chute and had to be distributed evenly by manual shovel work.

The two large propellers powered by the steam engines allowed the dirigible to choose its course, rather than rely upon unpredictable winds to bring it to its destination. The propellers allowed the *Golden Mary* to reach speeds of over twenty miles each hour. Steam power changed the world. Land, sea, and air travel, all at constants, and faster than man had ever known. It was an amazing age.

Captain Micawber sent Daniel up the mast so he could use a glass and get a better view of the city as they approached. Kimberley was getting better, he had been assured, even from when the *Golden Mary* had docked there a few months before. Over the last few years, the town had progressed from chaos to a large city.

Last porting, some men had tried to jump ship. This time, Captain Micawber said he prayed no one would be so tempted. Daniel, though, believed they would be. The *Golden Mary* did not have the luxury to stay at length and see to those men who would test the captain.

From the lookout came a shout, "Ship ho!" and that led to scurrying about. Daniel turned his glass to that part of the city the lookout was pointing towards.

"Where away?" Lieutenant Gay had the duty below and called up to the lookouts on the mast.

"She hovers near the city center. She's large, sir." As they neared, the image became clearer and Daniel saw in his own glass what he had not thought to see.

The German ship, the *Frederick*, that they had heard was operating in Africa, moored at Kimberley. The *Golden Mary* had twenty-four guns. There were thirty-six twelve-pounders aboard the *Frederick*. It was longer and had one more deck than the *Golden Mary*. Daniel believed the *Mary* much more maneuverable, though.

Captain Micawber called the crew together as they neared the square where they would drop to the ground and the coal stores. "The enemy is here. And you all know whom I mean. I am placing my trust in you, men, that you can enjoy your liberty without revealing what we are about. You all are in our confidence about how important this mission is. The Germans must not find out, for if they do, I would hazard they would interfere. They should dearly love for us to fight another war, since we just finished one. And the German Emperor would no doubt wish to add this very rich land as his own. Though his son is married to our Empress' daughter, I do not think that would stop the man and his minions, like Bismarck, from trying to take our diamond mines."

None of the men said anything. This wasn't a dialogue.

The captain's instructions, before they left the ship and got themselves into trouble, were to be followed. In hindsight, Daniel wondered why the captain had not kept secret his orders about the thieves and the diamonds. But aboard a ship, the only secrets were those that were unshared with another. The ship, as big as it was, was still small, where the only privacy one had was when at the heads.

And in the Dirigible Corps, naval architects had to modify their design. Since the quarterdeck had moved forward, the heads were no longer positioned there, nor were they free to the open sea or air. One could not take care of their needs as if on a sea-ship for an airship could be traveling over a city or village.

"Let me leave you with these words, men: you will be tempted to spend what monies you have. I hope the city shall open its arms to us as it did when last we ported here, but it may not. The amenities you seek may be quite costly. Annual income twenty pounds, annual expenditure nineteen pounds nineteen and six, result happiness. Annual income twenty pounds, annual expenditure twenty pounds ought and six, result misery.

"Watch that which is in your pockets, for we have other ports we shall reach, and we shall return to our berth in Cape Town, where you can acquire nearly all that you find here, and much the cheaper as well."

Lieutenant Gay pulled Daniel aside. "Copperfield, you and Jarndyce will be refilling the coal bins during our first port watch. You will have liberty during the second, as will Dawkins, who shall be overseeing the coaling operation. I advise you that Jarndyce might be inclined to test the boundaries one finds at a port like Kimberley, yet he can well-afford to do so. However, I caution our other midshipmen to spend such leave with most of their money left here with the quartermaster, and with their hands shoved as far down their pockets as able."

Sub-lieutenant Dawkins had overheard. "If you will allow, lieutenant, I shall take Daniel under my wing. You will recall that I am somewhat familiar with the town, and should be able to steer our young friend to places where he shall be in only the best circumstances."

The older lieutenant looked to Dawkins. "Mind the captain's words. This time, we have made few preparations and may not have the same kindness extended to us as our last liberty here."

Dawkins nodded and it seemed all arranged.

Two hours of hard work after they ported saw the hold filled with coal. Enough to get to Pretoria and return to Kimberley, should such be needed. And more than an hour for him to clean up and make himself presentable. Working with coal left those in the deepest part of the hold as black as night. The coal dust inevitably flew all about the confined space.

When Daniel and Dawkins made their way to the gantry and down the stairs, they noted several of the airmen from the *Frederick* nearby, clustering at their own gantry. Two Royal Marines stood at the foot of the *Golden Mary*'s stairs and came smartly to attention as he and the older officer left.

"I shall show you around, Copperfield. And though none can consider themselves truly at home in such a rough and tumble environment as Kimberley, I know of some few places where the innkeeper shall sell us liquor at reasonable prices. A man in uniform is sometimes very good to be seen through the window having a drink, for it calms the clientele. Other times, it is not so good, but our uniforms are a novelty, at least, anywhere inland."

The two men soon made their way through streets, which were really just dirt that had rivulets of mud throughout, to the Three Cripples Tavern.

"Now, I ask you, young Copperfield, where are our rights? We are Englishmen and here we are in the furthest reaches of the Empire. Were we not in uniform, we should be treated lower than low where the only thing of value is the money in your pocket. And I have lived like that before."

"Sir?"

"London, Copperfield. London. You are familiar with the place? And call me Jack, when we are off like this."

Dawkins and he forked over near a pound for a pitcher of beer. Foul-tasting as beers go, the stores onboard ship were better. At eighteen shillings, it cost nearly ten times more than Cape Town. Not that Daniel had much time to have noticed, having only been in that city for two days himself before ordered to report aboard the *Golden Mary*.

"Not as good as we would find in London," Lieutenant Dawkins said. "And not as cheap either."

"Is that where you come from? London?"

Dawkins smiled, "I did. Born there and lived there for most of my younger life. I knew the streets as well as I know my hand here. But my old guv'nor shook me hard one day and got me a place on a ship. Cost him and me a fortune, then. A veritable fortune. He made an atonement and I will state I am the better for it."

Daniel knew that London had many areas that were less than gentle. He suspected that Dawkins knew of them. His own grandfather, David, had spoken that he had been sent to such by Mr. Murdstone in his youth.

"Do you think that we shall see much action?" Daniel asked.

Dawkins looked about before answering, "A war having just concluded here against the Zulus, I am not sure we shall, and then, who would we fight? The Germans do have their airship, as you have seen, and the Belgians, I believe, are also close enough that they could reach us in a day or two with their own dirigible. For there is naught but a dirigible that could challenge us. Unlike the Navy, we have an entire new dimension—height—that we deal with. Aside from some raiding that the squadron in Cairo is doing, the RDC has yet to be placed in combat."

"I understand that, Jack." Daniel said. "Captain Micawber talks of his friends who fled the Confederate States of America, and how they once fought an air battle."

"I should not wish that on anyone. Or to be below it, should it occur. Things have a terrible habit of falling from the sky to the ground, including men swept off ships. No one—no one at all—survives such a plunge. Whether there is water below you, or something you pray will break your fall, no one survives. Even if we are landed, there is forty feet from the deck to the ground, and that would kill you as well, should you fall over the side."

Daniel knew the dangers in the RDC, like dangers elsewhere, but they had built ships with guns to fire on other ships. The *Frederick* here in Kimberley showcased that.

"Blast," Lieutenant Dawkins said, and used his head to indicate Daniel needed to look somewhere.

Turning, he saw German airmen had entered. "Sir, those men were at the airfield when we left." There was another man, dressed as a gentleman, with them.

"Yes, they've followed us. I expect all our crewmen on leave have been followed. I should advise the captain to cancel our leaves, but there is now really no way we can. Best we finish our drink and head back. Captain Micawber will want to ascend at dawn, and if the Germans are going to follow us all night, I expect the evening is ruined."

Daniel nodded. "That is fine, sir. Even with an allowance, I am not sure that I can afford these Kimberley prices for more than one pitcher."

A moment later, instead of reaching for his drink, Dawkins half rose and waved. Daniel turned again and saw Midshipman Jarndyce and Bo'sun Weller. The bo'sun said, as he sat, "Good, beer for us'm as well." Then he leaned quietly in. "Noticed 'em sauerkrauts following ye from the airfield and thought us'm should be following 'em. Mr. Jarndyce was kind enough to join us."

Dawkins said, "Good for you, Jarndyce. I thought we should finish here quickly and then return to the ship. Tell the captain."

The bo'sun shook his head. "Do ye notice that cove, dressed all fine? Do ye be knowing 'im?"

Dawkins looked—stared, actually—at the Germans and the well-dressed man, and then he nodded. "Manuel Antonio de Sousa, Gouveia. The Portuguese poohbah."

Daniel noted a sour look on both Weller and Jarndyce's faces. "That rum cove again. He's at the root of every evil there be here in Africa! And traveling with the sauerkrauts . . ." Weller said.

"The captain will want to know," Jarndyce said

"Yes, he will, but first we are going to have to get back to the ship, and I think those airmen, and Gouveia, have other plans for us." Dawkins said. "Drink up, and then, well, we will have to disrupt their plans, one way or another."

Daniel tried to think what Lieutenant Dawkins meant. How they could disrupt what plans the Germans would have for them? Aside from the richly dressed man, there was one junior officer and four airmen. Six to four, and from the way the bo'sun looked, and cracked his knuckles, the near future likely would hold some sort of rough-housing.

By his upbringing, Daniel believed that the lower orders engage in such. But, Dawkins, Jarndyce and he were officers, and the bo'sun a leader who set an example for the airmen of the *Golden Mary*. The look on Jarndyce's face showed that he was looking forward to a brawl as well.

Dawkins eyed him. "You look apprehensive, Mr. Copperfield. Have you not had your share of fights in this lifetime already? You did go to school, did you not? I did not have that luxury, but my friend Jarndyce has often told me that the boys of the lower forms learn to defend themselves over time."

Daniel shook his head. "Yes, of course I learned to defend myself. I placed third in our pugilist championships last year at school. But I suspect there will be rather fewer rules. And there are more Germans then there are of us."

Jarndyce chuckled, and Bo'sun Weller cracked his knuckles again. Then he reached for his mug of beer and drained it. Dawkins rose and said, "There are only two rules. Don't get killed is the first. The second, don't kill them."

Daniel smiled, joining the others in rising from the table. "So, there is some sportsmanship involved?"

Weller laughed, "Sportsmanship? No, young mister. The

lieutenant just doesn't want to be answering the hard questions to a magistrate should there be any bodies left about." And then the bo'sun seemed to find his hand stuck under the table where the Germans sat.

Dawkins had a hand on the lip of a chair that he was picking up. Jarndyce had the empty pitcher in his hand. A moment later, Weller's hand forced up the table, and pandemonium ensued.

Dawkins crashed the chair against the back of one of the German sailors. Jarndyce brained another with the pitcher.

"Even odds now, eh, Daniel?" Jarndyce said.

Daniel did not have time to respond as one of the airmen stormed toward him, easily three stone heavier, and with longer arms. Daniel took a hurried step backwards to avoid being hit, even crushed, by such a punch. He waited for his moment, the best offense against such a large opponent.

The man Daniel faced raged that two of his comrades were down, and would make mistakes. Howsoever unprepared, Daniel and his friends had the element of surprise.

Daniel kept his forearms up like gates of a fort that blocked the enemy's battering ram. Pain shot through his forearms each time his opponent hit, but he preferred that to strikes in the face.

In less than thirty seconds, the man had swung several times. With another blow coming high, Daniel would have a moment to land a solid shot to the man's solar plexus. From there, all sorts of combinations might become available.

Daniel blocked the incoming blow with his left forearm, and

then wound back and shot forward into the man's middle. The German gasped for air even as Daniel recovered his defense.

From the left, Daniel heard Jarndyce yell. "Blast. You damn sauerkraut!"

Daniel couldn't spare a moment for his fellow midshipman. He thrust at the German again. With his left fist, Daniel jabbed a punch. The German had left an opening.

Daniel aimed for the chin. He would use leverage, the chin extended, to apply torque. The man would spin to the left when the face went that way.

Daniel, though, found his aim off, or the man had moved his head a little. Daniel hit the man in his right orbital socket. He could feel the give of the German's eye as it rolled back. A sickening feeling in his stomach and something he knew caused as much pain or more as any other solid blow.

The man staggered back a half step, and Daniel knew it was best to follow through. One, two, three hits to the ribs. Then two solid blows to the face, and this time one connected with the chin, forcing the man to start turning.

Daniel did not think his opponent would fall, but the man came crashing down. Bo'sun Weller had put out his leg to trip him. Weller's opponent hugged the ground, crawling off. The fight looked like it was over.

"There now, Mr. Copperfield, ye has done well, sir. Better than Mr. Jarndyce who will be favoring 'is side there." Weller said.

Dawkins put the man, de Sousa, in a chair. "You just sit there and rest, Mr. de Sousa. Rest and think about spying on Her Majesty's officers. We both know that you are not supposed to be doing that. And consorting with these Germans. Men who instigated a barroom brawl with airmen of the RDC.

"Barkeep, Mr. de Sousa has agreed to pay for your damages, though should the constables come; these men might need a night in the city cells to cool their tempers."

Dawkins had a small billfold and took some currency from it, then gave it back to the hands of the Portuguese man. He looked in his late fifties when Daniel could see him closer.

"I am sorry that we cannot join you for a round of drinks, Mr. de Sousa, but you will understand if we return to our ship." Dawkins smiled again.

Then they hurried to the *Golden Mary*.

"Did ye manage to get anything worthwhile, Mr. Dawkins?" Weller asked as they raced back to the ship.

"Bo'sun Weller, you do not think that I would resort to my former trade? I am one of Her Majesty's officers!"

"Aye sir, and of course, them leopards ain't be losing any spots, now."

"Well, we shall just tell the captain that certain items fell from the pockets of Mr. de Sousa. I might have picked them up when they fell, and plumb forgot to return them."

Lieutenant Dawkins removed from his jacket a sheaf of papers and proudly waved them about. Daniel had to wonder exactly what kind of education the lieutenant had gained in the streets of London.

Captain Micawber wasted little time in recalling the crew from leave and readying the *Golden Mary* for flight. He retired to his cabin to look at the papers that Lieutenant Dawkins had retrieved.

Two hours later, the captain paced on the starboard side of the quarterdeck. He ordered Weller, the bo'sun, to compile a roll of who had not yet returned to the ship. Daniel noted twelve missing the last quarter hour before the watch ended. One of those, a man who had tried to jump ship the last time the *Golden Mary* was in port in Kimberley.

Lieutenant Gay called Daniel over. "Aloft with you, Mr. Copperfield. It will be day soon and we will ascend. Your station is in the crow's nest. There might be enough light for you to look about the streets of the city and see if any of our lads are trying to reach the ship."

Daniel climbed up to his post. He learned later that a short debate had occurred amongst the captain and his officers. They could prepare to ascend promptly at dawn, or start preparations to ascend immediately, giving stragglers a few more minutes to return to the ship. The captain chose the latter, yet when the mooring lines were cast off and steam raised in the balloons to send them aloft, four men hadn't returned to the ship.

Daniel did see from his glass two large parties of Germans struggling back to their own ship, with men in the groups clearly drunk and being carried. That had not happened amongst the men of the *Golden Mary*, though a few were unsteady on their feet.

Daniel and the lookouts reported what they saw. It was fairly evident the *Frederick* prepared to make way, as well. It was the laws of science that it took an idling steam engine a quarter hour to more than two hours to fill the balloons. A good deal of time to where they would create hot air to lift a ship to reach the highest it could go. The German ship would be left behind.

There was much speculation on the *Fredrick's* capabilities, for it was a larger ship, and of course had a heavier weight of shot. That could be telling, for even should a good part of the broadside hit, they would feel it. Though gunnery practice, which Daniel had yet to partake of, had showed the inertia a ship of the Navy displaced was absorbed by the waves of the ocean. In the sky, the blast of a cannon pushed against the ship and caused it to alter its place in the sky.

To those on a dirigible, it felt much like jumping about on the ground. And the more guns firing at the same, or near the same time, caused the ship to take much bigger jumps.

That they had seen the German getting up steam, even as the *Golden Mary* made way, warranted gunnery practice that day. The captain briefed the officers after the course was laid in. A slight change to course had been made. They steered not for Pretoria, but for a bank of clouds.

The Captain said he hoped the clouds would be big enough for them to get lost in, else, he said, "We shall have to lose these fellows this night, which is easily done, just as if we were at sea. We shall have to run with no light, of course, for here, in the sky without clouds on such a night, a light can be seen for miles. We do not head for Pretoria directly, gentlemen."

The captain pointed to a spot on the chart. "Lieutenant Bagnell and I have thought that we need to patrol this area. The men who have taken the diamonds should be reaching this area sometime no sooner than tomorrow. I know it encompasses a lot of empty space, but we have a great platform that can see for scores of miles from the sky. I intend that we should espy any caravan of men, and then set down and question them. Even search them, should it be necessary to do so."

Lieutenant Gay spoke up. "Sir, such men will have rights, and they will be armed."

"They do have rights, but we shall be armed as well. Cannister and grape will play hell from our twelve pounders. The Marines also have a few sharpshooters, I believe. Is that not so, Lieutenant Bagnell?"

"Yes, sir," the Royal Marine commander replied.

"We shall make it seem innocuous enough. Ensign Baldrick, Mr. Copperfield, and Mr. Weller shall head the party." Why Captain Micawber chose him was a mystery. The man said he did not plan to play favorites based on their ancient connection.

The captain explained. "Can't afford any of you lieutenants should we have to fire, and you young gentlemen, Copperfield is the oldest man amongst you. These Boers, I expect, will be older still. Even older than Mr. Bunsby."

That brought a smile, but it did not bode well for the junior warrants' mess, where the midshipmen ate. Daniel knew that the rest of the midshipmen would be upset. He also knew, if they could not see it, going amongst the Boers they found would be very dangerous. Perhaps a chance to win glory, but more of a chance to win a bullet. He had not been in country a week, and he knew the Boers were considered excellent marksmen.

They shot from greater distances than soldiers of the Army or Royal Marines, with much better accuracy. With the Zulu War over, perhaps it was expected that there would be a war against the Boers.

Daniel had three hours sleep before he was crudely awakened by Jarndyce. "Hurry, you bleedin' nummie. The call is clear for action and you've already lost three minutes!" Jarndyce was laying it on.

All the other midshipman had to do was get aloft with the top-men. Jarndyce had bruised ribs from the fight at the Three Cripples, so had light duty. Daniel oversaw the gun crews' readiness, clearing the decks of all the crew's dunnage in the middeck. Midshipmen lived a deck below that, and their space, if needed, would be turned over to Mr. Sawyer and the surgery.

During gun practice, few injuries resulted for the doctor to respond to. With a few seconds to spare, Daniel joined Lieutenant Dawkins in the middle of the deck, and saw that Wemmick had taken care of the starboard side of the ship. Gunner's mate Tartar had taken care of the port watch, the half of the deck that nominally reported to Daniel. All was well and ready with them.

Sub-Lieutenant Dawkins said to him, "Right. The captain is going to look for two things: accuracy and speed. We don't have an up-roll; no seas to contend with. Just the wind and the force of our own making. If we could, we would fire guns on opposite sides of the ship at the same instance. The force would cancel itself out, but then half of the ordinance would fly off to no avail, and we already have spoken about those on the ground below, if there should be anyone below, are apt to not appreciate such gestures. A twelve-pound ball makes a small crater when it lands on the ground. The higher up we are, the larger the crater."

New books were being written about gunnery practice in the sky, and more math was used to triangulate where the guns were to be aimed. Simple balloons, with weights, often were sent off and the ship moved a little further on, before doubling back for the practice. But should shot hit the balloon, as it frequently did, then another launched from the ship. Hence, triangulation and mathematics. The captain asked that shot be aimed for a space, often a hundred yards ahead of the balloons, and all would train their glasses to see how well the crews achieved this.

Daniel had participated in gunnery practice while at sea, in transit to the South African station. He found it shatteringly noisy on the dirigible, as it had been aboard a seagoing vessel. Yet with care and attention to detail, the shots rang truer. One less dimension of calculation that was more art than craft. There was no effect of waves upon the shot.

Captain Micawber's displeasure at the results was noticeable. His foul mood showed in his appearance and choice of words. He had much to say to Lieutenant Gay. They did this in the captain's cabin, the door closed. Yet ships are built thinly, so what was said was overheard by one crewman or another.

The captain asserted that their accuracy was fine, but the

British Navy ruled the waves, and, he hoped, the sky, from the speed of their delivery of such shot. The British always got away three or four volleys, outpacing their enemies' two. It meant that a ship with fewer weight of shot could defeat a larger ship.

That, every schoolboy knew to be true.

Something Daniel turned his mind to. Six gun crews were his responsibility on the middeck. He talked to the gun captains that evening after supper, and also the gunner's mate for his watch. Daniel worried action might be soon. Throughout the day, they could not shake the sight of the *Frederick* tracking them.

Night came, and darkness. Every five minutes, give or take, the captain ordered a light be put out. It took two hours, the ship becoming blackened. Three lights remained, and the captain ordered the apparatus that the carpenter had put together.

The *Frederick* followed three or more miles behind. They could clearly see lights on the ship which followed them.

"Light the decoy, and prepare to douse our lights," Captain Micawber ordered.

The three lights on the decoy were set, and the last lights aboard the *Golden Mary* then doused. The decoy was set to go forward on the course they had been heading with the wind, and generally towards Pretoria, while the ship went helm over and rose higher, with the making of more steam in the last of the six balloons.

To curb the noise the ship made, when they reached their new elevation, the propellers were turned off, and the steam engine idled. The ship lost altitude but was now on a new course. The sails also were brought down to eliminate the sound of their flapping in the wind. For three quiet hours they watched as the *Frederick's* lights passed on the old course, on its way to Pretoria.

Daniel, once more in the crow's nest, noted even with the looking glass, after the third hour, he could no longer see the lights of the German ship. Captain Micawber walked the bridge and nodded when he was apprised of this information. Daniel sought his bunk and sleep. He would wake with the first light and the landing duty, should there be any Boer parties to stop.

In the morning, their position was hundreds of miles south of Pretoria, along the route that the Captain seemed sure the men who had stolen the diamonds would travel. Captain Micawber confided in Ensign Baldrick, and him, "I did not question Mr. Rhodes, but he seemed well-informed as to the makeup of the thieves and their plans. That he knew this in Cape Town two days after it had occurred in Durban is due, of course, to the telegraph. That he knew so much can only be due to what Mr. Rhodes has made it his business to know. More than three hundred Boer men voted for annexation of the Transvaal. One can believe Mr. Rhodes has friends amongst them."

Daniel though thought Mr. Rhodes might be quite dangerous if he tried to keep one foot in each camp. "Sir, twelve men, heavily armed—that shall be a challenge."

"Yes. But I have confidence in you young men. And when you return with the diamonds, I shall invite the wardroom to my cabin where I shall make punch and we shall have a toast, eh?"

Two parties passed below, traveling north, while there was

one traveling the road south. The northern-bound two had cattle, wagons, kaffirs. Captain Micawber ruled them out, though Daniel thought it could be the enemy they sought in disguise. Then the lookouts called out that another party was sighted fitting the description of the vagrants they looked for.

Captain Micawber took them to the ground, and Daniel, with the search party, quickly moved to encounter the riders, a group of people not happy to be met, but they had little to hide. A family party, and most of them were British—something not easily ascertained from miles away in the sky.

Less than an hour later, another party was spotted, and once again, the *Golden Mary* and her crew sank from the sky to investigate. This time, a party of Boer men, but they were farmers. Daniel realized that almost all Boer men were farmers, but he felt certain those who stole diamonds would seem much more guilty than these.

Three hours later, another group of travelers looked as if they could be the ones they were searching for.

The *Golden Mary* descended, with the sun directly behind them, allowing an element of surprise. Circling over the riders, Lieutenant Gay ordered the dozen horsemen, once more Boers, to hold fast. Some cannons were trained on them, and a few Marines with their guns aimed towards the party. Ensign Baldrick and Daniel descended ropes to the ground, with six marines, six airmen, and the bo'sun, Mr. Weller.

"I say, you men, we are conducting a search and must ask you to empty your pockets and show us what is in your saddlebags. I am afraid it's quite important," Ensign Baldrick called.

One Boer on a horse closest to the party from the *Golden Mary* said, "Damn Englishers. You have no right." The man then spoke in his own language to the other riders.

Daniel spoke up. "We have a ship with more than two-hundred men and twenty-four cannon that says we do have such a right. We do not want to use force against you, but there are men of your nation who want us to be at war. They have done a thing to provoke such. And as you are aware, war causes men such as us to become killers. It is rather unpleasant." Daniel had pulled out his sword. "Be a good man, now, and empty your pockets."

The man on the horse looked once more to his cohorts and said something in Afrikaans again. He then spat a large gob to the ground.

Daniel had advanced on the man close enough that he could smell him. The Boer stank, as if he had been living rough for some time. It reminded Daniel of the sick, sweet smell of decay, when the vegetables aboard ship went bad.

This close, Daniel could see the man's skin was hardened leather from years under the African sun. A scar ran from his forehead down the left side of his face towards his ear.

"What's in your pockets?" Daniel asked once more.

"Nah. I shall not show you, damn Englisher," the Boer said, and reached into his coat.

Daniel saw a pistol being pulled forth. He jumped forward and slashed against the back of the man's right arm with his sword. A shot fired from the gun. The Boer screamed in agony and gripped at his wounded arm. The gun dropped to the ground as blood from the slash sprayed in the air. The muscles in the Boer's forearm were severed. He would never hold anything in that hand again.

The airmen and marines instantly brought their own weapons to bear, yet, the Boers pulled their guns as well. Shots rang out.

Daniel stood next to the horse, which gave him cover. The men from the *Golden Mary* took their shots, then crouched down as they reloaded.

A second round of shots began to ring out. The man that Daniel had wounded kicked him in the shoulder. The horse jumped. Daniel could not tell which side was shooting. Both, no doubt!

Daniel struggled with the Boer, who aimed another kick at him. Daniel struck the foot with his sword, then slashed at the stirrup leather once, twice, hitting the horse as well.

The injured horse jumped, and Daniel knew he could become badly injured. More than a thousand pounds of horse could crush him. The Boer kicked at Daniel's head. Daniel reached up and pulled the man's foot. The Boer fell out of the saddle and Daniel threw him to the ground.

Daniel could see how the battle was progressing. Four other Boers remained unwounded. The landing party readied to fire again. The Boers, still able to fight, defied the overwhelming odds.

Or perhaps they wanted to be martyrs.

One enemy aimed, fired, and hit Ensign Baldrick. Baldrick's last order had the Marines firing into the air. Calling for them to 'put up you damn fools! Put up your arms!'

All but two Boers surrendered, then. One of the last Boers pointed his rifle straight at Daniel and was shot dead. A marksman from the *Golden Mary* had exceptional aim.

Beside Ensign Baldrick, the Boers wounded three others in the landing party. Five of the thieves lay dead, with nearly all the other Boers injured.

Dr. Sawyer and his assistants came quickly to the ground, as did the remainder of the Marine contingent. Dr. Sawyer patched those that needed patching.

Daniel started a search for the diamonds. Then Lieutenant Bagnell took charge.

They found the large gems in the saddle bag of the very man that Daniel had engaged. Captain Micawber commended his men in a loud voice. "Justice has been done here. We shall bring these men aboard and return them to the Cape and Governor Frere will decide what to do."

Hustling up the Boers to the *Golden Mary,* the bandaged leader turned to Daniel. "Bawh, you Englishers are fools. You think this we do alone, without friends? You big country. We have big friends. We are not so foolish like you make picture of Oom Paul."

Wilkins sat in his cabin, taking a rest. The *Golden Mary* now headed back to Beaufort West, bypassing Kimberley. He did not know if the Germans would interfere over British territory. They had followed him the previous day, and the presence of Manuel Antonio de Sousa aboard the *Frederick* worried him.

The ship had enough coal, and the winds were favorable as well. He ordered the speed of the propellers be reduced. Wilkins worried about the Germans. What were they doing in Kimberley? Why had they followed them towards Pretoria? What did the old Boer mean when he spoke to Copperfield?

It was all a bother. He knew after a few sips of the punch he had mixed and things would seem better. A few glasses and his rest would become sleep, and he could use that. He had spent the previous night without any, manning the bridge and ensuring they lost the pursuing Germans.

". . . to the bridge. Lieutenant Gay's compliments, sir, and would you please come to the bridge!" Obvious striking at the door. "Captain Micawber, you are needed on the bridge . . ."

"Yes. Yes. I'm coming."

He slipped his feet into his shoes and then quickly buckled them. His sword hung on a peg near the door, but if he needed it, he would send for it. He opened the door and the Marine snapped to attention. Midshipman Copperfield waited for him. "Lieutenant Gay's compliments, but with the sunrise we've spotted the *Frederick*, sir. They came from the east with the sun at their back, and three thousand feet of altitude as well."

"High and behind, with the wind as well, I have no doubt." Wilkins did not like having lost the advantage of height. He felt the angle of the ship below his feet and knew that Gay already tried to regain some of it. Not that it would be easy.

He had three of his seven coat buttons closed when he reached the deck. Wilkins looked back and high to see if he could locate the enemy.

"There, sir," Copperfield pointed for him and Wilkins saw. No, he did not like it.

"Lookout," he called. "Has the *Frederick* cleared for action?"

"Aye, sir. They've run out their guns!"

"Then action stations. Lieutenant Bagnell, prepare for action!" he said to the marine commander, who would relay the order to his drummers. Wilkins knew his officers must make ready for war.

He saw Lieutenant Gay looking at him from the bridge, who nodded. "Well done, Gay. I think that Boer referred to the German Emperor as his special friend. We need more height. But I fear they shall be close enough for a volley before we are above them. And they are ready? Where have they got such speed?"

Lieutenant Gay nodded, "I do not think, as you previously espoused, that the *Frederick* is as maneuverable as the *Mary*. I think we might have something to show them."

Wilkins climbed the short steps up to the bridge. "We have our work laid out for us. The cannon on the middeck won't reach at this angle, so we are effectively half of our weight; but then, he may have the same problem. Now, prepare the gun deck for firing at the angle. But, below, where we can puncture his hull. Get at his engine room. Maybe see a shot that holes him and bleeds him of all the coal in his bins."

He had studied a fight of one such ship lost by the Union that way. The only time that dirigibles had dueled was the American

Civil War. The Confederate States ship *Richmond* had scored a hit on the Union *Samuel Adams*. Nine-tenths of the coal leaked out, falling to earth.

In all probability now, a new battle would take place.

But would it? The Germans would not want a war to occur over the Boers of the Transvaal, or would they? If Mr. Rhodes was right, the more land each European nation claimed, the more chances for great wealth, and many other advantages that would accrue because of such ownership.

In the distance, the sound of a cannon firing. One cannon, and all eyes turned back to the *Frederick*. "Ranging shot, or warning shot?" Wilkins asked aloud.

Looking below, there was nothing but the veldt and occasional farm lands. Still, farms meant that there might indeed be people below. Good luck to those souls. It was going to get messy. Very messy.

Wilkins stiffened as he realized that this moment was important. The pressure drew into his center and he felt taut. Was he a dried tree branch that would break? Were the men, most of whom had never faced an enemy in battle, ready for this?

Were he and his officers ready to lead under these circumstances?

When no cannon-shot flew in the air, sailing in the sky was rather pleasant. When the chance of being felled by a twelve-pound ball, or the damage it would do to the ship, existed, would the men stand firm?

Would Wilkins do his duty, as well? Or would all fall into quivering scared men, cowering and clamoring for safety?

"Sir, too far to hear if they are hailing," Lieutenant Gay said.

"It is that, isn't it? Well, we are certainly over the land of the Empire. Our Empire, not theirs. And either way, a shot at us is not something we shall let go by without response in kind. That they fired first provokes us and causes this to be an incident upon their heads. Are we cleared for action yet, Mr. Gay?"

"Sir. Momentarily, sir. Momentarily." Wilkins looked below to the gun deck and saw hurried activity as the crew ran about, some pulling on ropes that pushed the guns into position. Loaded and ready to fire.

Shouts and curses resounded as the men struggled to prepare to fight. If he could keep them busy, then their minds would be full. Not left to ponder on being killed by the enemy.

Wilkins stepped over to the helmsman, where Mr. Bunsby stood, as well. "Here are my plans, and you can add to it should you wish, Mr. Bunsby. We shall not have height, but we are rising at an angle, and the *Frederick* certainly looks to be falling at one, as well. I think we can turn sharply should we cut the starboard propeller just shy of crossing the line, then hard to starboard, and the port propeller will push us further and faster. We have practiced this," he reminded them. The helmsman would shift the rudder, and the propeller would be shut down by the engineers.

Mr. Bunsby said, "If we're lucky and can cut beneath the enemy, our deck guns all may fire up at the Germans."

"This is my intention, though I believe we shall launch one volley first, perhaps two, before such a maneuver can be executed."

The two men nodded. They understood his plans. When the

time came, they would do what was needed. He heard reports relayed that the middeck was prepared, although Wilkins did not think those guns would see action unless a great distance was maintained, or they reached a more level altitude relative to the Germans. Then the gun deck reported they were ready. He ordered the *Golden Mary*'s own guns run out.

Looking at the German, he saw that the enemy fired a full broadside, then heard the sound of attack. He ordered the helmsman to put the ship hard over to port, and shouted in a speaking cup to the engine room. More speed to the propellers.

That, however, did little good, as the cannon shot from the enemy reached where they had been.

And Wilkins smiled.

Where they had been. The Germans had not counted on how far they would travel when they sped along at over twenty miles an hour.

"Mr. Gay. Take note that they are ill-prepared for such gunnery when their target is in motion. You may respond to their aggressive attack at your pleasure, sir!"

Lieutenant Gay smiled back and then went to each of the six guns that had the enemy in its sights. On two cannon he made adjustments, and then commanded all to fire.

The noise was deafening. Much worse from the *Golden Mary* then the report from the enemy. His ears rang with the sound.

The ship rocked and moved sideways with the attack. It had taken dozens of gun drills for Wilkins to not be unnerved by such a motion. Still, it left him unsettled.

He worried that one day the ship would move, and he would

not. Then, for only a moment, find himself suspended in the air, with nothing below him. A second later, Wilkins envisioned he would plunge to the ground.

Lieutenant Bates, who watched the shot as it sped to the enemy, called out, "Two hits. Two solid hits."

The young man then clarified that one was against the hull, and another had scored in a balloon bag of the enemy.

Wilkins estimated that the larger ship had eight bags to keep it aloft. If the hit they had just given the Germans was solid enough, the enemy might now only have seven with which to continue the battle. That would make it harder for the Germans to maintain the height advantage they currently held.

The smoke would increase with each attack, so acrid and vile that it would cause his throat to dry and itch. Wilkins knew from many hours of gun practice that this would become the case.

"Mr. Wemmick, ensure that the gun crews have water for their thirst!"

Lieutenant Gay saw to the reloading of the six guns that had bore, the rest unable to shoot. Wilkins kept a careful watch, ready to alter course once the German ship fired again.

Such a moment came.

They turned to starboard, then reduced altitude quickly as the cannonballs flew past. The ship shuddered as one ball struck the bulkhead.

Sub-lieutenant Bates called that it had hit near the rear of the ship, and then clarified that the ball had hit the wall of his cabin. It had not penetrated, but splinter damage inside near the joints of an interior wall that had buckled would need repair. He would see to it after the battle was finished.

If he survived.

"There, men. They have hit us, and we still fly. Let us give them a response!" he called down into the waist of the ship. The men shouted their defiance as well in a hearty cheer.

Lieutenant Gay pulled men from the middeck crews for even greater speed on his reply volleys. The six guns that had shots on the Germans crashed out again. Three hits scored: two on the balloon bag and one clearly had hit the enemy's gun deck.

The two dirigibles had been angling in the sky, reducing the height advantage that the Germans' had. Of a sudden, the *Frederick* definitely lost a much greater degree of altitude. At least five hundred feet more loss than Wilkins' math projected.

"Reduce our ascent level by three degrees on the ailerons, if you please, Mr. Bunsby. We are having a great effect on the enemy and I should not like to lose the ability to place a volley up his backside!"

"Aye, sir. That is a right good description." Bunsby passed on the order to trim the propeller planes to the desired level.

Before the Germans could fire their third volley, Lieutenant Gay responded with his six guns again. Two of the guns, with Mr. Copperfield standing near, had a line of shot standing ready, with two rails that had been laid down between. Wilkins would have to investigate that after the battle was concluded.

"Three hits. Again, three solid hits, two to the hull, one to their quarterdeck."

Then the enemy fired, and Wilkins once again ordered maneuvers. He felt three hits by the enemy, one crossing the gun deck. The shot nearly obliterated one of his own gun crews.

Wilkins saw a man down. No, half of a man. He had no legs beyond stubs that had been his thighs. Another man was buried under the truck of the cannon that had been destroyed by the enemy shot. Two hale airmen tried to reach the wounded man, but the trapped man didn't appear to be moving.

The gun captain, Booth, attempted to pull a two foot piece of wood from his left shoulder, a splinter that had taken him. With luck, Dr. Sawyer would see to Booth, and he would live.

"Those wounded to Dr. Sawyer as quick as you can." Wilkins ordered two men. The enemy shot had destroyed one gun crew and part of the next, though on the port side of the ship.

Losses. Men he had known by name, now wounded, some dead. It did not look like any man had been thrown over the ship. In the RDC, the cry of 'man overboard' conveyed a far worse image than it did in the senior service.

Gay called to him, "Captain Micawber, we approach. Sir, we need time to set up the port battery again."

Wilkins looked at the spatial relationships. "I can give you a few seconds; that is all, Mr. Gay. Then you will have to shoot with what you have."

"Aye, sir. Aye. Copperfield, to gun three with your men. Get that gun up and pointed at forty-five degrees, do you hear me! Jump to it, you men."

Wilkins turned his mind to buying more time. "Hard to port

and down planes ten degrees." He started counting. If he had time, he would have worked the math. Instead, he went by feel. He counted and eyeballed the distances.

Then, "Hard to starboard. Up planes twelve degrees, cut the starboard propeller." He raised his voice and shouted towards the waist of the ship. "Mr. Gay, we begin our attack run!"

"Aye, sir. Fire as you bear. Aim at the forward hull!"

And instead of a volley, one after the other of the *Golden Mary's* guns rang out. Eleven shots sounded, and so Wilkins knew that Copperfield had gotten the damaged gun back into service.

He turned his eyes to the enemy, and helped Bunsby with the helmsman, as they guided the ship below and behind the enemy. A blind spot from which the *Frederick's* guns could not attack.

The enemy faced some problems. Several of the shots—Bates said eight hits—damaged the hull above them. And there, as he had hoped, a trickle of coal began to stream. "Let's rise behind them, Mr. Bunsby, and then turn to a heading for Beaufort West again. We shall see if they follow us. Mr. Bates, Mr. Dawkins, have the men see to repairs. Mr. Gay, we are still at quarters."

But over the next few moments, the tactic of crossing under the *Frederick* and then falling behind and below had worked. The enemy did not pursue when they broke to port. The battle— and the Germans—were finished.

Wilkins wiped the sweat from his brow. The Germans may not have been destroyed, but they had been defeated. He watched them steam slowly away. He could not see the vented steam from their balloons, but the slowing of the *Frederick* clearly illustrated the effect. They would need days to limp back to the Bantu lands that they tried to seize suzerainty over.

He waited a few more minutes until he was sure.

"Mr. Gay, you may stand down the men. Gentlemen, I think such a victory, and we have had one, means a double ration for the crew and for us; you must all join me in my cabins. I believe some of my grandfather's famous punch is called for once again."

Punch would make everything right.

AUTHOR NOTE:

I first encountered Mr. Micawber as portrayed by WC Fields. A charming interpretation. Since then, I discovered that his first name was Wilkins. Courtesy of an immigration officer, my last is Wilkin, no S. Then when this story came to mind, I discovered that the second most beloved comic figure in English literature is Wilkins Micawber, just behind Falstaff.

A story with a Steampunk flavor followed. It is thought that Micawber is modeled after Dickens' own father, and that the original David Copperfield was born about 1820; so, here, in 1879, the grandsons of both men meeting up and serving the Empire seemed logical.

Styled after David Copperfield by Charles Dickens

Little Boiler Girl

SCOTT WILLIAM TAYLOR

Heat from the boilers made the sweat on Pia Hansen's skin evaporate almost as soon as it left the ten-year-old girl's pores. She moved quickly in the room. Prolonged exposure to the inhuman temperatures guaranteed a gruesome death—something even a child knew. With the tasks done, she raced from the room, only daring to breathe after the massive metal doors clanged shut. Her act guaranteed the city two more hours of power.

Pia wiped the grime from her hands on her dirty work clothes and picked up her clipboard. With the hard part of her duties finished, she turned her attention to an equally important job. The duty should never have gone to a child; laws prevented it. But on this night—New Year's Eve—the law bent to the will of Lars Rasmussen.

New Year's Eve—the one night of the year when the government looked the other way and allowed its subjects to escape the captivity of their homes past midnight. Soldiers and civilians alike spent months in preparation for their only chance to break curfew and experience a brief period of celebration and unabashed revelry.

New Year's Eve—the one night the intense heat churning the bowels of the power plant barely satisfied the city's need for energy, and no one knew more about harnessing the beneficial properties of fire than the Rasmussens.

To hear Lars tell it, he began working with steam technology before he could walk. His family carried the knowledge in their blood. The first Czar appointed his great-great-grandfather, the city's first hydronic engineer, a century earlier. From that day, Rasmussens ran the power. Systems had evolved much since the first crude machines powered only mills and basic modes of propulsion. Now, the very existence of humanity itself owed everything to the proper balance of heat and water.

For eons, the gods jealously protected this knowledge, but the Rasmussen family forever deprived Deity of its greatest gift when Lars Rasmussen invented the great equalizer; he invented the Kalt Afdeling System.

No one knew exactly how Lars came up with the Kalt Afdeling System. Some said it came to him in a dream, yet others thought the man sold his soul to the devil himself in order to unlock the almost unlimited power the new system provided. Somehow, the idea came to him, and he realized that heat alone could not produce the kinds of power the growing populace needed. Heat worked fine for singular functions, but could one heat source run an entire city? No, it could not. For his society to survive, the city demanded more power, more energy.

Lars found the solution to the centuries-old problem, invented the system, and by so doing, forever changed the face of history, cementing his name as one of the great inventors of all mankind.

He ran the city's power concern as its own kingdom, with himself as sovereign. A dictator in his private realm, Lars treated his employees much worse than the inhuman equipment that served the city. Those close to him knew never to cross him, for only his memory surpassed his evil nature. Netta Hansen never had a chance.

Netta's husband never met their daughter. The soldier died while in the military. Without income, the pretty mother applied for various jobs, finally securing employment with the Rasmussen Power Company. The still-youthful woman toiled in the plant, earning barely enough to cover food and shelter costs for her struggling family. She would return home after many long hours, exhausted, but the sight of her daughter's beautiful face washed away the memories of the plant. As long as they had each other, they were happy.

But those days lived only in the past, a past forever changed. Now Pia worked for Lars Rasmussen, a tyrant who forced her to risk death every time she entered the boiler room, a place so hot it only compared to the very caverns of Hell in intensity.

Only two more shifts tonight, Pia thought, as she gathered her clipboard and walked from the torturous room. She could still feel the searing heat emanating from the door as she walked down the hall, finally stopping at a small metal panel near the floor. She knelt and turned a latch; the panel swung wide. She crouched, crawled into the space.

Once inside, Pia turned to a bank of twelve switches on a far wall, one switch for each one of the enormous boilers in the plant. Looking at the numbers on her clipboard, she clicked each switch to match the number she recorded while inside the inferno. She hurried the task and scampered from the room, closing the panel door as quickly as possible. She stood alone in the hall, a solitary figure in the massive power plant. Her face awash with anguish, thoughts of her mother came to her mind as she walked to her living quarters.

Years had passed since the days when Netta walked those same halls. Everything changed the day Lars Rasmussen met Netta Hansen. When she stepped outside during a rare break, he was immediately smitten. That very day, he hired her as his personal assistant.

The Spartan life Netta and Pia had shared disappeared forever. For the first time in her life, Netta could afford to buy her daughter more than the necessities. The humble family enjoyed the fruits of her many hours of labor.

With her new income, the two moved from their meager existence into a nice house, one where snow didn't blow in from ill-fitted windows, and where the vermin remained outside. Pia came to know the feeling of a full stomach and a warm night's sleep. Netta watched with grateful eyes as her daughter at first began to smile, and then laugh. Finally, Netta felt worthy of true happiness. The feeling did not last, due in part to Lars's machine.

Lars invented a machine so advanced it replaced the human labor force at the plant. He called his machine the Kalt Afdeling System, and no one knew how it worked. He even barred anyone from seeing the revolutionary device. Many believed the claims of his invention impossible—a self-sustaining power plant. They called him a fool, they called him crazy, but the insults died the day everyone walked out of the plant, and the power remained on.

Netta felt the pain of watching scores of friends leave the plant, their livelihood removed. She remained one of the few employees left at the company. After the successful launch of the Kalt Afdeling System, Lars turned his attention to Netta—attention she neither requested nor desired.

As Netta continued working for Lars, Pia noticed changes in her mother. Netta stopped laughing, and then, she stopped smiling. She nearly collapsed at the end of each shift, but not from physical labor, like when she worked long hours at the plant. Then one night, Netta never came home.

Pia Hansen never knew what happened to her mother. She left for work in the morning and disappeared. Police opened an investigation, questioning everyone who last saw the woman. They directed many questions toward Lars, her employer and one of the last people to see her alive. The police found nothing. With no leads, the investigation turned stone cold, and eventually closed.

As unanswered questions mounted, Lars acted. He announced that he would adopt Pia and raise her as his own daughter. The little girl moved into the Rasmussen mansion.

Without her mother, no temporal possession could restore the loss in Pia's life, and the girl grew despondent. She also found that the person she thought Lars to be never existed. The man who spoke so kindly with others changed into a vindictive bully. Three weeks after moving into Lars's home, he told her of his decision to move her from the mansion.

"Where will I live?" Pia asked.

"You're going to work for me," Lars replied.

"In the mansion?"

"No. You'll be working in my power plant."

"Doing what?" she asked.

"Work," he told the frightened and confused child. That day, Lars himself drove her to the gates of the power plant. After informing her of her new responsibilities, he left her alone, with only her memories for companions.

Always the resourceful child, Pia found living by herself a much better situation than the time she spent living with Lars. In the vast expanse of the factory, no one yelled, no one threatened, and no one hit—living without love the price she paid for those meager comforts. Lars needed someone inside, someone to do this important job. In her, he found the perfect candidate—perfect, because she had no other options.

Pia turned her attention to her duties and the long night that awaited her. Normally, the law required the boilers power down after eight o'clock, but tonight, the people's need for energy required the plant operate well into the night. That meant two extra shifts for her; one at ten o'clock, and another at midnight. After that, she could finally take a well-deserved break and sleep. She checked her timepiece; it showed 7:50 p.m., ten minutes until her next shift.

Shadows from endless pipes, walls, and wires cast eerie patterns on the dark hallway leading to the heart of the building. Pia approached the room slowly. She could feel the heat, even through the thick metal doors that stood between her and the inferno beyond.

As she walked, the sweat already forming on her small hands made it difficult to hold the clipboard and pencil she needed to do her job. She stood on her tippy toes and hit the button releasing the door. It crawled open and, as she had done hundreds of times before, she entered the room.

She worked as fast as she could, recording the information from each of the twelve boilers, then recorded the numbers into the crawl space. Only two more shifts, and she could finally stop for the night.

Pia took longer than normal to return to her room. The one-time private living quarters for the plant's security guard contained a bed, bathroom, and a small eating area. The girl slowly climbed the large steel staircase to the room surrounded by windows. These gave the plant's only occupant an unparalleled view of the vast conglomeration of piping and vents, hallways and secret passages. Lars Rasmussen might have owned the property, but Pia oversaw it all.

Her bare feet ached as calloused flesh touched the cold metal of each step. The day she came to the plant she had shoes—good shoes—but she long ago outgrew them.

Once in her room, Pia lay on the thin mattress of her bed and closed her eyes. As her tiny body tried to recover from the torment inflicted upon it, her mind began to swim in a sea of unconsciousness.

Her breathing slowed and her mind filled with dreams. She saw an entity made entirely of heat, not only physical, but also spiritual in nature. This mysterious being pursued her, and she tried to get away. Pia's legs began to thrash on the bed as she tried outrunning the horror that progressively gained on her.

She ran endlessly through the plant. The chase ended when Pia saw an area she did not know, a place where she had never been. When she turned back, she expected the monster to consume her. Instead, she saw nothing, no phantom, no threat. Something more deadly, yet welcoming, replaced the dread. The thought jolted her body awake, and she quickly sat up in her bed.

The calmness of the dream replaced her sense of fear. Pia cursed herself for falling asleep, something she could not afford to do between shifts. She'd done it before, and the repercussions were swift and severe. She quickly checked her timepiece and exhaled in relief. She still had time to make the ten o'clock round, but she must hurry.

Pia flew down the stairs. With clipboard and pencil in hand, she reached the boiler room with only a few minutes to spare.

She stepped on her toes, hit the button, and entered after the door rolled open.

The blast of heat overwhelmed her. She thought it could not possibly get any hotter inside, but she thought wrong. It wasn't until the large metal door clanged shut as she left, her readings taken, and she wiped the sweat off her face, that she realized the increased heat burned her exposed feet.

Only then did she feel the searing pain. The floor inside the furnace room reached temperatures hot enough to burn. She sat on the floor of the hallway and tried massaging the pain away. After adjusting the switches, she sat and wondered how in the world she would be able to check the wicked engines one more time.

The red glow from the boilers cast a long shadow of the sad girl on the hard concrete floor. Pia imagined those outside the high plant walls, the children and their parents, and what they planned on doing for their one night of extended freedom, the one night everyone could stay up and welcome in the New Year. She struggled to control her emotions. Ultimately, fatigue and exhaustion overcame her, and memories of better days, happier days, with her mother came flooding back, as if a dam had burst.

For years, she, too, celebrated the New Year's arrival, when soldiers put down the weapons of death and honored life. She remembered the parties, the delicious food, the joy of laughter, much of it her own. And the fireworks—oh, the fireworks—that filled the sky with millions of points of brightly colored light. She loved the fireworks most of all.

The thought of parties and laughter and fireworks for every-one else but her caused her to sink deeper inside her cocoon of inner anguish. She wished New Year's would not come, or if it did, she wished she could just disappear before it arrived.

Dejected, Pia finally stood and began meandering around the empty plant, not returning to her lonely room atop the stairs. Each step proved a painful one, but she felt a greater pain inside her heart. She kept walking.

She wandered the empty halls, passing places she visited hundreds of times. She continued until coming to a part of the building foreign to her. Looking up, she read the words: KALT AFDELING.

Pia knew as much about the workings of the plant as any normal ten-year-old child. She understood the boilers somehow made it possible for everyone in the city to have power, power to do the things they needed to do. However, her mind could not comprehend Lars' system, other than it made possible a ten-fold increase in power from the existing engines. She did know she stood just outside the room housing Lars's greatest contribution to humanity.

Pia looked at the sign that loomed overhead, and a chill spread through her body. That part of the plant felt strange, foreign, unknown. Pia glanced about her furtively, as if someone lurked in the shadows, watching her. She felt as if a presence would run at her, screaming at her for her obvious disobedience. The silence echoing throughout the building only added to Pia's trepidation.

She waited, but no one came. Pia checked her timepiece.

She had one hour until the next shift, until she again faced the tormenting heat.

Instead of leaving as she knew she should, Pia remained and studied what she saw. She noticed a wall with no indication of an entrance. The hallway simply ended, and where a door should be, nothing. She read the words of caution on the sign and said the words out loud. "Kalt Afdeling."

The natural curiosity of the ten-year-old overcame the previous fear of being caught trespassing in a restricted area, and she remained, transfixed in front of the silent wall.

"Kalt Afdeling," she said again. "Kalt Afdeling . . ."

A ping somewhere in the bowels of the plant brought Pia out of her hypnotic trance. She checked her timepiece again and cursed when she realized how much time she had wasted standing before the metal barrier. She turned to leave, but her body disobeyed. And when she finally moved, her motion took her toward the unknown, not away.

Pia stepped closer to the wall and felt a presence, an entity that hid somewhere beyond. She recognized the presence—it was the same one that came to her in a dream two hours earlier. Somehow, Pia *had* to get beyond the partition. It called to her.

Pia extended her hand and touched the smooth surface of the wall. The moment her finger made contact, a light appeared just right of where her finger touched. She touched the wall again, this time where the light seemed to be coming through the metal.

For a few seconds, nothing happened, and then she heard a faint hum coming from behind the metal wall. She took a step back. Suddenly a panel began to move slowly and silently until it disappeared, leaving only a black space where it once stood.

Pia froze. The beating in her chest increased as she stared into the nothingness before her. The black scared her more than her dream, more than her memories of Lars. She shivered with cold even though her body remained warm from the boiler room. An urge to turn and run washed over her. Instead, something inside the space issued an inaudible call to her, and she answered by slowly walking into the darkness.

Once Pia crossed the line where the hallway ended and the unknown began, a flash of brilliant light flooded the chamber, whiter than anything Pia had ever seen in her short life. She shielded her eyes. The brightness of the room overwhelmed her.

Something else hit Pia as her eyes adjusted to the almost painful light—cold air. It swirled around her, comforted her. The freshness also soothed her soul.

A moment after Pia fully entered the room, the panel silently slid back into place, sealing her inside. She didn't notice. She did notice the stale metallic air of the plant no longer filled her lungs when she breathed, as well as the absence of any sound in the space, only a faint hum felt through her shoeless feet.

Finally, Pia's eyes adjusted to the point where she could see. What she saw overwhelmed her. She stood in a foyer with a larger area beyond. The floor-to-ceiling windows allowed her to see inside. Huge metal tubing crisscrossed the ceiling, all converging at a single point in the center of the room.

The conduits led to a large machine, but it was unlike anything Pia had ever seen. The vibrations came from the apparatus in the other room. She saw a small entrance door to her left, and she moved toward it.

She unlocked the door, and the silence disappeared, replaced by the hum now audible as well as felt. It came from the contraption. Something else came from the room . . . cold air. It cooled Pia's body, even her clothes, still warm to the touch from the overwhelming heat of the boilers. It rushed at her, comforting her with a smothering pillow of relief. The open door invited her in and she answered the call.

Pia entered the room and her blistered feet touched a frozen floor. She recoiled. The frozen atmosphere slowly wrapped itself around her. Her feet burned, but not from the fire; from ice.

Pia wrapped her thin arms around her body. She knew she should leave, but the same prompting that drew her to the room begged her to stay. The frosted air reminded her of the times spent with her mother, years ago. Their ill-equipped home provided poor shelter from the bitter winters; somehow, they survived. She remembered huddling around the home's only fireplace, listening to Netta tell stories of her childhood.

Pia slowly ventured further into the room about twice the size of her living quarters. Shaking, she approached the machine, but as she drew near, something in the corner of her eye caught her attention. Behind a silver tube, she saw a shoe—a shoe attached to a foot. She recognized both immediately. The child took another step and came within full view of the perfectly preserved corpse of Netta Hansen.

"Mother!" Pia screamed, and ran to where the woman lay on the frozen floor. She knelt beside the lifeless body and touched her shoulder. She didn't move. Pia placed her hand on her mother's cheek and jumped back. She touched skin as frozen as the room around her.

"No," Pia whispered. "No." She began to back away from the vessel that once contained Netta's soul. As she stared at the body, all lights in the room went out, leaving the terrified girl in complete darkness, except for the faint light coming in from the inner room's door. Pia turned and ran as fast as she could out of the room and into the bowels of the power plant.

She stopped at the bottom of the stairs leading to her quarters. Instead of going to her room, she sank to the floor and drew up her knees under her chin.

She didn't know how long she sat and cried. A part of her knew she had a responsibility to check the boilers at midnight and register the levels, but the overwhelming horror she felt at finding her mother dead inside the cold room immobilized her, numbed her as effectively as if she had stayed with her mother's body in the room.

After what seemed like an eternity, Pia rose and walked back into the plant. However, she did not continue to the boilers, but absentmindedly walked to where the words KALT AFDELING hung above her mother's tomb.

Pia knew what would happen if she failed to do her job and report the readings on time. Mr. Rasmussen lectured her over and over again about the consequences. He warned her if she failed to enter the boiler readings every two hours, the emergency override would shut the boilers down, and the city would lose its power. If she failed to do her job tonight, hundreds of thousands of revelers would suddenly be without power.

However, that night, her boss's threats no longer held her hostage. She no longer cared about the power plant, the people enjoying themselves on New Year's Eve, or, especially, Lars.

This time, she approached the room, no longer frightened. She calmly touched the smooth wall, revealing again the secret entrance to the room, and entered. The door slid silently closed behind her. Once inside the inner room, she maneuvered around the pipes until she came again to see her mother's body prone on the floor.

Pia approached the body. She wanted to be close to the corpse. The sight no longer instilled her with fear. Shaking, she sat on the floor next to the body, drew her legs under her chin, and wrapped her arms around them. She lowered her head onto her frozen knees and tried to think of what to do next. She looked again at her mother's face resting on her arms. She looked so peaceful, as if she were sleeping.

Pia touched her mother's cheek again. This time she did not withdraw, but caressed the skin that belonged to the woman who had loved her with all her heart.

As before, the lights in the room shut off. Without light, the darkness and cold seemed to conspire against her. She began to imagine demons and ghosts somewhere in the black. Instinctively, she reached for her mother's hand in the dark. She could not move it from the floor.

However, next to it, she felt an object the size of a coin purse and picked it up. With only the sense of touch, she immediately identified the object: her mother's match case. Her father gave the metal box to her mother years before Pia was born, and Netta wore it around her neck on a string. A conversation returned to her.

"What's that?"

"It's a gift from your father."

"What's in it?"

"Only matches," Netta said. "But this reminds me of him, and those memories are much more valuable." Pia held the frozen memento in her hands and felt a connection to a man she never knew.

Pia opened the case and touched three wooden sticks. The slim shafts offered the shivering girl a chance to once again see her mother's face in the darkness. She lifted one of the matches and struck it against the ridged edge of the metal case. The black space around her retreated and a small light blazed.

She extended the match to illuminate the face she loved more than anything else in the world. She held the match close and the peaceful look warmed her heart. She watched until the flame descended and threatened to burn her fingers. The light went out. The darkness returned to occupy the space it so deeply coveted. She sighed. This time she couldn't see the cloud of condensation rise in the blackness.

A short time passed. Pia began to lose feeling in her limbs. As she sat, she began hearing voices and imagined seeing people in the room with her, speaking to her, trying to reach her. She wondered if one of the voices could possibly be that of her mother's, offering love and comfort, or could it be voices from others, from ghosts wishing to haunt and terrify.

With great effort, Pia opened the case and drew out her second to last source of light. Her shaking hand barely applied enough pressure to the side of the case for the spark to ignite. Again, Pia extended her shaking arm. She focused only on her mother's beautiful face.

Suddenly, the cold room grew bright. The vibrating machine vanished. In its place, Pia's childhood home appeared and her heart nearly burst from her body with happiness.

In her mind, Pia saw it all: the frosted window near the front door, the worn, braided, rag rug which they had made together on the floor, and the entryway where winter winds slithered between small cracks and stole the heat from the room. She continued looking until her tired eyes rested upon Netta—no longer lying next to her on the floor, but smiling brightly before her, a smile yearning to be shared with her daughter.

Pia remained where she was, a wide smile spread across her frozen face. She held out her arms, almost willing herself to cross the span that separated them.

But she remained seated on the floor. The match in her hand burned down and finally died. Before the flame went out, it burned her fingers, but Pia never felt the pain. The moment the flame died, so disappeared the scene before Pia's iced-over eyes. She had to get them back. She could not allow herself to lose her mother again . . . not again.

The dying girl found the last match and struck it against the side of the case. She dropped the object on the floor and never heard the echo as it hit the ground. The light from the last match intensified her previous vision. The room of her past returned but with a greater force.

The aroma of a roasting goose wafted throughout the room and into the girl's nostrils. The hard floor transformed into a warm wooden chair situated close to the meat slowly turning over the fire.

This time, she heard laughter, like music from a symphony, or the sound of birds in the spring air. She heard the lilting sounds of Netta's voice echoing throughout the small space. Pia longed to remain at home forever.

"Pia," Netta softly said. "My beautiful girl. Join me and we'll be together forever."

"Mommy!" Pia whispered. "Please take me with you. I want to never be apart again. When this last match dies, you will disappear, like you did before."

"No, darling," Netta said as she crossed the small room and picked up her most precious possession. "I will never leave you again."

Pia melted in the warmth of her mother's embrace as the last fibers of wood burned to nothingness.

※

Lars Rasmussen sat in his study as he looked outside his window at the city lights below. The man loved New Year's Eve.

He loved seeing a world powered by his brilliance. Through the frosted glass, he heard the masses making as much noise as possible. His anticipation grew as he waited for midnight to arrive. He longed to hear everyone celebrate together. He checked his timepiece. Midnight was only seconds away.

As sirens blared and bells atop government buildings rang, Lars slowly sipped whiskey from his private stock. As he lifted his glass to drain the remaining exquisite drops, the lights in his study began to flicker. A moment later, the house went dark. He watched in horror as lights all over the city faded and eventually died.

Lars ran to his desk and hit the button on the communicator. "Peter!" he screamed into the metal box. "What the *hell* is going on?" Silence met his angry words.

"Peter!" Lars hit the button repeatedly until he remembered the contraption only worked with power. Lars yelled into the darkness. "Martin! Martin!" The door to the office opened revealing a lone figure holding an oil lamp.

"Yes sir," the obedient servant said.

"I'll be at the plant!" Lars slammed his fist on his oak desk. He grabbed the lamp from Martin's wrinkled hand and raced from the room.

It took Lars thirty minutes to reach the plant. Others arrived before him. The security gates had been forced open and he cursed to himself as he ran inside.

He ran through the empty hallways of the plant. The sound of his patent leather shoes echoed through the cavernous space.

He ran first to the boilers. *Just wait until I find that girl,* Lars thought, as he wondered why she failed and embarrassed him on this, of all nights. He then checked Pia's living quarters.

"Where is she?" Lars spat. When he found her, she would pay. Would everyone now know the truth of his experiment—that his plant was not self-sustaining and required at least one person to run it? Would the authorities find out he employed—no, forced—a mere child to work for him under inhuman conditions? The implications raced through his mind as he descended the stairs from Pia's living quarters. Though humiliating, the damage could be repaired, especially if he acted quickly. Yes, that little brat would pay.

As Lars reached the last step a single word came to his mind: Netta. He stopped. A visceral fear gripped him and caused him to retch the contents of his stomach on the plant floor. After regaining his composure, he ran.

The man responsible for the city's power ran through the plant. His aging heart screamed its displeasure at being pushed to such a level of exertion. He wheezed as he continued toward the one place in the building he never wanted to visit again. As he rounded the last corner, two stone-faced policemen halted his progress.

"Mr. Rasmussen?" the first guard said, his voice as unfeeling as the cold floor on which he stood.

"Yes," Lars said trying to catch his breath.

"I'm afraid you're not allowed beyond this point."

"Excuse me?" The officer met his words with silence.

"Listen!" Lars screamed. "I can go any place I damn well want to! This is *my* plant, and not you or anyone else can stop me!"

He walked toward the men who moved to block his path. He stopped and wiped the sweat forming on his brow on the sleeve of his designer jacket. He tugged at the collar on his tailored shirt and his legs went limp. The hardened guards watched as one of the most powerful men in the country fainted in front of them, falling into a heap on the floor, his breath raspy and shallow.

Lanterns illuminated the areas of the plant occupied by police officers, the bodies of the dead, and one unconscious Lars Rasmussen. The city's power extinguished, the men worked by the light of simple flames encased by glass as they tended to the gruesome scene before them.

The security team had discovered the bodies of Netta and Pia Hansen twenty minutes after the power system failed. A wrong turn led the men straight to the tomb. None of the officers knew anything of the Kalt Afdeling System or how it worked. They only knew nothing could survive the extreme temperatures generated in that part of the plant.

Silence filled the room as hardened men worked at the crime scene, the somber tone a fitting tribute to the departed. A detective delivered the news of the positive identification of the woman to his boss. It took a moment to find him—he had his hands full gathering up Lars Rasmussen and sending him to headquarters for questioning.

The girl's identity remained a mystery, as did the reason for her being in the plant itself. The officers wondered why someone would voluntarily stay in this room to die.

"It's freezing in here. Why didn't she just leave—the door was unlocked when we got here."

"Don't know . . . damn shame, such a young girl," one of the officers said.

"Can you believe this?" another man said as he held up a spent match. "She actually tried to keep warm with a couple of matches."

"You see how she was treated?" The men noticed her malnourishment, the filth on her skin, her hair brittle and crisp. Finally, they saw the burns on her feet. Every officer watched as the men reverently transported the body from the room that killed her. As her body passed before them, everyone noticed the smile that lingered on the dead child's face. Somehow, her cheeks were rosy.

The officers removed Pia from the black halls of her prison. The walls stood as silent sentinels, while the flicker of lights danced from the men's lanterns. Fire bid her goodbye. Men placed the small body next to that of her mother in the wagon. They shut the doors and it slowly rolled from the power plant to the deserted streets of a darkened city.

The officer in charge lingered behind. He remained in the room and shivered from the cold. With so many questions, the events of the night signaled only the beginning of his search for answers.

He knelt at the spot and touched the floor where life evaporated for two souls. He felt the frozen ground through his leather gloves. His fingers began to numb, and he slowly lifted them to his face. The gloves frosted his cheek.

The thought of the girl's face, forever etched into his mind, haunted him. She didn't have to die—not with an unlocked door. Why did she stay?

He took out a small notebook. With shaking hands, he began jotting notes of the case. He recorded the location of the bodies inside the room and the condition of the victims. Hoping he had enough information, he turned to leave the room, but something urged him to say, to find a message . . . a clue.

"What?" the man asked himself. The sound of his voice disappeared in the machine's hum. He took a final look and noticed the match case—evidence even he overlooked.

Holding his lantern high, he picked up the case and studied it. Delicate etchings decorated the polished metal. He shook it. It responded with silence. He held the lantern closer and noticed something wedged into the bottom of the case. Using his pen, he fished out a small photograph.

The firelight jumped across the picture. Even in the darkened room, the man immediately recognized the face of the girl who perished where he stood. Turning the picture over, he found writing.

My dearest Pia, I pray this note finds you so you'll know of my love for you. Whenever you see this match case, remember me and know that I will always be with you. Please keep the knowledge of my love in your heart. One day we'll reunite and my joy will be complete. Pia, never forget that I love you more than life itself. Goodbye, my daughter, until we meet again.

The officer pocketed the evidence and left the room. The sound of his boots against the plant floor echoed as he made his way out of the labyrinth of walls and pipes and vents and rooms filled with secrets, finally emerging into the night.

As he stood staring at the stars, thoughts of a mother's final wish swirled in his mind and he recalled the look of serenity on the child's face. He hoped to God the mother's prayer was answered. He climbed into his vehicle and made his way through the darkened streets of the sleeping city.

Styled after Little Match Girl by Hans Christian Andersen

The Clockwork Ballet

M. K. WISEMAN

The blessed silence, the reprieve from the damned ghost's haunting presence, lasted a brief three years following the untimely and dramatic departure of the Opera's Prima Donna, Mademoiselle Daae. But in late 1884, it became abundantly clear that Monsieur Leroux's fantastical tale contained at least one incredible falsehood—namely, the Ghost was not dead.

Oh, the management was in on the misdirect. They still paid his salary, obligingly kept Box Five for his exclusive use, and kowtowed to his every whim. The ballet chorus still kept on their metaphorical toes, shrieking at the occasional odd sound or strange happening—as excitable young women are wont to do. But, perhaps most importantly, the murders stopped.

Yes, it was a quiet truce. One could argue that it bordered on comfortable. The theatre was enjoying a resurgence of popularity, now gained through the quality of its productions, rather than the sensationalism of its apparent haunting. Messrs.

Armand Monchamin and Firmin Richard even begrudged little of the stipend they were forced to pay their resident spook. After all, the Opera Ghost was now earning his keep . . .

Christine's kindness, her kiss, had changed Erik, the man known to most only as *Le Fantôme de le Palais Garnier*, or simply, the Opera Ghost. Still a recluse and a figure of terror, he kept to his subterranean hermitage, making his wishes known via the ever-servile Madame Giry. The ghost now worked in the background to assist the company through his many talents.

And by background, I mean literally. The wonders of a Palais Garnier production were a sight to behold. Audiences came expecting theatre and left talking miracles, magic. It has been expounded upon elsewhere, the natural genius that the phantom possessed for engineering, mechanics, and illusion. His myriad of secret doors and passageways, the nerve system of the already magnificent Palais Garnier; his own lake-bound dwelling-place beneath the seven stories of basement catacombs, an unsung modern marvel.

It only followed that, in his newfound fit of goodwill, Erik should lend his talents to the prop, scenery, and stage effects department. At first the contributions were subtle, but as initial mistrust faded, the aid became more . . . *outré.*

Combined with his talent for writing, original and marvelous productions soon graced the stage of the Paris Opera. Audiences soon spoke of modern effects not seen elsewhere— scenery that moved itself, props that soared over the crowd.

The age of the machine was in vogue, and Paris was leading the way.

And Messrs. Richard and Monchamin knew exactly where to invest their sizable profits.

"How? How does this happen?" M. Monchamin, a portly and florid gentleman of the desk, threw the morning paper down on the credenza, startling his partner with his brash entrance.

"Beg pardon—how does what happen?" M. Richard, as thin as his partner was thick, middle aged and generally the more impassive of the two, looked around wildly. They'd enjoyed their reprieve for too long, it seemed. *Please let it not be a cast member,* he scanned the page, feeling a headache threaten.

"This. This!" Armand jabbed a finger at a small article below the fold. It read:

LONDON OPERA HOUSE FITTED WITH NEW ELECTRIC LIGHT, AUDIENCES IN DELIGHT

"Audiences are in delight, dear Firmin," the manager sputtered. "*In delight!*"

"Hmm . . ." Firmin was mostly unmoved, wheeling as he was from relief that the headline heralded no disaster. "I suppose we'd better look into this ourselves."

"Look into it? Goodness, I've already told Mme. Giry to handle it."

As if on cue, Madame Giry appeared in the doorway, her wiry

frame doing little to block the light, but somehow dimming the small office with her presence.

"Ah! Madame Giry," Armand motioned her in, eyeing her nervously. "We were just discussing—"

"He won't do it." She wasted no time, delivering her message curtly, with a tone as flat and colorless as her austere attire.

"Oh, but surely he must—" Firmin began, calm as ever.

"Must what?" Giry cut in. "Must be your houseboy? Must waste his time with your projects—all so you can turn another tidy profit?"

"We meant no disrespect, Mme. Giry," Armand soothed, "but with his talents, we thought surely that—"

"You thought wrong," she looked from one man to the other. "The Ghost does not wish to have his opera bathed in the garish and vulgar light of Mr. Swan's infernal invention." She bid them good day and swept out of the room.

"Well!" Armand put the full effrontery he felt into that one word. Firmin was already scribbling furiously on a piece of stationary, one finger held up to request silence.

"There," he put the final flourish on the note then passed it over, "I suppose we'd both better sign it." At Armand's puzzled look he explained, "We'll send it today—M. Garnier surely must know someone who can aid us in this endeavor."

"But the ghost—"

"Hang the ghost! If all he's willing to contribute is clockwork trickery and cheap smoke and mirror illusions—we're looking at the future here, and I'll be damned if we get left in the dark."

❧

The lights flickered and grew dim. Shrieks filled the brief space of time that it took the gas to right itself and return the room to steady illumination.

"O-oh! The ghost! The ghost!" A dozen fear-filled girls surrounded Meg, who winced and shushed the skittish dancers.

"Ladies, ladies," she called for order. Though not the principal ballerina (not yet anyway!), Meg Giry commanded special attention in the corps. The last of the original chorus to perform alongside the famous Prima Donna Daae, and daughter of Mme. Giry, the Opera Ghost's own messenger, the girls looked to the tall, dark-eyed beauty for answers.

"It's just an air bubble in the pipes caused by the workmen," she sighed, giving the explanation for the eighth time in a week. Flickering lights, tools gone missing, small accidents amongst the electrical crew—such things had become regular occurrences during the opera house's fitful upgrade to the new electric light. However, having lived through the horrors of three years prior, Meg was ready to believe these small hiccups for what they were: natural delays in a complicated process. That she'd once in a while seen a pensive, worried look flit across her mother's face never bothered her—Mother was always worried.

An urgent knocking on the door nearly brought the room to chaos again. Cracking it open to see who summoned, one of the young ladies—a back row girl by the name of Brigitte—nodded rapidly at the unknown visitor then turned to Meg, eyes bright with apprehension, "Meg? It's your mother—"

With a frown, the young lady wove her way to the door, her

grace making even the short, utilitarian journey a lovely sight to behold. *I really don't need an interruption right now*, she glowered inwardly as the girls lapsed into one more round of ghost-induced tittering.

Meg stopped short. The man at the door was clearly not her mother. With a puzzled glance and growing unease in her chest, she thanked Mademoiselle Brigitte who obligingly left Meg to her conversation with the stagehand, a ruddy fellow who nervously fingered the grey shapeless cap he held in his hands.

"Mam'selle Giry? Your mother's had a small accident. If you could please come with me." The words were gruff, but not untinged with kindness. Meg followed the roughhewn stagehand down the hallway with alacrity, leaving her corps to gossip and invent reasons for her swift and sudden departure.

It was not the ghost that'd brought Mme. Giry to the attentions of the prop master's ministrations, but something rather more ominous: sickness. Laid up on a small and ridiculously over-decorated settee, Madame Giry awaited the doctor's arrival with customary sharpness. This alone helped put Meg at ease as she arrived on the heels of her obliging messenger. If her mother had the strength to be impatient, then it couldn't be all that serious.

Still, the concierge had fainted, and, at her admittedly advanced age, any illness could become serious. Meg knelt by her mother's side.

"Do not let the doctor treat me," Mme. Giry clawed at Meg's arm, her voice husky and whispered. There was a feverish tinge to her lips, a brightness in the eyes that recalled Meg to her earlier alarm. *Not call the doctor? Nonsense. He was already on the way.*

Meg informed her mother of this and was promptly shushed. Drawing near, the old woman hissed, "In my room. A small bottle with a dropper. Fetch it, my darling."

Eighteen years of knowing better than to argue, Meg complied with the strange request, returning from her errand to find her mother having regained her feet, albeit with the aid of her cane. Madame's eyes positively glowed as she espied the stoppered brown bottle in Meg's hand. "Come, come," she toddled away to a small dressing room in spite of there being no one about, the crowd having dispersed now that Meg had been fetched. It wasn't that the old woman was disliked, rather the consensus was that nobody necessarily wanted to deal with the shifty old crone and only tolerated her because . . . well, because of past events.

One small drop. Three minutes time. And Madame Giry was very much herself once more. Perhaps paler, perhaps frailer than other days, but it was hard to tell. Meg watched her mother's satisfied sigh as she re-stoppered and pocketed the rather miraculous cure with reticence.

"Mother, what was—?"

"My medicine," Mme. Giry snapped then softened, "Thank you, my dear, for fetching it for me." There was a loud bang, a rushing noise, then the lights went dark—this time for good.

ই৩৬

"That was some excellent quick thinking on the part of your foreman," M. Monchamin mopped his sweating brow with already damp handkerchief. It had been an exciting half-hour since their narrow avoidance of a true crisis—nay, disaster.

The accounts were different from half-a-dozen of the workers, but consensus was that a sudden shower of sparks from a worker's tool had come dangerously close to one of the opera house's multitude of exposed gas lines. One of the men had leapt to action, closing off the valves—which led to the flushing of the system, and the subsequent plunge into darkness that the entire opera house had suffered.

"Someone get this damned thing out of the way." Firmin was taking the crisis with much less calm than his florid partner. Taking an ill-tempered swipe with his cane at the heavy fire curtain now blocking his entrance onto the stage, the frustrated manager paced the apron, ignoring the explanations from his prop master that the very thing that made such a safety feature work was its hard-to-remove nature after deployment.

"Cut the ropes if you have to, I want it down!" Firmin reasserted, frowning with satisfaction as a muffled "Stand clear!" sounded from the other side and the curtain descended into a heavy heap upon the stage.

"Monsieur Richard!" a white-faced Meg Giry stood center stage, a gaggle of slack-jawed stagehands and flighty ballerinas surrounding her. She held out a plain envelope to the theatre's owners in hands that trembled slightly. "We found it when the lights came back on," she offered tremulously, "along with these." Firmin now noted that not all the figures he'd at first taken to be members of the dance corps were indeed human. Eight full-sized mannequins, dressed in the taffeta trappings of a ballet troupe, stood arrayed in fifth position, the stage workers pointedly leaving them alone.

Firmin snatched the letter from Meg's slack fingers, raising his eyebrows at M. Armand as he sliced the seal and began to read the letter within:

Dearest Messers. Richard and Monchamin,

Please accept my sincerest apologies for the misunderstanding under which we currently seem to be operating. It would appear that my initial message as regards how I wish my theatre to be illuminated was misinterpreted. I presume that, if you are reading this letter, the gas jets have been re-ignited with no great harm and you'll have noted my peace offering—to be implemented in conjunction with the enclosed new opera.

Let me make absolutely clear that I in no way wish the garish and harsh electrical light to make a permanent home within my opera house. You can see from my ballet corps that I am not a man opposed to progress or ingenuity—quite the opposite, in fact. However, I will assert that, if this outfitting of electrical illumination continues, you must be prepared for, shall I say, consequences of an unfortunate sort.

Please again understand that I desire nothing but the best for our theatre and appreciate your efforts to improve relations of late. I am, as ever, cordially yours—

The Opera Ghost

P.S. Future communication may be relayed through Mlle. Giry—I wish her mother the speediest of recoveries.

This postscript immediately turned scrutiny from the ghost's corps de ballet to poor Meg herself.

"It just appeared. Right outside the room where my mother was recovering. I—"

"Goodness, my dear girl. Nobody's accusing you of anything." *Not yet anyway,* Armand harrumphed. He moved, not to comfort the poor ballerina, but rather to M. Richard's elbow to peer critically at the note. It was genuine O.G., at any rate.

The familiar spidery script made his skin crawl. Still, nobody had died—at least not as far as he knew. And it appeared they'd a new opera—always a good thing. And those life-sized dolls—if they worked—would likely merit a larger headline font from the press than any electrical light ever would. These last two observations he said aloud for the benefit of his wan-faced audience, drawing an impromptu burst of applause and a hearty "Bravo!" from Firmin.

❦

Out of safety precautions, the work crew was dismissed for the rest of the week. They still couldn't come to a consensus on whose work had caused the shower of sparks that had led to the gas shut-off. The chorus of dancers had their suspicions— "The ghost!"—and for their part, Mm. Firmin and Armand, and Madame Giry, couldn't disagree.

And so, until a better working solution was hit upon, work on the electrical upgrade was halted. Besides, rehearsals on the new opera had begun almost immediately. Construction would only get in the way as the company attempted to work with the Opera Ghost's newest "members" of the dance corps.

While at first the new mechanical marvels mingling amongst his very human dance corps excited M. Munier, the reality of dealing with mindless automated actors began to wear upon the dance master. He had taken an immediate shine to the mechanized mam'selles. Their precision was a dream come true, they weren't prone to fits of hysteria and gossip, and were (almost) always ready to rehearse. However, M. Munier was a man used to being obeyed, and the first time one of the clockwork corps was found out of place nearly threw the man into a fit.

A missing ballerina one could bark at and bring running. A missing machine, one that required three stage hands to move if not wound properly, was a touch more difficult to call into line.

It was odd, really, how these mindless machines managed to wander off—but then again, nobody, save the Phantom, really knew how they worked. And these random occurrences would have likely inspired more suspicion than exasperation had the roving set pieces been found in more compromising circumstances. Instead, such eccentricities as finding a clockwork ballerina pacing the dim corner of a room, the fire from its electrical circuits glowing out of the dark, were simply marked off as glitches.

Unfortunately, with the added efforts required to keep the clockwork coryphée in line, Dance Master Munier could not rehearse certain scenes to his heart's content. The entire performance had to be run from start to finish. Curtains had to be incorporated into rehearsals, and the entire company was made to schedule more dress rehearsals than normal.

One benefit of this: they were becoming an extremely polished and cohesive company. The only problem: a complete halt on the electrical retrofit.

But for the most part, everyone was too busy to notice, most especially Meg, who now pulled triple duty as senior dancer, opera ghost intermediary and, perhaps most importantly, nurse to her increasingly ailing mother.

The aged concierge, always mobile but never sprightly, had now taken to resting whenever and wherever possible, limiting trips from the front of house to back. Obstinate as always, she refused to relinquish her position, and neither M. Monchamin nor M. Richard asked that she do. After all, her work was not physically demanding. Most of it was deskwork, and they didn't dare risk the Opera Ghost's wrath with such a dramatic personnel change.

It was a shame, though, that someone so headstrong and vocal be robbed of her vitality through lungs that simply no longer worked the way they ought. Unnamed and unexplored,

Mme. Giry's ailment progressed so that she could no longer be without her little brown bottle of elixir, a steady supply of which was now being delivered to Box Five alongside the Ghost's communications.

The first instance of Meg's discovery that her mother's preferred physician was none other than the Opera Ghost himself set the young woman into a fit of stubbornness nearly equal to that of Mme. Giry. For once, the familial resemblance was acute as the young lady refused the patient her cure of dubious origin. Instead, she called upon the company's physician, in order to save her mother from the aid of the fiend.

Too many years in the ballet corps, succored on tales of the Phantom, Meg saw not a kind physician but a madman. Even so, after five days of watching helplessly as her mother's condition deteriorated at a new incredible rate under the doctor's ineffective care, she capitulated.

Luckily, re-introducing the phantom's cure halted further degeneration, and Meg found herself free to concentrate on her duty to the dance corps.

❧

The Phantom's latest was a smash hit. The papers swooned, the audiences wept with awe, and there were no empty seats—save for Box Five.

A modern piece, the tale followed the tumultuous relationship of a boy and his father, a toymaker who turned to his craft when he couldn't bend his son to his ambitious visions.

Resplendent in effects wrought by new scenery and props lovingly rendered, the story brought to life the toymaker's magical workshop.

In spite of its novelty, some were not entranced with the Phantom's latest work. One critic called to question the whole production, unique and heavily mechanized as it was:

"While undoubtedly a solid performance, the company of the Palais Garnier Opera must temper their ambitions if they are to expect audiences to believe their fantastical undertakings are the genuine article. One comes expecting Art and finds a Circus, chicanery of the worst sort. I half expect we'll see the bearded lady in their next performance.

"The singing was fair to excellent, however."

Armand could not care less about the artistic merits of the production. A businessman first and theatre manager second, he could have laughed at the highbrow criticism they received were it not for the potential chilling effect it could have on ticket sales. "There ought to be laws against this. Libel and slander," he paced the office while Firmin chuckled, rather inappropriately, over the harsh review.

"Chicanery," Firmin snapped his fingers, "Bah. Someone probably paid him off to say that—just jealousy."

"Jealousy or not, this mechanical mayhem is driving me mad," Armand interjected, "All I hear from the staff is how deucedly hard this stuff is to work with—"

"I've heard no complaints."

"Yes, well, they've filled my ear," Armand grumbled. "'The

clockwork ballet is making my dancers look sloppy.' 'The props need winding and oiling.'" he did a fair imitation of each complainant.

"They're just lazy," Firmin waved the concerns away. "'Course some of these things need maintenance; of course M. Munier's corps looks sloppy—they are. Even that Giry girl. How many times has she been passed over for prima?"

"So you side with the ghost?"

"I'm not saying that—"

"But you do—"

"I'm not saying that, Armand. Though I find it interesting that the staff seems only to complain to you."

The heated debate raised both tempers and voices, the final exchange leaving the two men in discomforted silence.

Firmin bent his head and began scribbling upon a piece of stationary.

"What is this then?" Armand cocked his head, glancing uneasily at his partner.

"Tendering my resignation as I've just discovered we've a shocking redundancy of management around here," Firmin was brusque in his reply. With a final flourish he handed off the crisp sheet to his partner then donned his coat, "Good day to you, sir." He left the room.

Armand glanced down the page, eyes widening for a brief instant before he mastered himself. "'Suppose I'd better go after the fool," he muttered under his breath, donning coat and hat and scurrying after his fellow manager.

కుఖ్

The managers made their peace, though it was a shaky one, and the company suffered for it. If Firmin said white, you could count upon Armand to say black. M. Richard's instruction that they double the number of Saturday performances would result in M. Monchamin cutting all Sunday matinees. Everything from the length of intermission to the speed at which the orchestra should play was suddenly a bone of contention.

"I knew, I *knew* those two would be a bad idea. I said it from the first," Mme. Giry was heard to gripe to the prop master.

"There were co-managers before Mm. Richard and Monchamin," had been the counterargument.

"Yes. But them, I liked," Giry had sniffed haughtily. Then, she tottered off to find a more receptive audience for her gossip.

As the Great Managerial Row raged on, much of the old company's scenery was stripped away, ushering in a new era of rich, complicated designs that complemented the ghost's latest operatic brainchild. Dioramas and engineering designs for a new configuration of stage trap doors and secret compartments were delivered and adopted (with contention, of course).

What is more, in the midst of the harried readying of a new set, stage, and score, the phantom found no small bit of time to inquire as to Madame Giry's health via his intermediary, Meg. Hurrying down the hall on one of her never-ending errands for her mother, Meg unconsciously placed her hand upon her breast, her thoughts caught up on a different sort of thrill.

Her cheeks flushed, she bowed her head, feeling as though every eye were upon her. If they knew what she carried over her heart, beneath her bodice . . . She blushed anew, trying valiantly to ignore the letter concealed upon her person, a note penned to her in the Opera Ghost's distinct hand and delivered alongside her mother's latest dose of medicine.

All young women are fools at one time or another, and Meg was no exception. The ghost's kindness to her mother forced her to admit, at last, that perhaps Mme. Daae hadn't been wrong about the mysterious, though temperamental, benefactor.

The opera ghost's latest production followed the life of an engineering prodigy, called upon to build a new manufacturing facility for two merchants. The plot outlined the commissioning, building, and subsequent betrayal of the artist by his benefactors who, in the end, turn on their architect, throwing him from the smokestack of the newly-built warehouse. The story ended with the triumphant return of the hero who, by luck, falls not to his death but into the river that flowed alongside the building, his machines rising up in his defense to turn on their masters.

To perfect his vision, the opera ghost delivered additional dance corps members and "extras" to supplement the cast, clockwork creations that far outstripped their predecessors in that an operator could remotely control them from behind the curtain.

Wild with delight over this gimmick, sure they would attract yet another sold-out run, Messrs. Richard and Monchamin pointedly ignored the covert threat being leveled their way by the storyline, especially once a hushed consultation with Madame Giry revealed the phantom's opera to be more autobiographical of events before he settled in Paris. Though, with what followed, perhaps the managers should have been worried.

A small cluster of ballerinas stood at the end of the hall, not daring to pass, watching in suspense as M. Munier and M. Armand argued not forty paces away, the former gesticulating wildly, his face red and dangerously apoplectic. Rehearsal had, once again, been delayed by a mechanicorps gone missing. But this time, nobody yet had managed to find said machine.

Whilst the ballet chorus tittered in their dressing room, stagehands had searched high and low for the missing "cast member." They discovered one of the control panels in a storage room, the device crackling with life and seemingly abandoned in haste, judging from its overturned state upon the ground. It sent M. Munier over the brink at last.

Bunned heads swiveled in unison, a movement that would have pleased their teacher had he noted it, the girls gawked as a newcomer puffed down the hallway in haste. The portly stagehand hailed the two arguing gentlemen with an apologetic shake of his head. Though they still huddled at the far end of the corridor, the young ladies could hear the news relatively easily: the missing mechanicorps had been located.

And it appeared that the timely discovery of its control device had averted true disaster, for the errant machine was found in one of the subbasements; most particularly, in the room selected for installation of the new electrical controls for the theatre. Tangled in exposed wiring, the machine's methodical sabotage had apparently been arrested by the severing of the signal, saving more than just the better part of a month's work.

A curious Meg Giry now joined her fellow dancers, having used the delay in rehearsal to minister to her mother. True to form, she was quickly caught up on the news, the excitable girls adding rapturous and dramatic assessments of the danger they'd narrowly avoided. With a frown, Meg took in the girls' disordered description of events, wondering how close they were to the mark—a seventeen-story honeycomb of a building riddled with gas piping was not the place to spark an electrical fire.

Oh, Erik, please tell me you had nothing to do with this, she pleaded inwardly, her mind's eye picturing two glittering eyes and a wicked smile that gleamed in the dark.

The curtain fell on the first act, and soot-faced industrials exited the stage, transforming immediately into the fresh-faced young ballerinas they actually were.

"This blasted ash is ruining my complexion," little Brigitte complained, espying herself in a mirror.

"It's not ash, it's stagepaint," Meg chided, "And the whole thing's rather brilliant."

"Yeah, if you're a smokestack-worshiping roast beef. I hear they're positively clamoring to get this new opera," one of the other girls piped up, pulling a face at one of the automated actors as it clomped past.

Meg turned to the long mirror on the wall. The inky smudges actually didn't look all that bad, really. An added drama, a deeper contrast to rosy cheeks, it brought out the ebony hues of her hair and eyes. Wickedly, she wondered if the phantom watched tonight, if he approved of his having turned blushing young ladies into bedraggled industrial symbols. Such was the magic of theatre.

Still . . . with a sigh, Meg thought back to three years prior. Christine, with the voice of an angel, the handsome comte with his endless bouquets of expensive hothouse flowers, the corps talking ribbons and silks instead of rivets and steam.

Movement in the hallway caught her eye. Meg turned to espy a rough-looking gentleman who simply did not fit in with the usual flurry of activity occurring backstage of an opera's intermission. He appeared to be in hushed conference with someone who stood in greater shadow, unidentifiable at this distance. Curious, Meg crept forward, staying near the wall and out of the speakers' line of sight.

"It is done then?" the figure in shadow spoke, his voice immediately recognizable to Meg as that of M. Firmin. *Who, by rights, should be out front,* Meg frowned.

"No, sir. I mean, we're prepared and ready, but my man below said that the opera ghost was not at home. He reported scarcely half-an-hour ago that the phantom had apparently decided to view this evening's performance in person. Said he came up passage 9B."

Meg concluded from his manner of dress that he might be one of the electricians who had been re-assessing the Palais Garnier's grounds. For the past several days, they had worked overtime—even during performances, so long as they did no electrical work.

"Show me," a new voice sounded, that of M. Armand.

Interesting . . . Are they no longer on the outs, then? Meg snuck a peek in time to see the electrician pointing obligingly to the aforementioned passage on a leaf of opera house plans. The managers certainly looked chummy as they gazed together at the schematics.

"And we can't just take him now?" Armand suggested, his tone indicating he did not quite believe it a viable option but felt it needed voicing all the same.

"No," Firmin shook his head, "Not without endangering the cast or audience. You remember Faust, my dear Armand. No, we stick with the plan until we seal that deformed rat in his hole. Your man is standing by, then?" This last he addressed to the electrician, who'd since furled his blueprints and clearly awaited further orders.

"Yes, monsieur. Soon as the phantom returns to his lair, we seal him in," the man nodded smartly.

"Well, my dear Firmin, it appears I must quarrel with you a while longer," Armand smiled, "Appearances, you know."

"Quite right. Divide and conquer." Firmin adopted a stern look. "Well then, we've about two minutes to curtain. Gentlemen, to your posts."

Meg retraced her steps back along the hallway. She directed her most disarming smile at Monsieur Monchamin as he strode past.

"Positions. Positions!" M. Munier hissed out of the darkness, startling Meg out of her reverie.

So they plan to seal the opera ghost below? She mulled the thought over in her mind as she took her position, unsure of what she thought of it. For all his apparent kindness of late, the opera ghost was a murderer, a sick and twisted fiend who suckled on fear. Or so they said.

After all, her own mother had agreed to serve him and received nothing but kindness from the poor wretch. And Christine—hadn't he done her any number of favors? While Meg knew very few particulars, she had heard something of tenderness at the heart of the terror, reverence for the man, Erik, amongst the revulsion.

You must warn him. This last thought flashed through Meg's mind as the final notes of the overture struck and the curtain opened.

There were no words to describe the agony, the abject and total mortification poor Mam'selle Giry felt, especially as she alone suspected why she had turned her ankle during the final piece of the evening. In front of a sold-out audience. While *he*, of all people, was watching.

It all had happened so fast. Chassé-ing and leaping, the corps twisting and weaving a complicated pattern amongst the gleaming clockwork coryphée, Meg had lifted her eyes for one instant. Intended as a stagy gaze into The Beyond for a final transcendent moment of beauty, Meg had instead found her eyes directed to Box Five where two glittering eyes in a death's head stared back at her. It was in that moment that shooting pain informed Meg of her error, and she landed in an indecorous heap upon the brilliantly lit stage.

She still wasn't sure if she'd simply landed wrong or if she'd caught her toe upon an imperfection in the boards. And what's worse, her rapidly swelling ankle had necessitated a quick rescue by one of the burlier extras, his rough chastisement as he dumped her in the wings doing little to dim the reddening of her cheeks, nor stop the flood of tears now brimming in pain-filled eyes.

The company really did function at times like an extended family. Full of all the bumps, fits, and starts of a real family, they weren't perfect, and none save the props master came to see to her needs until the final curtain fell. But that was understandable; the performance did not stutter just because an errant dancer twisted an ankle.

Oh, you silly, silly goose! Meg cursed herself through gritted teeth, more than slightly aware that, from her perch, she was mere inches away from craning her neck to espy one more time

Box Five's ghostly inhabitant. But no, she resisted bravely—after all, her error was sure to have displeased the spectral spectator. It occurred to Meg that her one glance at the man was likely to be the last she'd ever have. They'd sack her for sure after this, and that'd be the end of it. No more ballet. No more Palais Garnier. No more Opera Ghost.

A new thought entered her head as the first of the curtain calls began and more of the crew now found themselves free to tend to Meg's needs. If Meg was removed from the corps—and therefore relieved of her duties as the phantom's interlocutor—how would her mother continue to receive her treatments?

Despair at this new dilemma only served to heighten her pain, and she smiled wanly at the few ballerinas who now hovered around her. She could see the hunger in their eyes—already the politics of vying for the coveted first row position were stirring.

The growing crowd parted and Meg blushed anew to see M. Richard approaching, the look of concern somehow better filling the lines on his face than that of cheer.

"Mademoiselle Giry. The doctor tells me it is a sprain, yes?"

Meg nodded confirmation of the fact. Already the doctor had seen, assessed, and dismissed her injury with the bleak prognosis of a couple weeks rest. The damage to her pride seemed likely to be more permanent than that of her ankle, though both hurt equally at present.

"Yes, well, good," the manager looked troubled and he appeared to struggle to find the words. "Am glad to hear it is nothing worse. Would never have forgiven myself, you know?"

Meg heard herself saying some nonsense about the inherent dangers of live theatre.

"Well said, my dear. Well said. I, ahem, must be off—" He jerked his head towards the front of house, nervously tugging at his gloves.

"Thank you for your concern," Meg smiled through gritted teeth, touched that he'd came backstage just to check on her well-being when he was so clearly needed elsewhere.

Firmin's tone grew businesslike, "Gentlemen, see to it that Mlle. Giry is given the utmost care. I've been—I've been informed that Lady Christine's old room is quite comfortable—" His voice broke on this last sentence, and he hurried away without a backward glance, one black dinner jacket amongst many now milling about the dressing rooms. A sea of gentlemen admitted backstage to call upon their paramours.

Madame Giry arrived in time to see Firmin's hurried exit. "Come, child, let's get that foot up and out of harm's way." She shot a mistrustful gaze at the back of the retreating manager.

Meg was grateful that she'd not have to sit, miserable, immobilized, and exposed amongst the graceful and lively corps of ballerinas as they flirted and teased the male suitors, men more interested in girls than opera. However, she was chagrined at the idea of being exiled to the long-disused dressing room of her former friend. Somehow, the isolation, while she changed, a blessing to her throbbing ankle, seemed redolent of her fears that her on-stage tumble meant expulsion from the company.

As she followed her mother down the hall, past the current

prima's rooms, Meg suppressed a shudder—she wasn't sure whose progress was more labored, hers or her mother's. *Relics of a time past, like the ghost who'll soon be sealed in his lakeside tomb*, the young lady hobbled along, grimly assisted by a stout stagehand that looked like he'd rather be elsewhere.

The journey was short, even with their snails' pace. Dismissing the stagehand with a grateful smile and heartfelt thanks, Meg sank to a small settee and allowed her mother to fret over her. Assuring her at last that she was fine, Meg demonstrated her capabilities by moving to loosen her ties. With a curt, no-nonsense nod, Mme. Giry agreed to fetch a carriage, leaving Meg to her arduous task. Luckily, the last act of the opera required a plethora of raggedy factory workers, instead of a bevy of young ladies, making her costume one she could remove with no help and little trouble.

Smiling at the tidy heap her clothes made on a nearby table, Meg again was reminded how painfully slow their progress down the hallway must have been if someone had found the time to be so thoughtful as to fetch her clothing in anticipation of her needs. "I should thank M. Firmin again later for his kindness," Meg remarked then emitted a started "Oh!" as she nearly knocked over a diminutive glass bottle that had lain nestled amongst her garments.

A small note fluttered to the floor and she froze, very much aware of where she'd seen such a shade of stationary before, such a small brown bottle.

Heart pounding, her mind's eye on the glittering visage she'd seen in the instant before she'd taken her ungainly tumble, Meg fumbled through dressing. Numb fingers working furiously on an uncharacteristically stubborn set of buttons, Meg found herself straining to hear the sounds of the hallway. Perhaps her mother had found luck in securing a carriage in the post-opera throng, perhaps she was approaching the door now, perhaps . . . Meg's eyes darted to the abandoned note. She'd delivered countless letters to and from Box Five over the past several months, why should this be any different?

"Mademoiselle Giry, why do you reject my gift? It is perfectly safe, I assure you. It only dulls the pain, lessens the swelling." The voice spoke in masculine tones, smooth, deep, commanding.

Glancing wildly to the still-shut door, Meg found her tongue, "Who's there?" The question was unnecessary, she knew full well who it was. *Where* he was, was another question entirely.

A low chuckle sounded behind her, and she felt the hair on the nape of her neck prickle. "Come, you are far too in command of your faculties, and we know each other too well, to prompt such a fearful reaction, Mlle. Meg. May I call you Meg?" honey-sweet and flecked with notes of danger, the voice soothed and seduced.

"Yes," Meg breathed her answer—an answer that came too quickly, really. She turned around, eyes darting to the dark corners of the room. Half of her wished, prayed, for someone to come, half-dreaded someone might. "And I'm to call you . . .?" she led, suddenly reluctant to address him as the Opera Ghost, when he sounded so like a man.

"Erik. Call me Erik," the ghost's reply was equally quick and contained an element of relief.

"Erik," Meg repeated, savoring the privilege. With a start, she recalled the events preceding her accident, *I must warn him.* "Do not return to the lake beneath the opera house," she blurted the warning, giving the words a touch more womanly fear than intended.

Her words were met with silence. A silence punctuated by one small noise—it could have been a moan, a snort, or over a suppressed cough. Meg waited.

"Your . . . concern is noted," the disembodied voice spoke at last. "But neither can I stay here, among men."

"Is it because of your—" Meg stopped herself short, blushing. "I mean, I've heard that there are reasons you might wish to remain apart from—"

"I'd ask you to step to the mirror, but in light of present circumstances . . ." Erik suddenly sounded much less ghostly, much more corporeal and near.

From the corner of her eye, she saw him appear. Not from the door but from a rather well-lit corner of the room. She did not know why it surprised her that he be dressed for the opera—white gloves, cape, and all—for she had seen him in his box scarcely half-an-hour prior. Perhaps, the bone-white masque that covered two thirds of his face served as a marked contrast to his very conventional formal dress. Meg tried to look away politely but found she could not.

"Yes, I don't much blend in with 'regular men.'" He spat the term. "Although I've made great strides," he added, as if to himself. "Little Meg Giry . . ." The eyes beneath the mask glittered as they had in Box Five, as she'd always imagined them, as if a deep fire burned within. "You wish to save me then. May I inquire as to the nature of the danger?"

Meg swallowed, glad she was sitting, else she'd have sunk to the floor long ago. Even so, she felt near swooning, "They want to s-seal you in. Keep you from ever leaving. I heard them say they'd a man reporting when you returned to your . . ." She searched for a proper word, for "home" didn't evoke the right image in her mind.

"I was aware they'd been poking about—exclaiming boorishly over this and that trapdoor." Erik turned to face the dressing mirror, the resulting multiple reflections magnifying his presence in the room. "But, no. They don't seriously believe they've identified all passages that lead into the theatre. No." This last seemed to be a reassurance to himself, the rich voice sinking to a near whisper.

"And the medicine . . ."

"Somewhat different from what your mother has been receiving, dear Meg. Both come from the finest physician I've ever had the pleasure of knowing. A man, who, through his studies, is an infinitely better study of the human condition than I. He has taught me all I know."

"A teacher?"

"A father . . ."

Intrigued, Meg turned to the ghost, the man, Erik. There'd been a different sort of catch in his voice when he'd spoken just now, and she'd found that her heart had responded with an equally different sort of thrill than what she'd felt of late. The Opera Ghost, no longer an idea, but a man of flesh and blood. A man with motives and fears like her own. Meg hungered to know more.

"I'm just fetching my daughter and then I'm off," Mme. Giry's voice sounded clear and sharp outside the door. "Poor thing's ankle's swollen to the size of a cabbage." There was a grunting male reply, and Meg turned wide eyes to the phantom only to find she was again alone in the room.

"And thank you, once more, for your kind concern, little Meg," the ghost's voice sounded in her ear and then faded.

The door opened, Meg's mother clomping in. "Are you in much pain, dear? You look flushed."

"'The Wasp and the Butterfly,'" M. Armand read the title with relish. "Based on the Aesop's fable of the same name, the story follows the conversation of two reincarnated souls—a, ahem, butterfly and a wasp, obviously. Through their narration we discover who they were, how they were connected, how they died—"

He paused, giving his small audience a dramatic raise of eyebrows. "Stylized as a Chinese fairy tale, it follows the first lives of the main characters—that of an Empress and her forbidden lover. We're working on the necessary changes in instrumentation.

"To that end, the Empress and her lover . . .Their parts are somewhat demanding; *however,* I've been assured that the parts were written especially with our own Mme. Allemand and M. Voland in mind."

He paused and cleared his throat, clearly bracing himself for the next words. "The parts of the wasp and butterfly have similarly been reserved for our principle dancers, but I've been instructed there should be a change—a change in prima ballerina for the duration of this next production. Mlle. Giry?" All eyes turned to the girl, many tainted with ill-concealed animosity.

"I cannot yet dance, M. Armand," Meg stuttered, not quite sure she understood, a rumble of discontent from the cast backing her claim.

"Yes, well," Firmin piped in. "That, too, has been a matter of much discussion between the prop master, acting manager Mercier, and myself. It appears the role requires some . . . interesting . . . stage effects that remove the seemingly insurmountable barrier of requiring an injured dancer to, well, dance."

A multitude of people now spoke at once, each outshouting the other in an effort to dissect Firmin's interesting, yet puzzling, response. A prima ballerina role that does not require the dancer to dance? They would not stand for it! Could they not, for this once, ignore the Opera Ghost's eccentric demands?

"Here, here. People, calm yourselves," Armand thundered through the protests. "Yes, this is an Opera Ghost piece, and yes, these instructions have come directly from him. But rest assured, when I tell you that Firmin and I have looked over this production and agree *of our own volition* that these demands are by no means excessive and are, in fact, some of the best ideas we've ever seen put to paper. Please, trust us."

The rumblings began again, this time carrying a current of excitement, for they had seen the twinkle of enthusiasm in their managers' eyes and now were more intrigued than irked.

Meg felt certain the topic wasn't entirely closed, however. She self-consciously lifted her eyes to the vacant Box Five. *Thank you, Erik,* she silently spoke to the ghost, *Why you put your trust in me, I'll never understand . . .*

Never before had the ghost light seemed so aptly named as Meg stepped into its aura, heart pounding in her chest. The theatre was not the most welcoming place to be alone at night, and, in spite of the illicit thrill, she felt apprehensive.

Movement in the shadows caught her eye, soft and non-menacing in spite of the oppressive darkness. Erik smiled at her from beneath his ever-present mask, clearly pleased with himself for not having startled her. He commented, "Your grace, dear Meg, is as beautiful as a song."

In the dim solitary ghost light, Meg wondered if the phantom could see her blush. She deflected the compliment. "Only some of the time . . . Erik."

Her reward was the approach of the opera ghost, clad in dark, well-tailored clothing, most appropriate for dusty backstage work. It suited him, though Meg still had a difficult time tearing her gaze from his mask.

Meg again felt her heart beat fast. She'd seen the schematics for the phantom's plan and knew full well that he intended his butterfly should take to the air, but . . . she fought the urge to confess her fear of heights. Behind the mask, Erik's smoldering eyes shone at her and she knew, oddly, that she was safe.

Feeling suddenly self-conscious, she accepted the ghost's gentle assistance as she stepped gingerly into the waiting harness, carefully avoiding stressing her still-tender ankle. Light, but strong, the straps and buckles of the contraption would easily be concealed beneath her costume, her butterfly wings.

Meg averted her face to hide her renewed blush in shadow, as the phantom's sensitive, but no-nonsense fingers, worked at adjusting the harness to her lithe dancer's form. *Silly goose, you wouldn't blush if it were a stagehand*, she scolded herself. She released the breath she hadn't realized she had been holding.

Erik stepped back, admiring his work for a moment, before positioning himself in the wings. She saw that he waited for her nod, some sign that she was ready to take flight. She hesitated.

"Would it be permissible to light a few of the house lights first?"

"Embrace the darkness, Meg. Let it lift you so that you soar over the world, not just the empty seats of a dim and lonely theatre. As prima, remember it is *you* who'll light the stage." Erik's answering chuckle sounded through the blackness.

Meg nodded, gasping as she felt the ground fall away beneath her. Soaring out in a gentle arc over the vacant house, Meg could sense the grandeur of the space as she'd never had before. She marveled at the sensation, the sweet night air breathing gently upon her face.

Released from her fears and worries, Meg allowed herself to fall fully under the spell of the mad genius of a man who pulled the strings in the shadows, a man who bent the very laws of nature to his whim.

"Another note, Meg. The ghost has left another note," Brigitte squealed. She scampered past the tiny room where Meg tended to her mother. Giry had, once more, taken a turn for the worse.

"Go see what he says, child." The pale and skeleton-thin concierge waved her daughter off with a weak smile. "Mayhap he's left more of my medicine . . ." This last was delivered with a small note of hope, and while Meg pasted a kind smile onto her face for her mother's benefit, the ballerina turned to the doorway with eyes radiating hurt.

The doctor had explained to her the previous day her mother's dire situation. Her lungs were dying, slowly, inexorably. He'd said the hard words kindly, had expressed frank surprise that frail Mme. Giry had hung on as long as she had.

But three days ago she'd turned poorly; three days ago, she'd run out of the phantom's cure.

Legs carrying her fast as they could down the myriad of backstage hallways, Meg muttered black thoughts against the Ghost. *How dare he disappear, sending nothing save useless notes of encouragement and improvement for the new opera, neglecting my mother's care!* Meg glowered. *How could he have forgotten?* She calmed herself. She'd look in Box Five. Maybe this time he had left something.

As Firmin's strong, warm voice read proudly the opera ghost's review of the previous day's performance, the penultimate of their current production, one rather wondered if the manager mightn't pop buttons off his waistcoat, puffed with pride as he was. He and Armand both. And as the words of laud for their rehearsals of "The Wasp and The Butterfly" were exceptionally strong, Meg, too, had felt herself carried along on the tide of good humor and high spirits.

Tomorrow evening, she would fly. In spite of her anger at the non-delivery of her mother's medicine, her remembrances of Erik, the private rehearsal in a dark theatre, warmed her thoughts.

Heart pounding as she fervently searched Box Five, Meg prayed that the phantom had seen fit to remember her mother in the midst of putting his rapturous praise to paper.

She found nothing.

"So that's it then? You're just going to let her die?" she muttered, temper as black as the empty box she searched. "You could save her and yet you do nothing. Erik, you really are a murderer. Just like they all said."

"Meg! Meg Giry . . ." a voice in the hallway startled her to standing.

It was M. Mercier.

"Meg?" He entered Box Five, eyes darting about curiously. "Goodness, girl, what on earth are you doing in here?"

"I—" Words failed her, but it didn't matter. M. Mercier spoke over her.

"Never mind," he waved away explanation, and motioned for her to follow. He was clearly in a hurry, his eyes radiating kindness. Too much kindness. Heart in her throat, Meg followed with alacrity, not even giving the abandoned Box Five a backward glance.

The old woman lay groaning upon the divan. Perhaps rasping might be the better word, for Mme. Giry's lungs appeared to be expiring at long last. Meg knelt by her mother's side, listened as the guttural whimper changed tone, became words: "Take me to the lake. Take me to *him*." Meg could barely understand the utterance and leaned in close.

"I'm sorry, I don't understand." She held her mother's shaking hand.

"Erik. Erik will know what to do. I need Erik."

"She's asking for the damned ghost." One of the stagehands lingering in the doorway spat on the floor. M. Mercier shot him a look so that Meg didn't have to.

"Mother, mother, you're delirious. Please, let me get the doctor," Meg pleaded. "Someone fetch the doctor," she turned to the small crowd gathering in the doorway. Seeing the tears in the young woman's eyes, shamed at having gawked over another's misfortune, the crowd scattered, Mercier promising he'd fetch the doctor himself. Nearly crumbling with relief, Meg turned her gaze back to her mother and was startled to note that the woman, weak as she was, was attempting to rise.

"Must . . . see . . . Erik," she gasped.

"Mother, you don't know what you're saying. Please, lie back down," Meg cooed, crossing the room to fetch a damp towel.

"I know plenty," Mme. Giry's voice regained some of its customary sharpness, "I must—I must go . . . to Daae, to Daae's rooms. Take me there, Meg."

Meg turned sharply, memories of her conversation with the phantom coming back full-force. *They don't seriously believe they've identified all passages that lead into the theatre . . .* She understood at last. "There's a passageway in there . . . to his underground lake."

"Daae . . . Daae's room . . . " Mme. Giry gasped, lying back down against the cushions. "Go to him. Tell him—"

"Yes. Sh-sh-sh . . . Yes," Meg kissed her mother's forehead and hastened from the room.

Hefting a lamp, knowing she had to work quickly, lest her actions inspire suspicion, Meg peered about Christine's former dressing room. *If they didn't insist on such ostentation, this would be easier,* she lamented, pushing aside a large wall hanging for the third time, exposing the same blank wall. If there was a trapdoor in the room, it was well hidden.

A flicker out of the corner of her eye caught Meg's attention and she turned to find herself facing the room's full-length dressing mirror. The wavering reflection of the lamp in her hand tore at her eyes, and Meg assessed the thin and none-too-happy-looking young person that stared back at her.

"Oh, Erik, how did you sneak up on me that night?" She addressed the dim copy of herself, pausing as if it might give answer.

It did.

A sudden thought entered her mind. Meg leaned in close and examined briefly the elaborate gold-leaf frame. Something of its design seemed familiar, an elegance, an overwrought heaviness . . . like a stage prop. Like something the phantom would design. *There!* She saw the catch, gingerly reached out a finger to give it a stroke.

Somewhere inside the mirror a small click could be heard. The looking-glass swung outward, revealing . . .

A blank wall. No, not a wall—a brick barrier. Meg's arms broke out in gooseflesh. She ran a finger along the rough masonry. Someone had bricked up this passageway. Recently. A new idea hit her—what if the opera ghost hadn't been sending the messages Firmin and Armand had shared with the cast, glee evident in their faces? What if, instead, he had indeed been imprisoned below as the two scheming managers had planned?

"Which would explain why my mother hasn't received any new medicines from Erik . . ." Meg breathed the conclusion, hands exploring the new brickwork, her frustration growing acute.

Tomorrow would be the opening of "The Wasp and The Butterfly" and the phantom *would* attend. Tonight . . . tonight she was breaking him out of his subterranean prison.

❧

Meg moved through the wings of the active production, her mind elsewhere. Her ankle still too weak for dancing, Meg's only duties since her sprain had been in rehearsal for the new piece. Frustrating at first, this now proved to be a blessing in disguise, as it meant she might work out how to free Erik and fetch his assistance for her mother without shirking her duties to the company, and, therefore, draw attention to herself and her activities.

Eyes darting to and fro, she summarily saw and dismissed any number of tools that might help her break through a wall of solid brick. *What I need is something big and strong. Preferably something that even these useless little arms of mine might wield.*

Again she looked about the bustling backstage. Her eyes lit up as she scanned a rather large item that stood forgotten in the corner. One of the original mechanicorps, phased out for the new and improved remote-controlled style brought in for the phantom's second opera.

Meg nonchalantly wove through the jungle of curtains, counterweights, and ropes that hung in the wings. She avoided eye contact with the men bustling about in the half-light. As long as she stayed quiet and kept out of their way, they were perfectly happy to ignore her. She made it to the storage cabinet unimpeded.

The door swung open on silent hinges, and she peered into the locker's interior—a deeper blackness set in the surrounding gloom. There. She spotted one of the individual control mechanisms on a shelf. While one trip into the small props storage would be overlooked, a second foray might excite comment. She made for backstage, just another dark figure flitting about the wings, breathing a sigh of relief when she once again found herself alone in the labyrinth of storage areas in the back of the theatre.

With all the moving about of scenery that had been done in the past few weeks—movement that Meg now correctly assigned to the emptying of lower basements as part of the plot against the Ghost, rather than the usual changeover occurring with the start of a new production—she wondered whether she'd be able to find any of the newer models of mechanicorps. *They couldn't have gone all that far, they're so irksome to move without the aid of the controls,* she reasoned. She felt encouraged by the fact that one of the remote controls had been so ready at hand. She looked down, trying to gauge if it was in working order or not.

She turned the corner and found herself face to face with no less than twelve impassive figures who stood blocking her path. "Oh!" she exclaimed, both startled and elated. Standing in a darkened room full of mechanical dolls, she suddenly felt small, frail.

Immobile and stern metal faces glinted in the half-light from the hallway. The mechanicorps dancers seemed to frown at her, laying harsh blame at her feet. She had the power to save their creator, a man with a mind finer than any other she'd known. She could not let their genius inventor die in the dark beneath the opera house.

Flipping the switch on the top of her device, she chose a mechanicorps doll at random. She snapped a control on the back of one of the hulking machines and an answering low hum emanated from both machines. Signal established. Breathing a sigh of relief as the clockwork dancer lurched forward at her command, Meg turned to lead. Help was on the way.

A human-sized machine made of metal is a heavy thing; even so, Meg was unprepared for the ease with which her abducted dancer broke through the brickwork behind Christine's old mirror. Before her yawned the dark and menacing passageway known only to a handful of beings on God's earth.

The thought chilled her more than the damp and unhealthy air that issued forth. Still, Meg moved quickly, lest her noisy actions bring anyone running. She snatched up the lantern she'd brought, and moved to lay aside her corps controller. Pausing, she debated the wisdom of her next act.

Think, girl, think how hard they worked to trap poor Erik, she reasoned, trying to force her reluctant feet into forward motion. She turned her mind to thoughts of her mother as she'd last seen her: lying sedated upon a divan, her frail sickness a terrible foil to the fluffy and ornate stage prop. It was the story of Meg's short life. Everything beautiful was a lie, a fakery to please the shallow world's sensitivities. All was gold leaf and face paint.

Galvanized by the sheer unfairness of it all, both in regards her situation and that of the opera ghost, Meg worked the controls for the clockwork doll once more, guiding it into the dark passage ahead of her. Then, with one tremulous backward glance, she loosed the ties on a nearby drapery, the heavy brocade swinging down to hide the entire scene—mirror, broken brickwork, and all.

Cold, damp air caressed her face as she turned to the illicit passageway with her flickering lantern. The bland metallic face of the mechanicorps dancer looked menacing in the chill corridor, and Meg shuddered, feeling for the first time that her intrusion might well be unwelcome. Hurriedly putting such thoughts aside, she hastened her progress down, down into the darkness beneath the Palais Garnier, careful not to turn her ankle on an errant stone or uneven flag.

While she knew the opera house supported seven stories of sub-basements, all poised above an underground cistern that doubled as ballast for some of the larger set pieces, the journey to the phantom's subterranean lake seemed painfully long to Meg's overworked mind. The floor endlessly sloped down, down . . . the ceiling gave the impression of having receded high off above her head long minutes ago. And still Meg found herself in a winding, twisting passage of stone, with no sign of Erik anywhere.

As if in answer to her worries, and without warning, the passageway suddenly came to an end, opening out into a large cavern bathed in an eerie blue light. Though her experience with such things was small, she was the daughter of the theatre and could sense the dramatic space that lay before her in the dark.

She could feel, rather than see, that it must hold heart-stopping beauty. The ballerina hesitated, suddenly afraid that in the inky blue-black of the cave, she might step over the banks of the nearby lake and sink to a watery death.

Luckily, Meg's lengthy walk in the winding corridor had pre-pared her eyes for such dim surroundings, and she soon could pick out the dark form of a small boat lying on the banks of the water she could now see, as well as hear.

Climbing into the vessel without so much as a second thought, and praying she wouldn't overturn the thing as she grabbed at the oars, Meg peered about the dim cavern to see where she might direct her efforts. Alarmingly, she soon had her answer.

"Ah, Baroness. Sweet Meg." He spoke to her out of the black water, Erik's now familiar voice sending shivers up Meg's spine and nearly prompting her to drop the oars. A chuckle echoed around her, the mocking tone of his address a burden on her shaken nerves.

"Am I to take this as a social visit? You'll find me rather unprepared to receive visitors at present—I so rarely have them and have been busy with . . . other matters . . . of late."

These last words fell oddly flat on Meg's ears, and she felt a tremor of guilt that she should be affiliated with the men who would imprison this remarkable man, a part of her whispering that she was only here to secure aid for her mother, and was therefore as in the wrong as if she'd laid the confining brickwork herself.

"I'm sorry for what they did to you," she whispered, as if the paltry apology would exculpate her from the crime of federation with the wicked deeds of men. "I know that—"

"You know, do you? I don't think you *quite* understand, dear Meg," the ghost's voice echoed in the half-light, sounding both near and distant at the same time. "And I do believe it is time you do."

At his words, the small boat jolted into motion and Meg grabbed the rowlocks to steady herself, lest she be thrown over-board into the inky water. Peering into the darkness and seeing nothing but a light ripple in the water before her to hint at what might be providing the locomotion, a wildness seized her mind, and she considered leaping into the water and swimming to the not-yet-distant shore.

But, no. That would leave her nowhere but wet on the edge of a lake thirty metres below the Paris Opera House and, as she truly felt that right was on her side, she must see it through, no matter how terrifying the phantom's revelations might be.

The boat slowed, approaching the far shore of the under-ground lake, revealing a colossal structure of stone. Before her, she could see the dark silhouette of a mechanism churning and whirring on the lake's edge, a chain threading through the series of pinions, leading up from the water and clearly having its origins at her boat's prow. The mystery of her craft's propulsion solved, she now eagerly looked about for the phantom.

"Meg Giry, I bid you welcome to my humble abode." Erik was again clothed in all black save for his bone-white mask, and a gloved hand reached out to help her in exiting the boat. With unaccountable eagerness, she took it and allowed herself to be handed gently onto the waiting shore, her own dark eyes locking brightly with the glittering ones that shone out from beneath her host's luminous mask.

Sure of footing, even in the dark—for the ghost still held her gently at his side—Meg crossed the short space between the lake and the phantom's home. Struck with awe that such a large building should exist beneath the opera house, with little rumor as to its existence, Meg allowed herself to be led through the massive front door, little noting the smell of death and decay that emanated from within the hulking edifice.

"How long—?" she began, choking on the words as she looked up into the blank masque of the opera ghost. They passed through a grand foyer resplendent with finery. Had the journey not been harrowing, the darkness without near complete, and her host equally enigmatic and terrifying, Meg would have paid her surroundings due attention.

"On the evening after our last meeting, Monchamin and Richard's men erected barriers of stone and mortar over each and every one of my outlets into the world above."

The ghost supplied the answer to her ill-framed question, his pace quickening as they progressed through a large sitting room lit by no less than a thousand candles. Meg now compulsorily swiveled her head to take it all in before they hurried into the next, equally opulent room, this one graced with a large pipe organ. The grand instrument was truly an ornate piece of art, such a one might have been seen in churches a hundred years prior.

"So the night I flew for the first time . . . "

"Was my last night of freedom." The bitterness in the phantom's voice carried a new menace and Meg gasped, partly out of fear, partly out of pain, for their rapid pace and her lengthy sojourn had greatly taxed the still-sore appendage and she found herself longing to rest her poor ankle.

Either they had arrived at their destination, or the opera ghost became cognizant of her needs, for he now let go of her arm and bade her sit, offering her a glass of very old, very expensive wine. Perching gingerly on the edge of a large overstuffed armchair, for this room was singularly ill-lit in comparison to the prior one, and the couch smelled faintly of disuse, Meg waited numbly with glass in hand as the ghost moved about, lighting lamps and asking questions.

"And your mother, how is she? How goes the current production? Has your own rolé in The Wasp and The Butterfly proved sufficient?" His rapid-fire collection of inquiries startled and baffled her, and she stammered to answer each in turn. It struck her suddenly that the opera ghost seemed nervous, anxious.

"You're here to ask for my assistance in your mother's

recovery, yes?" The sharp eyes turned back to her, demanding honesty.

"Yes," she breathed and took a sip of the reassuringly aged wine that swirled darkly in her glass. Dismayed at her own simplicity, knowing it was her own exhaustion and fear making her speak so, she moved to explain, "I didn't know what to do. And when I found out that Firmin and Armand had trapped you through their treachery . . . They've been passing the company notes these last few weeks as though the instructions came from you."

"Ah!" the ghost turned his back on her now, doubling over, his gloved fingers picking at his mask, as if he might rip it from his face. His voice radiated a pain that nearly moved poor Meg to tears. "Say no more, dear Meg. I should have known. I should have known you would not prove false to me—you or your dear mother, who has served me so faithfully all these years."

Meg moved to rise, was forced into stillness by the ghost's cries, "Stop! Come no closer."

Pacing like a caged animal, Erik strode the room, the violence in the delivery of his next words matching well the manic energy in his movement, "Meg, you must know that I never meant for you to make this choice. But these past weeks have proven disastrous to my plans. My father is here, in Paris. Quite nearby, in fact. But he—" his gait caught a hitch and he appeared to consider his next words before continuing "—he has fallen ill and it appears my hand is to be forced."

He stopped his frantic pacing and turned to her, his eyes losing their menace for once, instead appearing to glitter with tears, "The medicines that I had given Mme. Giry. My father has told me that she—that she is the only one who might save him, and him, her. That the treatments once meant to cure them both have now become the only thing that might allow me to rescue one of them from the jaws of death."

Frozen with wonder, knowing that in his raving the opera ghost was trying to explain something very, very important, Meg fought through the fog of fear that had begun to enshroud her mind, "I'm not sure I understand. Your father, is here, in Paris?"

"Listen. Listen to me," the crazed energy returned to the opera ghost's voice as he crossed the room to her. "You have a choice. I—I'm giving you a choice, though it may mean my imprisonment here forever. Meg Giry, only one may be saved— as your mother's lungs are failing, so is my father's heart. My father has assured me that the medicines coursing through each of their veins is enough to guarantee compatibility. Should you wish to save your mother, my father will die. And with him, my chances of his healing me of this . . . this . . . " his hands now made good on their promise from before, tearing off the masque and flinging it angrily at her feet "—this disease, this deformity with which I am cursed."

With a shriek, Meg found herself mere inches from the truest nightmare she had ever dared to dream. Old Joseph Buquet, chief scene-shifter dead these four years, had not even come close to describing the horror when he'd terrorized the ballet corps with his stories.

Yellow skin, like parchment, flaked away from the edges of

ragged wounds, sores weeping angrily at the world. Unmasked, the glittering eyes turned sunken, falling back into the depths of the man's skull-head, as if to escape affiliation with the crooked nose that was barely present in the center of the broken monstrosity of a visage.

He continued. "My father. My father has within him the power, the medicinal know-how to fix this." He jabbed a finger at the abomination that was his face. "This face that would imprison me at the hands of 'good men' such as your Firmin and Armand." His voice dripped sarcasm at these last words, and he seemed to gain some modicum of control over himself. Turning, he appeared to have forgotten that he'd flung his mask from him, and he looked wildly about, flinching like a whipped dog when Meg bent and picked up the ghost's discarded guise and held it out to him, tears in her eyes.

"I cannot. You are wonderful, but I cannot," she choked. Surely he understood? Understood that she could not seal her own mother's fate. "Please—"

"Then you must stay with me," he stepped back, voice low. "If you are to consign me to this fate—"

"No."

"No? Come, come. If I am to save your mother at the expense of my father, surely you owe me something in return." He cocked his head to the side, seemingly surprised at her boldness and more than a little bemused.

"There has to be another way," she shook her head, the motion making the room spin around her.

"I eagerly await your erudite suggestions, dear Meg Giry," as he stepped backward into the growing gloom, "But I fear we—and you—are almost out of time. I shall fetch your mother while you sleep off your wine."

Something, some unknown instinct in her, had bade her imbibe no more of the phantom's cloying vintage, but it seemed that the insight had come too late. Meg's last conscious thought rang with the stomach-churning echo of the phantom's laugh.

Waking in near darkness, Meg sat and waited, fearful of the ghost's return, but somehow sensing that he'd left the cavern entirely. There was an emptiness, a dullness to the phantom's house. She tremulously rose to her feet, surprised that he should have left her to freely roam about his dwelling-place in his absence. Perhaps he had no fear of her escape—after all, every passage into the opera house, save one, were sealed.

A small, clattering noise arrested her attention, and she froze. Echoing through the dark, in a room beyond that which she presently occupied, the miniscule sound repeated itself. Scrambling to lay hands upon a lantern, she hurried toward the noise, heart pounding in her chest so as to nearly drown out the faint utterance she so anxiously followed. Meg quickly arrived at a closed door, light bleeding out from underneath. She tried the handle—unlocked—and found herself in the presence of the phantom's other captive.

"Oh! Thank God above. An angel!" the man cried out, half-rising from his chair, still keeping his voice low, but full of unchecked emotion. Painfully thin and pale, he seemed more skeleton than man. A shock of white hair fell over his shoulders and the sunken cheekbones and dark eyes bespoke a grave illness. His first reaction had come from involuntary impulse and he grew still, eyes betraying a cunning that Meg had seen before.

"My son did not send you, did he?" the question was blunt, mistrustful, and Meg was moved with pity.

"Oh, sir," she quickly set her lantern aside, its brilliance redundant in this, the first splendidly illuminated room she had seen thus far in Erik's lair.

"Olivier. Please, call me Olivier. The world should know my name before I die," the old man spoke with a bitterness, a despair, which broke the girl's heart.

"What can I do, Olivier?" Meg looked about the room, eyes dancing across all manner of clockwork schematics, bits and pieces of machines, vials of chemicals, and complicated instruments of the medical profession. Her eyes widened, *It was in this room that the mechanicorps had undoubtedly been born.*

He followed her gaze, "My other children, yes; I am the one behind many of Erik's inventions, but his is the real genius. My talent lies in potions, medicinals. Or at least it used to." He shifted uncomfortably, the clink of a chain betraying the true state of his imprisonment. "Erik blames me for his . . . affliction. And I suppose he has a right to. But you must understand me, *I never meant for any of this to happen.*" A gnarled hand reached out to clasp her own, and Meg shivered, unable to break away from the mesmerizing eyes of the old man. "His mother was dying. Dying! The medicine I administered was meant to save her," he hissed, breath pungent and stale through broken teeth. Meg moved to back away, and found herself unable.

"And I did! I did it. But at the cost of my son's dignity." He released her, moaning to himself, "I still don't know what went wrong. He came out of the womb a monster." He looked into her eyes once more, pleading, "I wanted to fix him. Cure him. Really, I did. And I've tried for the two years since I found him here, rotting beneath this accursed theatre. But his very soul is twisted, and I fear there is no help for him. Please help me, Mlle. Giry. The choice he gave you is no choice at all. Please let me escape, and in exchange—" he pressed a small phial of liquid into her hands. "When Erik thought himself to be trapped, I made this for your mother, in hopes I might yet save her. Please, administer this to her—one drop per day—until it is gone. It should help."

Nodding, shocked that a man so kind could have so cruel a son, Meg asked where she might find the keys to Olivier's chains.

"You'll find his ring of keys by his organ. I've seen them but once, though I know he rarely moves them," he explained, eyes bright with gratitude.

The keys were where he promised, and within moments Olivier was free, staggering on long-unused muscles. "I thank you, Meg Giry," he wheezed weakly.

"Come, let me help you," Meg moved to support the man's frail form, and together they made their way arduously out of the phantom's mansion, towards the lake, towards freedom. The boat was, miraculously, still pulled up tight against the dock, and the two escapees quickened their pace.

"What have you done?" Erik's words rang out across the rippling water, a promise of murder in his voice.

The shock alone would have been enough to bring Meg's attention to the dark figure that now strode towards them along the silent shore, but it was another movement entirely that now arrested the young woman, that of the violent twisting of her arm. A knife flattened against her throat, its cold blade startling her into immobility.

"Ah, Erik. The prodigal son returns," the figure at her back laughed deeply, maniacally.

"Let her go." The phantom halted his own forward progress at the sight of the gleaming blade.

"Why? So I can spend another two years rotting in your dungeon of a house?" Olivier spat back, his words hissing angrily past Meg's ears. She struggled to remove herself from the close embrace, was stopped short by a meaningful press of the knife's blade, "Not so fast, dear Meg. You're my ticket out."

One slow footfall followed another. The ghost crept closer, bright eyes on the blade at the ballerina's throat, "You know why I kept you here. Once you followed me to Paris, to the Palais Gar—"

"You thought that by holding me here, by forcing my hand in your cure, you might win retribution," Olivier screamed, spittle dotting his lips as he took another step back towards the waiting

217

boat, his iron grip on Meg's arm inhumanly strong, though perhaps not as strong as the fear which gripped her heart.

Don't fight him, Erik. Let him go, her eyes pleaded, a meaningless gesture in the dark cavern. She could almost hear the pop and creak of the clockwork buried deep within her captor's imprisoning limb, and she wondered absently how much of him was man, and how much of him machine. The voice at her back taunted further, "You, my greatest creation, hiding from the world in a cave, writing operas! Misapplied genius . . . together we could have the world. You, Erik, are a perfect fiend, and my triumph that will be complete when I finish what I started—"

The opera ghost lunged, cloak sweeping out in a dark arc and revealing his own weapon, a cane black as midnight, a bright metal skulls-head at its top.

"Run, Meg."

She did indeed run, as Erik's father turned to defend himself, letting go his hostage. Throwing her weight to the boat-winch's lever, she was rewarded by the heavy clink of metal on metal, the chain reversing its progress to carry the boat to the farther shore. A sharp gasp punctuated the heavy tumult on the water's edge, and she turned involuntarily to the scene behind her as the boat began to glide silently away, carrying her towards blessed freedom.

There was a pause, a sickening, wet sound—one redolent to Meg of stage battles, heroic deaths by daggers through the heart—as the smaller, thinner of the two dark silhouettes fell, and then . . . silence punctuated by the sound of quiet sobbing.

❧

Meg ran past the myriad of concerned and startled salutations from the cast and crew of the Palais Garnier. She'd emerged from the hidden mirror passageway in Christine's former dressing room moments ago and discovered the company to be in frenzied preparation for the evening's début of the phantom's new work.

"Meg! Oh, Meg. You missed him, you silly goose!" Brigitte caught her up as she hurried down the hall. "The Opera Ghost was here. Someone said they saw him with your mother—"

Spurred on by a new fear, Meg hastened through the backstage area, ignoring all attempts by passersby to ascertain where she'd run off to today, of all days. Brigitte, kind in spite of her flightiness, stayed at her side, guiding Meg to where her mother was resting, thoughtfully staying outside and keeping shut the door as the prima ballerina tentatively entered the sickroom.

"Mother?" Her eyes were met with an unexpected sight.

Madame Giry sat calmly in the little room, arguing with the company's doctor. Thumping her cane demonstratively on the floor, she was in the middle of insisting that she resume her duties when her daughter entered. Knowing himself to be dismissed, and relieved to be rid of his troublesome patient, the doctor removed himself from the room with alacrity.

"Erik—"

"Was here, yes, child," Meg's mother completed the sentence

219

and opened her hand to reveal a tiny glass bottle, a twin to the one Meg had lost in the dark below the opera. "We had a good little chat, he and I." Her eyes twinkled and she patted the couch beside her. Meg sat. "We've long had an arrangement, the details of which you're not needing to know. Suffice it to say, I am happy to report that he is keeping his end of the bargain," the old woman sniffed, clearly pleased with herself.

"But his father, he—"

"His father is a bastard," Madame Giry's eyes grew hard. "If it weren't for him and his infernal experiments, none of this ever would have happened." She paused, grew thoughtful, "Though, without it, Erik might never have become the remarkable genius he is today. And when you think on what some of his creations could be capable of in the wrong hands—the government, the military . . .You might say he's done society a great favour, resigning his clockwork marvels, his smoke and mirror illusions, to the humble theatre, where no real harm may be done."

"But he's a murderer!" Meg blurted out, unable to help herself from assigning blame, in spite of all she'd seen.

"Accidents, my dear. For which poor Erik is quite sorry, I assure you," Madame Giry shook her head sadly. "It's taken a long time for our opera ghost to find his way in our dark little world. He has had little of the comforts that you or I take for granted. A mother's love, a father's approval . . . He has loved and lost and been left with nothing but this opera house and its colourful asylum of inmates. Even developing out of such circumstances, you'll find he's infinitely more honest and trustworthy a man than our own Mm. Richard and Monchamin are. But they, too, are products of their world . . . " She patted Meg's hand. "I trust that the wonders you saw in his world below will serve as a reminder someday when you, too, leave all this behind and are tempted to forget your humble origins, prima ballerina Meg." She smiled sadly.

"Oh, but I don't see that—" Meg shrugged off this last insinuation.

"Shh . . . " Madame Giry turned, fished a small letter out of her pocket, "He asked that I give you this."

Dearest Meg,

I confess that your trueness took me quite by surprise. I am not often faced with such honesty in another—in fact, I can count the occurrences on one hand. But I am not without conscience, and, after our discussion a bit ago, I have found myself unable to go through with the plans I had been forced to consider in my long exile beneath the opera house. You and your mother deserve that much from me, and so I beg your forgiveness and hope that we might be friends henceforth. With such a hope, I do believe that I might find contentment with my place in this world. For you've managed to show me that, in the words of a very wise butterfly, "It does not matter what we used to be: the important thing is what we are now!" I am, as ever, your humble servant—

Erik

"Put on your gayest smile, my dear. I hear that M. Baron de Castelot-Barbezac is to be in attendance tonight." With a sly smile, Madame Giry kissed her daughter lightly on the cheek and disappeared into the growing throng to deal with the arriving audience.

Styled after The Phantom of the Opera by Gaston Leroux

His Frozen Heart

AARON AND BELINDA SIKES

E'benezer stood, head bowed, a single tear chilling on his cheek as the bearers lowered Rose's wrapped body into the waiting earthen womb. He stood as the prayers were said, wincing at the first handful of dirt scattered across the shroud over Rose's face. He stood, cold and rigid, until they'd all gone. Until the gravedigger had left the last shovelful of earth, as Ebenezer had requested. The gravedigger nodded respectfully and reached a shaking hand to collect the sovereign Ebenezer held out to him.

Ebenezer watched the man disappear into the gloaming. And then he began to dig.

With each gentle push of the spade into the earth, he felt his memories peel back to reveal the long march he'd taken to that dismal hour. If only he and Rose could have afforded cleaner lodgings. If only he hadn't been so quick to disobey his father. If only his father had been less fierce, more prone to forgiving than forbidding.

"You are to be wed to Miss Catherine Howlett and I will hear no more trifling over this Rose Bennet. My son, to wed a dollymop . . . a woman of *that* standing!"

"Father, a fine woman Miss Howlett may be, but she would have me as half a man and all the price. She knows me only as heir to the family fortune, which you have worked so hard to build. And she would have no more knowledge of me than that! I love Rose and she loves me, inheritance or no. And she—"

"Ebenezer, I have seen that Bennet woman enter a public house, and unaccompanied at that! She is but a lowly strumpet! I won't have you throw your life and my fortune away by marrying her. If you marry her, your services will no longer be required at the firm."

"No, please. You misunderstand the situation, Father—" but his words rebounded from his father's disappearing back.

Rose had loved Ebenezer from the first time he walked into her uncle's public house. He treated her like a lady, not a barmaid. Whatever pains his father might have taken to instill in him a disbelief in her virtue, they had not worked. She assured him of her purity, despite her standing.

As he spent time at the pub and grew to know her, he knew he had been right to believe in her. Her rosy cheeks and sparkling gray eyes reflected her sunny, sweet disposition. She cast dispelling sunlight on the fog that had surrounded Ebenezer for most of his life. As the only son to a fierce-tempered patriarch, Ebenezer had had his share of gloomy days, but with Rose by his side, he'd seen a more cheerful future stretching out before him, like the open sea.

His father, alas, held fast to his convictions, and he dismissed Ebenezer from the family business on the day of the wedding. When Rose began coughing blood mere months after they spoke their vows, Ebenezer's future once again hung over him like the bleak, soot-black, smoky skies of London.

Rose's death came one year to the day after the wedding. Ebenezer shrank inward. No wintry weather could chill him; no summer day would warm him. He wrote to his sister, Fanny, with the news of his wife's death. Burial was not a pittance at six-pound-and-ten, and he would be damned if he'd let them throw Rose atop the pile in a pauper's grave. He hoped that Fanny might have more luck than he in warming the old man's heart enough to loosen his purse. But the elder Scrooge kept to his convictions, as only a Scrooge can do. Ebenezer's name had been stricken from the family.

All hope seemed truly lost until Neville Jameson, his mother's favorite brother, came to his aid with a gift meant to satisfy both the burial costs and a second chance at Ebenezer making something of himself. He would do both, he assured his Uncle Neville. He would leave the dirty streets of south London where he and Rose had lived and loved for that one painful year. But he would see her properly buried first, even if only in the farthest corner of the churchyard.

Rose's family accepted his gift with grace and understood his circumstances. Half of his uncle's money was spoken for. Jameson had made it patently clear that Ebenezer should invest the maximum possible. He felt half would be enough to establish himself. The remainder would go for better lodgings. And Hargreaves's invention.

Ebenezer first came across Hargreaves in the public house owned by Rose's uncle. He and Rose were ensconced in a cozy booth, daydreaming aloud about their future, when a ragged gypsy approached.

"Ah, 'tis a fine couple I see. Would you be wanting to know how many strapping boys you'll be having? Cross my palm with silver and I'll tell all." Rose giggled and held out her hand. The gypsy's face darkened and she muttered something.

"What? What is it?" asked Rose, her voice too high and tight.

"Ah, poor girl, poor, poor girl. You've found great love and he will give up everything for you, but death will claim you early." She walked away, head bowed, without her silver coins. Rose burst into tears.

"It's just humbug. Pay no attention, my dear," soothed Ebenezer. He watched as the gypsy approached a well-dressed man sitting with a small, dirty boy in scruffy, stained clothing. The gypsy raised her voice.

"You play with forces you can't hope to understand! Your machine shall be your undoing! And," the gypsy continued, turning to look with horror at the boy while still addressing Hargreaves. "You will kill this boy while you play about with the Lord's work." She turned and scuttled out of the pub.

Rose excused herself to attend to some duties for a moment, and as she did so, the fellow with the street urchin approached Ebenezer, asking if he might explain the gypsy's meaning.

"I do hope the fortuneteller's ravings have not put you of a suspicious mind, sir."

"Not entirely, though I would speak false if I said I had no questions for you. What explanation do you propose to offer? Perhaps we should begin with introductions, though. I am Ebenezer Scrooge."

"Roland Hargreaves. A pleasure, Scrooge. A pleasure." Hargreaves took a seat while the boy stood alongside the booth, eyes downcast.

"Scrooge, I am an inventor and my device is nearly complete. When ready, this machine, as the vulgar gypsy called it, shall be death's undoing. Think of it, Scrooge, to live forever. To no longer fear the grave's grasping hand at life's end."

Ebenezer had asked for details, fascinated by the inventor's talk, and, he admitted to himself, not a little entranced by Hargreaves's passion. The old scholar conveyed a sense of wonder and awe with his words. And also power—the power to defeat even the greatest challenge man could expect to meet in life.

But a haunting pall draped itself across Hargreaves' brow, shadowing his eyes and casting a grim atmosphere over his words. Something in the inventor's manner made Ebenezer wary of the man.

They parted amicably enough, Hargreaves leaving an ornate visiting card with Ebenezer. Rose asked about the man and the boy when she returned to their booth.

"Who is he? And what does he mean, treating a child with

such neglect? The boy shivered so. Why, his clothes had hardly enough stitching to be called garments."

"He is an inventor, my darling. A man of science, he says," Ebenezer replied. He turned the conversation away from Hargreaves, still feeling unsettled by the suspicions forming in his mind.

Ebenezer and Rose stayed together talking into the evening, until time came for Rose to help with closing up the house for the night. Ebenezer left with promises to return the following day, as he always did. He exited the warmth and went out into the chill London night. As he walked to his rooms, he slipped Hargreaves' visiting card into his breast pocket, not knowing why.

Ebenezer had no dreams of employing Hargreaves's device, not even when the first signs of Rose's illness made themselves known. But when the doctor confirmed their worst fears, Ebenezer made the trip to Hargreaves's home at the edge of the city.

They spoke in hushed tones over tea that Hargreaves poured from a battered silver service. Ebenezer took in the unkempt condition of the man's parlour. The cold hearth. The dust laden mantle. Fearing he would be turned out for it, Ebenezer admitted to his own poverty, but the inventor seemed not to care.

"We will manage matters of finance as they come. For now, rest assured that I shall help should your wife's condition prove as is feared."

Despite his worry for Rose, Ebenezer found Hargreaves' obsession harder still to swallow. "Why, Hargreaves? What prompts you to such toying with the Lord's work?"

Hargreaves drew forth two tattered scraps of paper from the pocket of his waistcoat. On one, Ebenezer saw an image of the inventor standing next to a pregnant woman. On the other, he and a young child stared, as though entranced. Their eyes seemed to follow Ebenezer's as Hargreaves held the images out to him with a shaky hand. The boy looked familiar. In the clothes of a street urchin, he would be the young lad Ebenezer saw with Hargreaves the day the gypsy accosted them both.

"Who are they? And what manner of trickery makes the pictures seem alive?"

"These are photoetchings, Scrooge. I had them made by a Frenchman, a fellow inventor of sorts. My wife and I spent summers on the Continent. Even in her condition, we traveled. A tradition, well, against the doctor's advice, but one we kept then, and which I keep, still. At least, until very recently. This," Hargreaves said, looking around the dismal parlour, "this is my only home now."

Ebenezer knew the pain of loss as well as any man, and his ears resonated with the sorrow in Hargreaves' voice.

"They were taken from me too soon, Scrooge. My wife, by seizures after our Robert was born, and the boy not some few weeks after my first meeting with you. I could not save them. My device was not yet ready. It could not . . . could not perform the task I'd set for it. I—"

Ebenezer sipped at his tea while Hargreaves regained his composure.

"I could not save them. But I will not see love stolen from you as it was from me. If your Rose should succumb, I will revive her. And death may go hunting for another sheaf!"

Ebenezer clawed through the final layer of earth, his fingers catching on the shroud that held his Rose. Hours after seeing her buried, he drove a horse-cart heaped with straw on top of Rose's body to the old manor in east London. He rapped gently on the door in the pattern of knocks he'd been advised to use. Tap-tap RAP, tap-tap RAP.

Hargreaves opened the door, peering out at Ebenezer from behind a candle flame.

"You weren't seen?"

"No," Ebenezer managed. His voice shook around the word, as though he'd confessed to murder before a judge.

"Around the side of the house. Go. I'll unbar the gate."

Hargreaves had built a laboratory in an old carriage house. Ebenezer carried Rose's body from the cart and, with Hargreaves's help, laid her onto a rickety table in the middle of the room. Hargreaves wheeled a heavy iron cabinet out from the shadows. He opened it, revealing a wooden case with a seat built into it.

Together, they placed Rose's body in the seat where she reclined in death, as cold as the iron jacket itself. Hargreaves arranged straps inside the cabinet to support Rose's torso and limbs. Feeling a chill course through his bones, Ebenezer pulled his gaze from Rose's face and cast his eyes about the room.

Thick curtains framed a threshold before the back of the

room which loomed in ominous shadow beyond the heavy drap-
eries. At the near end of the space stood two chairs of stout, dark
wood. Bands of metal on the arms and around the back sat open
on hinges, waiting to restrain a body seated there. Domed metal
bonnets lurked above the chair backs on slender copper arms,
hinged to an array of clockwork behind the chairs.

The mechanism linked into metal cabinets fastened on the
near wall, beside the door. The cases bristled with pressure
gauges and an array of softly illuminated dials, the whole appearing as if waiting for an infusion of energy to spring into life.
Thick coils of copper wire sprouted from atop the housings,
aiming towards a solitary gray iron post that hung suspended
from the rafters.

From the top of the post ran several tubes of copper and one
of gleaming brass. The copper pipes connected to more metal
compartments along the far wall. These, too, waited quiet and
cold. The brass pipe descended the far wall to a coupling that
bridged it to a solitary metal box faced with a series of levers.

A scattering of spanners and cutting tools lay across a
workbench beneath the box. A second branch of the brass pipe
extended from the box and ran the length of the wall and to the
rear of the space, ending at a hollow formed between two more
workbenches.

The whole brought to Ebenezer's mind the great steam-
works he had seen at the shipyards where his uncle had accompanied him the day prior. His future, he'd been told, lay in
international commerce, and the future of trade lay in steam

and its power to move great bulks up and down the Thames and out to the open sea. Ebenezer should have been a captain of those industries, like his father, rather than struggling to begin again as an investor. He took no delight from the irony that he might now be in a position to fund the very enterprises he once stood to inherit.

He shivered as the reality around him settled into his bones. There he stood, in a dusty carriage house. With his wife's corpse strapped into an iron cabinet.

Studying his beloved's cold, pallid face, Ebenezer begged, "Can you do it, Hargreaves? Can you bring my Rose back to me?"

"Of course," Hargreaves said, dismissing his guest's concern with a wave of his hand. Seeming to reconsider, Hargreaves turned a sympathetic gaze to Ebenezer. "I will do all I can. You must know I cannot make a promise in this matter. There is much to be done that I can and will do. And yet there remains much to learn, that I could not learn in time to save my wife and son. But, with the benefit of your investment, I may purchase the final pieces of equipment I require. And with hope, with luck, yes. Your Rose shall return to this life. Once again, you shall have her by your side."

Hargreaves clasped a hand to Ebenezer's upper arm as if the two were brothers setting out to make their fortunes together. A thin smile sought Ebenezer's mouth, but it could not wrest his muscles from the grip of sorrow, and so he turned to leave the laboratory. He gazed one last time at Rose, his Rose, left in Hargreaves' hands.

The inventor's words stopped Ebenezer at the door. "You . . . you made the deposit, Scrooge? As you'd promised, yes?"

"Yes, Hargreaves. The money is in your hands."

"Tomorrow then, Scrooge. Come after lunch. I doubt I will have made sufficient progress before then."

Ebenezer nodded to confirm and left the laboratory without the benefit of the horse and cart. Hargreaves had needed the nag, he said, forcing Ebenezer to walk back to his rooms. He did so, hiding his soil-stained hands in his pockets like a commoner. And what better manner of appearance could he affect? Regardless of his newly gained wealth, was he not still a commoner himself? Stripped of connection to his family's name, and for all intents, as empty of pocket as of heart.

Through the dank fog, Ebenezer stalked the empty streets of east London, a ghost among the mists, lost without the sun. Tomorrow, he told himself as he approached his rooms. Tomorrow would be a new day, and whatever may come of Hargreaves's tinkering with God's creation, Ebenezer Scrooge would begin tomorrow as a new man with a new station.

The next morning, Ebenezer stood outside his uncle's townhouse looking up at the elegant façade. He took a deep breath and mounted the freshly scrubbed steps. The butler held the door for him and announced him as they entered the breakfast room.

"Ebenezer, my dear boy, have you breakfasted? Come, come, help yourself. The kidneys are quite fine today." His uncle stood and vigorously shook his hand. Ebenezer tried to smile, but the chill, within and without, kept his face stiff and cold.

"My thanks, uncle," he choked out. The thought of eating gagged him, but he helped himself to some tea and toast.

"How can you keep body and soul together eating like that? I suppose yesterday must have put you off your food. Sad business, that, but we must move on, eh?"

Ebenezer inhaled sharply at the reminder of Rose's burial and unearthing, the loamy scent of freshly-turned soil filling his nostrils, and the feel of her cold, cold body in his arms as he laid her gently in the cart.

"Yes. We must move on, as you say. You mentioned a promising business venture in your note."

"Indeed, indeed. An old friend of mine, his son has need of a partner. Well, he is in need of funds, but with those funds comes a partner—you. Young Marley is waiting for us in the drawing room. If you are done with your breakfast?"

Marley stood as Scrooge and his uncle walked into the drawing room. His frame dwarfed the delicate gilt and wood furniture and his hand engulfed Ebenezer's.

"It is my pleasure to make your acquaintance, Scrooge! Your good uncle has been so kind and generous. My luck is sure to improve now that I have you by my side. I look forward to a long and prosperous partnership!" Marley's booming voice filled the room. His smile was infectious and Ebenezer smiled back, the ice inside him thawing a little.

"Marley. I, too, look forward to a most prosperous partnership." Ebenezer hoped neither his face nor his cool reply would betray the shock within his breast caused by the untoward announcement. This great blustering oaf of a man, his partner? But his uncle held the pen in this matter, Ebenezer knew. His own role was merely to be the ink.

With almost prescient grace, his Uncle Neville proclaimed the deal sealed. "Ah, good, good, then, it's all settled. I'll leave you two, must be off. Congratulations on the establishment of Scrooge and Marley. I bid you good day."

Left alone, the new partners surveyed each other, Ebenezer, with a hint of suspicion, and Marley, composed, but still appearing unsteady within, as if ready to burst in another fit of bluster at any moment. Finally, Ebenezer pulled his checkbook from his pocket, flinching as the coat lining tore slightly.

"Shall I write you a bank check for my share of the partnership? My uncle has deposited funds into my account, so the money is there, despite my outward appearance." Marley voiced agreement, an almost too-eager agreement, that the check be written promptly. Ebenezer thus took his time to print carefully before handing it over.

Marley examined the document and pursed his lips.

"Ah—I understood the sum to be higher, my dear Scrooge. Your uncle had promised more."

"Yes, but you see, I have certain expenses that must be met from the sum he gifted me. That is all I have left, though 'tis still a princely sum. I trust this will not threaten our venture? I am sure I can invest the money elsewhere."

"No, no, that will suffice to make you partner. I must have misunderstood. Shall we shake upon our partnership? Your uncle may take a spoken agreement as all that's needed, but I have always trusted the touch of flesh above the sound of speech."

Ebenezer, still wary of Marley's manner, lifted his hand and smiled at his new partner. Perhaps the man's left eye betrayed a tic at just the right moment, or perhaps Ebenezer's intuition chose that instant to assert itself in his favor, but he let his hand drop and allowed the cold within his chest to extend outward into the space between him and his new partner.

"Why, Scrooge, whatever is it? You look as though death itself would be a finer companion than I on this morning's meeting."

"You are no man of low means, Marley. And yet here you come a-begging funds. I will not partner with a man who treats the truth as the prize in a game of look-about. Whence your need, Marley? And speak plainly, with none of the gusting wind you used earlier, no doubt in hopes of concealing some duplicity."

Marley's shoulders sagged and he sighed heavily. The tic Ebenezer noticed a moment ago returned, the tremors coursing down Marley's cheeks until his lips shook as well.

"I . . . I am cursed, Scrooge. Cursed with a sickness that has twice before brought me a-begging." He spat the word as though the taste of it burned like acid on his tongue. "Your uncle owed my mother a favor for many years, and she has been kind, you can only pretend to know how kind, in not coming sooner to demand he make good his promise."

"What promise would this be?"

"To—" Marley began, but choked off his own words as he stifled a sob. "To provide for his son. At last, to provide for the child he sired with her."

Ebenezer felt the shock of Marley's revelation hit him in the chest, nearly forcing him backwards. He steeled himself and looked long at Marley's features, his round face and jovial cheeks. Given the means to reverse time, Ebenezer could be staring at his Uncle Neville.

"My word, Marley. Cousin Jacob," Ebenezer corrected himself. He again lifted his hand and took Marley's in a firm grip. His smile returned, and then waned as his own duplicity swelled full in his throat.

"Cousin Ebenezer, what is it now? Trouble haunts your brow as gulls above the fishmonger's stall. Come, tell me, please. I'll make no proclamation of refusal such as you did just now, but my interest in seeing this partnership succeed is as genuine as your own. If there is a matter . . ."

"Yes, cousin. There is a matter. The expenses I mentioned before, the disposition of those funds I am not able to provide for this partnership."

Ebenezer related to Marley his meeting with Hargreaves and told him of the device the inventor had prepared. He told Marley of the scheduled visit that afternoon, but not of his delivery of Rose's body the night before. Marley gave voice to the shock he felt, just the same.

"I cannot think how he might, but if he should succeed with this invention, do you hope to profit by some measure? But this is madness, Scrooge. Hargreaves can only be toying with you. I can think of no reason save true devilry that would compel a man to treat his fellows so poorly, with such disregard for their trials. Why, your Rose is not yet in the grave a full day and he has you—"

Marley cut himself off and stared full into Ebenezer's watering eyes.

"I beg your pardon, cousin, truly. I spoke in haste. I shouldn't have."

"Do not think on it, Marley. Forgive me this weakness. I assure you, my hands and heart are steady for the task before us as partners."

"And of that, I have no doubt. But let us agree on one point before the shingle is hung."

"Of course. What would you ask?"

"To protect your uncle and the integrity of our firm, we should refrain from addressing each other as cousin in the future. Better that we proceed on the understanding that we are no more family than we are generals in Napolean's army."

"Agreed, Marley."

The men shook again and made their exit. A cab, called by Uncle Neville, no doubt, waited on the street to carry them to the warehouse in Cornhill.

On the ride to the warehouse, Marley detailed for Ebenezer the nature of their firm.

"A small trading company, Scrooge. For now. We buy from the captains who sail to the Orient and sell the goods down the line. But we have our sights on larger game than this, oh, yes."

Ebenezer found it hard to concentrate on business, with his mind in riot with thoughts of Rose's corpse locked away in Hargreaves' laboratory. He fixed a smile to his lips and nodded at appropriate moments while Marley went on. They would acquire shipments of tea, spices, exotic wood, and furniture, stoneware, and glassware, as well.

"We stand to make a good living at it, if I dare say so. Eh, Scrooge? Scrooge, are you with me in this cab or have you only deposited a body in your stead while your mind wanders another route?"

At Marley's mention of a body, Ebenezer sat up, as though called to attention at his father's dinner table.

"Forgive me, Marley. It's this business with Hargreaves. My other investment. It concerns me."

"I'm glad you mention it, Scrooge, as I'd meant to ask your plans for the afternoon. You mean to visit this inventor, yes?"

"Yes, he expects me to call after luncheon."

"I would join you. Now, now, before you refuse me, hear me out. As you know, I am a man of no small means, but I am always in search of some way to grow my holdings. Might I at least see this Hargreaves' laboratory and his invention, to gauge whether or not an infusion of my own capital might be called for?"

"He is very secretive, I am sorry to tell you. It took months of my own begging before he would allow me a glimpse of his device."

"Well, a recluse he may be, but as partners in this firm, I see no reason why we should not be transparent about any ancillary behavior. I insist, Scrooge. You must allow me to accompany you on your sojourn there this afternoon. I promise I will make no missteps that might put your inventor off the idea of taking your money." Marley finished with a chortle, clapping a heavy hand on Ebenezer's shoulder.

"Well, if you insist. I . . . I suppose Hargreaves would not take offense to me bringing my new partner along."

Marley laughed again and the cousins regarded each other over smiles, Marley's easy and relaxed. Ebenezer hoped his appeared natural. He felt the muscles of his cheeks straining as he forced his mouth to convey the good humour he did not feel.

Later, over lunch at a nearby inn, Ebenezer and Marley discussed the wares already collected in their stores. As they compared notes, a crier approached waving a special edition of the paper.

"Missing lads, good sirs. Five gone from their beds in the orphanage. It's the third time this month."

"This is a grim business," Marley muttered, dropping sixpence into the crier's hand. The fellow stepped to the next table and repeated his story there as Scrooge listened to Marley recount the events described on the page.

"Early this morning it seems. Nursemaid went to check the boys' dormitory and found five empty beds. The five youngest are missing. Two older lads still present. None missing from the girls' dormitory.

"And just eight days earlier, another disappearance. A quartet of boys that time. A pair went missing the fifth of this month. Oh!"

"What is it?"

"A horse and cart were spied at this most recent incident. A black nag with a white spot on its cheek. What do you make of it, Scrooge?"

"I hate to think on it, to be honest. I've quite enough gloom to satisfy." Ebenezer felt his throat constrict around each word. Marley cast a look of calm appraisal at him and simply nodded his sympathy. Smiling, he said, "We should be on our way then. Hargreaves expects you after luncheon, and both my belly and my timepiece toll the hour."

Ebenezer stood, stony faced and with his eyes cast to the floor. Sensing Marley's curiosity, he raised his eyes and smiled before turning to lead the way out.

At Hargreaves' residence, Ebenezer and Marley stepped down from the carriage. The groom accepted Marley's coin and saw to the horses as the two gentlemen approached Hargreaves' gate. It stood open a crack, so Ebenezer only rapped gently on the wood before pushing through to the yard beyond.

The nag, still hitched to the cart, waited by the carriage house as it had on Ebenezer's last visit.

"The man has no groom of his own, no doubt," Marley observed. "Awful husbandry to keep the beast hitched that way, don't you say, Scrooge?"

Ebenezer had already begun moving to release the nag from bondage to the cart. As a young boy, he'd learned a groom's work at the school his father sent him. He'd never taken to riding, and so his relationship to mounts consisted only of soothing and cleaning them.

The nag whinnied as Ebenezer patted her muzzle, and the sound brought Hargreaves from his laboratory. The door opened and Ebenezer turned to see the inventor advancing on Marley with a knife in his hand.

"Explain yourself, sir! Interloper! What manner of business brings you into another man's garden unannounced? Well?"

"Hargreaves," Ebenezer called out. "He is with me. This is my c–, my partner, Mr. Jacob Marley. We have just today opened our firm together in Cornhill. I brought him with me at his insistence, but also with my approval. Marley would see your device to weigh the decision of injecting more capital into your work."

Hargreaves eyed Marley with a glare that would drop a weaker man, but which only served to further wrinkle Marley's brow into furrows of doubt and suspicion. Ebenezer watched the two men facing off across the yard, Hargreaves still wielding a lengthy knife and aiming it at Marley's navel. Then the inventor withdrew the blade and sheathed it at his side. An assortment of tools hung from rings along his belt, including, Ebenezer noted, two stout knives in black leather scabbards.

"A further injection of capital, as you say, Scrooge, would be most welcome. But I am afraid my device is not in a condition to be viewed. I have encountered some difficulty in establishing proper operation, and therefore must ask you to return two days hence. And no earlier than that!"

"Two days?" Ebenezer gasped. "But what of—"

"I must insist, Scrooge. Rest assured I have not forgotten our collective wish to see her returned, but my progress has been slower than I'd hoped. Please, two days more. And then we may celebrate my success together, just the three of us." Hargreaves finished, looking straight into Ebenezer's eyes, clearly meaning to indicate that Marley would add a fourth and much unwanted party to the affair.

Ebenezer and Marley departed the yard outside the carriage house. Hargreaves accompanied them and barred the gate firmly after shutting it behind them. They rode back to Cornhill in silence, Marley regarding the landscape and Ebenezer watching his cousin for signs of anger or any other emotion. But the larger man only stared out the carriage window.

"Pleasant company you've found, Scrooge," he said as they lit upon the street outside the warehouse.

"I do apologize, Marley. Our earlier meetings had nothing of what you saw there, I assure you. "

"'Tis grimmer still, Scrooge. I . . . I need excuse myself from any more business today. The memory of that madman's knife has me off my pins. I will see you in the morning."

Before Ebenezer could protest or offer further apology, Marley stepped away down the street and around the corner in a crowd of traffic.

❧

The next morning, Ebenezer arrived at the warehouse at nine of the clock. A full hour later, Marley entered in an agitated state. His chin needed a razor and his eyes cast storms in every direction. He closed the door and turned the latch before spinning to face Ebenezer across his desk.

"It is my turn to speak with a sterner tone than you may feel necessary, Scrooge. But you must tell me everything. What dealings have you had with that man, Hargreaves?"

"It is only as I've told you, Marley. He is an inventor, and I have invested a sum—"

"Yes, yes. As you've told me. Of whom did he speak when he mentioned your collective wish to see her returned? Tell me you have not done this thing. Tell me I am wrong when I suspect you of grave-robbing!"

But Ebenezer could not so tell his cousin, and so he told him the whole gruesome and damning truth of what he had done, and why he had done it.

"I loved her so, Marley. I loved her . . ."

Marley took his time in replying, calming himself and settling behind his own desk. When he spoke, he expressed neither revulsion nor horror.

"I know too well the lure of love and what a man will so easily part with to secure it, even if that parting is between himself and his mortal soul."

"But, I was given to know you a bachelor. Uncle Neville

spoke of no love in your life, nor of any want for love. Do forgive me, though, if my words scrape against a wound on your heart."

"No, Scrooge. Your uncle spoke well. In all my years, I have felt neither love from nor love for another. Not the type of love you knew with Rose. But I have felt love, and it is one that I find far stronger and more lasting than what may be had between men and women."

Ebenezer waited in the pregnant silence.

"Money, Scrooge. No one and nothing in my life has been so like love for me than the handling and possessing of coin."

"But this is mere avarice, Marley. Not love. Have you never felt the warmth of a woman's laugh? Her smile? Her hand in yours? You, who claim to trust flesh over speech as evidence of a vow? The love of money I understand well enough, but the loss of money is no comparison to the loss of love."

"Isn't it, Scrooge? Isn't it? Are you not the same man who lost both your father's love and his money in one stroke? And did you not find yourself without even a woman's smile to comfort your pauper's heart not two days ago? In that black hour, your uncle provided succor from his purse! Tell me you would still champ so hard were it not for the fortune we have joined to seek, and your uncle's coin that made it possible for us to so act."

"I—yes, yes, Marley, I would be far less the man you see before you were it not for Uncle Neville's timely gift. But this business with Hargreaves, this grim and horrible business—this is for love, not for money. And I would have given all I had if my uncle had not made this partnership a condition of the gift."

Regretting his words at once, Ebenezer opened his mouth to retrieve them. Marley spoke first, and he evinced no offense at what Ebenezer had said just then.

"I do not judge you a sinner, Scrooge. I do not call you damned, for it is not my place to make such proclamations. I leave that to the vicars and people in the street. Am I to be judged differently than you for choosing to love money as deeply and truly as you loved your Rose?

"Money, Scrooge. That is the only love worth pursuing, the only mistress who, when held, will never part from you unless you wish it, or are foolish enough to allow it. You believe Hargreaves will return your Rose to you, but I tell you that whatever he has promised, it can be only lies."

"What do you mean by this, Marley?"

"I followed him last night. After we departed his domicile, I took pains to recall the way. I returned late in the evening and observed him on his cart. A cart drawn by a black nag with a white spot on its cheek!"

Ebenezer felt his throat tighten and he attempted to choke out a reply, but Marley spoke over him.

"You are devoted to Hargreaves and would not see what I know to be true. Indeed, you did not see evidence of it upon our visit yesterday. But I did!"

"What evidence? What do you speak of?"

"The orphans, Scrooge. The ones gone missing. I saw small jackets in the back of Hargreaves' cart. And he has the nag."

"That does not condemn him."

"No, it does not. But the three boys I saw being marched out the kitchen door of an orphanage in the small hours, that, Scrooge, that is evidence!"

Ebenezer could only stare in disbelief, all the while knowing in his heart that Marley spoke the truth. The twinge of worry he'd felt upon first meeting Hargreaves nearly a year ago returned in full to weigh on Ebenezer's shoulders. His remorse bowed his head as if he were clapped in the stocks awaiting the end of a life's sentence. And yet, a mote of hope remained in his breast.

"You are certain it was Hargreaves?"

"The nursemaid took a small purse from him and I saw his face. He drove up and rapped at the kitchen door. The nursemaid opened it, collected the purse and retreated inside. Then she came out with three boys in tow; three lads, Scrooge, not one over the age of five. Hargreaves must be stopped. I only wanted to speak to you and hear it from your lips before going to the constabulary."

"But you can't, Marley! They'll find Rose's body there, and—"

"Then we must act, ourselves. At the very least, we must confront this madman and tell him to cease his kidnapping. Of whatever else he may be guilty, I cannot guess, and fear to discover."

"But he will accuse me of assisting in his crimes. With Rose's body there, he will have no trouble bringing me to the gallows with him."

"He has already done so. Clearly he has made use of your investment to purchase the orphans as cattle. If we cannot alert the constabulary, then we must stop him, Scrooge. We must."

❧

The cab driver took Ebenezer's coin and clattered away into the foggy afternoon, the air palpable and brown. To Ebenezer, London proper had never seemed more distant.

"We must hasten, Scrooge."

Ebenezer's thoughts quickly returned to his own worries about Rose, and he rapped on Hargreaves's door in the same pattern as before. No answer came from within, and they stood on the gravel until, presently, Marley suggested they approach from the side of the house.

"He must still be in the laboratory."

"Indeed, and the gate is surely barred."

"Hah!" Marley expelled the word as if it were a shot from a pistol. He stepped around Ebenezer to face the gate. The man stood nearly tall enough to peer over the barrier, and, leaning up on his toes, he could see the space within quite well. He gave a cry of surprise and began pushing on the gate with all his strength. Ebenezer did not seek explanation but leapt to lend his own strength to the effort, feeble though he felt next to the bulk of his cousin.

The latch across the gate strained with their pushing, but it came loose at the last. Marley stumbled forward into the yard and Ebenezer followed. They turned and quickly pushed the gate to. Marley's shout of surprise had carried also a degree of horror, and as Ebenezer surveyed the yard, he saw what had alarmed Marley so.

The horse and cart stood hitched beside the carriage house. In the cart, they saw clothing heaped in piles: jackets and boots, caps and shirts, trousers and knickers. All of it sized for children.

"Surely you believe me now, Scrooge."

A sound came to their ears then, a heaving and grunting from within the carriage house. Light as if from a fire flickered within the windows in the carriage house doors. The side door stood open and to this Ebenezer and Marley crept, careful not to disturb the silence of the yard more than they had already done.

At the door, Marley stole forward and chanced a look within. He dashed forward then, bellowing a cry of accusation. Ebenezer followed, prepared to join whatever fray might await.

"Devil! Fiend!" Marley shouted, leveling a stout finger toward Hargreaves, who held in his hands the limp form of a child, and crouched before the mouth of the boiler's furnace. Ebenezer could make out the shape of ashen bones among the embers and his gorge rose with his horror.

Hargreaves stood with the boy still in his arms. Ebenezer thought the child's face appeared too old for one of his size, too withered and frail. Wrinkles furled his brow, and his cheeks sagged into jowls like those of an old man.

"You disrupt my work, Scrooge! And this ox you bring with you."

"Better an ox than a devil!" Marley rejoined.

"Devil? Ha! I have only done as your partner requested. This is what you asked of me, Scrooge. And I have done it!"

"Lies!" Ebenezer shouted, his voice faltering as he finished.

"Lies. I made no such request as this, Hargreaves, and you know it. I only asked that my Rose be returned to me."

"And she has been returned. Regard, Scrooge. Your wife!" Hargreaves aimed his chin behind the two men.

Behind the macabre twists of pipes and machinery sat a woman bound within the iron cabinet. Her face glowed, her ruddy cheeks accented by sparks emanating from the coils of wire atop the cases along the near wall. The sparks flew to collect on the post hanging overhead where they wrestled with each other, coursing in a frenzied whorl as if alive.

The woman's eyes now glinted from within her reanimated face and reflected the flickering light, sending a haunting shiver through Ebenezer as he stared into her gaze.

A dressmaker's dummy caged her torso and leather straps held her limbs to iron bars linked with clockwork and tubes. Steam occasionally hissed from each joint, punctuating the demonic glare on her face. She lifted her head to stare more directly at Ebenezer, and a sorrowful, plaintive moan escaped her lips, though her jaw did not move to open her mouth beyond a thin crack.

"Rose? But who is this woman, Hargreaves?" Ebenezer said, slowly stepping forward to lean against one of the chairs. He saw the woman more clearly now, and knew it to be other than his wife.

A grunt and cry of pain from behind him spun Ebenezer around, and he held to the chair for support. Marley staggered forward and fell onto the second chair. Hargreaves stood behind him, grinning like the madman Ebenezer knew him now to be. The child lay on the ground at his feet. Hargreaves held a syringe in his left hand.

"Help me move him, Scrooge," Hargreaves commanded, indicating Marley's unconscious form and drawing a knife from his belt with his free hand.

"Help me, Scrooge," Hargreaves demanded. He stepped quickly to press the blade against Ebenezer's throat. Unable to think of anything but his Rose and where she might be, Ebenezer nodded his submission. Hargreaves removed the knife and pushed Ebenezer towards his cousin's limp figure, slumped over the chair.

Wrapping his arms around Marley, Ebenezer took comfort from the sensation of his cousin's beating heart, and then he fell to sobbing. Hargreaves shouted urgent commands again, and Ebenezer felt himself obey, tugging with every ounce of his strength to help lift Marley and turn him over to a seated position in the chair.

Hargreaves pushed Ebenezer aside and fastened the bands around Marley's wrists and chest. He finished by fitting the metal bonnet over his partner's head. Ebenezer stood to the side, watching in horror as Hargreaves worked. Only when the madman had finished did Ebenezer's senses return to him. He clapped his hands on Hargreaves's shoulders, crying for him to stop.

Hargreaves spun around, revealing far more agility than a man of his age should possess. He knocked Ebenezer's hands away and pounced forward, thrusting his left hand under Ebenezer's guard and stabbing the syringe into his belly. Ebenezer instantly folded over in pain and slumped to the floor. The room darkened and constricted around a vanishing circle of light. As he fell to Hargreaves's poison, his eyes swam in and out of focus around Marley's face.

Ebenezer awoke to the sensation of his heart being pulled from his chest. A great suction seemed at work on him and he could not at first discern its source. The sight of Hargreaves closing the furnace door brought Ebenezer's mind back to the present, though the dizziness persisted. He sat in one of the chairs, and Marley sat next to him. The madman, Hargreaves, stood facing the furnace, lost in thought and touching his fingertips with his thumb as if counting off a series of steps.

The restraints simply closed over Ebenezer's wrists so that the metal could make contact with his flesh. He took care to work silently as he removed his arms from the bands. He lifted the bonnet from his head, and the dizziness dissipated instantly. Doing the same for Marley, Ebenezer watched his cousin slump forward in the chair. Marley's face hung long and withered with age.

Ebenezer released the band around his own chest and stood, careful to keep his balance. Whatever sedative Hargreaves had applied, Marley received the lion's share. Ebenezer, hardly more than dazed, moved towards the inventor from behind.

Perhaps his foot made a noise, scraping against the earthen

floor, or perhaps Marley grunted, but Hargreaves spun on his heel and rushed at Ebenezer. Ebenezer leapt to his left and grabbed a spanner from the bench. He spun to face Hargreaves and felt his legs give way as a wave of dizziness blurred his vision. Ebenezer regained his balance only enough to make a feeble strike at Hargreaves with the spanner. He swung and felt it crash against the inventor's head. Hargreaves staggered to the side with a cry. Ebenezer slid to the floor, landing on his knees.

He twisted at the waist and brought the spanner up to defend himself from Hargreaves's next attack. But the inventor did not move from the floor. A ruddy puddle formed beside Hargreaves's head, leeching the madman's evil into the soil.

Ebenezer let the tool drop from his hand. He went to Marley's aid, then, releasing him from the chair and helping him stand. Marley rallied as Ebenezer had, and took his own weight as he stumbled to the door. Together, they staggered out of the hellish laboratory and into the yard beyond.

Marley slumped to the ground beside the door and held his head in his hands. Ebenezer went to the nag and hitched her to the cart once more. Helping Marley to his feet, Ebenezer led him around to the back of the cart. The horse gave a whinny of complaint as Marley's bulk put weight on the traces. Ebenezer patted its side and went back into the laboratory.

The boiler and furnace still burned and warmth filled the room. Hargreaves's body lay on the floor where he had fallen. Ebenezer regarded his own hands. An oily smear from the spanner stained his palm.

"Fitting that I should leave this place with a mark on my hands," Ebenezer said, glancing over his shoulder through the open door. Outside, Marley stirred in the cart. Ebenezer turned and went to the iron cabinet. The woman in the cabinet looked at him from behind a mask of stage paint. Glass orbs replaced her eyes. And even without these horrors, Ebenezer knew that his Rose had not benefited from Hargreaves' labors. The woman before him now was none other than the inventor's own wife, preserved somehow over time and here, in place of the woman Ebenezer had loved so dearly.

A bound volume lay open on the workbench beside the iron case. Ebenezer lifted the book and flipped through Hargreaves's notes. The inventor had, indeed, found a way to animate the dead. His device drew the essence of life from a living host and infused it into a corpse. But the dead, once revived, would expire each night unless recharged by more infusions of life essence each morning. Worst of all, Ebenezer saw, was that the corpse to be revived needed a newly dead heart. His Rose had surely burned away in the inventor's furnace, but her heart beat still in the mannequin before him.

Ebenezer went to the boiler and opened the gas jets full bore. Then he closed all the boiler valves and rushed outside to urge the nag and the cart bearing Marley away from that place.

Marley groaned with each step. When they'd gone some length along the road, Ebenezer turned to regard the carriage house. He felt a silent mote of satisfaction when, a second later, the boiler explosion leveled the building. The blast pushed against Ebenezer's chest and trembled in his belly as timbers and shards of metal and glass flew in every direction. The splinters of Hargreaves's madness rained on the landscape before him, and Ebenezer's ears rang hollow as silence rushed back to fill the night. A shriek of ravens sliced against Ebenezer's muffled hearing. Dark birds circled above him, slowly returning to their roosts in neighboring trees.

The horse spooked and nearly bolted, but Ebenezer calmed the animal as he had before. Only when he saw fire begin to spread to the manor house did Ebenezer mount the cart and begin the trek back to London proper.

Years passed and neither Ebenezer nor Marley spoke of the night in Hargreaves's laboratory. Neither their suppliers nor their customers knew Ebenezer and Marley as younger men, and so no surprise registered when they appeared as wrinkled and bent as ancient oaks.

Their business flourished as Ebenezer's keen eye for trading ensured they never wanted for goods to sell. Marley played the role of salesman in counterpoint to Ebenezer's knack for acquisition, and the two remained the closest of friends throughout their years together.

Jacob Marley died one Christmas Eve night. His landlady found him in bed, as if asleep. Ebenezer alone paid for and attended his burial. A simple stone proclaimed the resting place of *Jacob Finchly Marley, as dear in friendship as family.*

Each day, counting his coins, Ebenezer reflected on the sorrowful turns his life had taken. The loss, first, of his father's love and money, then, of the raft he'd built in his marriage to Rose. And, finally, the loss of his friend and cousin. It seemed that no amount of trying would prevent death from stalking him, and Ebenezer took to calling for it each night.

Every evening, as he laid his head upon his pillow, Ebenezer cursed the fates that had taken his wife and then his only friend, and he cursed himself for approaching Hargreaves and for funding the man's vile schemes. Unwittingly or no, Ebenezer had thrust a dozen children into death's hand, and so he wished to be taken, too. Each morning, the dawn came not as a reprieve, but as an extension to his sentence. Month after month, year after year, each new day encased his heart in another layer of ice, until his last hope froze within him, waiting for a love that might one day thaw him anew.

Styled after A Christmas Carol by Charles Dickens

Our Man Fred

A. F. STEWART

Fred crouched down, watching the dockside building from the shadows, the calm, rippling resonance of the Thames River at his back. He recognised the two men loading a crate onto the back of a mechanised wagon; they worked for the infamous madman, Rupert Muggins. The strange, steam-powered conveyance they used left no doubt this was an operation backed by Muggins, purveyor of all things clockwork and mechanical.

The tip from Fred's informant had been good. After tracking this man and his current scheme for months, he finally had a break in the case.

Fred drew his pocket watch from his vest and checked the time in the faint light from the morning sunrise. He frowned; his partner should have arrived. He couldn't wait much longer. He glanced back to his adversaries. They were securing the back of the wagon.

"Damn, they're leaving." Fred pulled his pistol and rushed

forward as the wagon began to roll away. "Stop! Cease what you are doing and surrender! You are under arrest by an agent of the Clockwork Department!"

The wagon driver cursed and pulled a lever. The wagon lurched, gaining rapid speed, spewing smoke and noise, while the other two men ran down an adjacent street. Fred made a quick decision and gave chase to the two men on foot, knowing the wagon could easily outdistance him.

The men had a head start, but he closed the gap and spied them slipping into an alleyway. Pumped from the chase, he recklessly pursued, only to be met with gunfire. Diving for his life, he barely escaped being shot as he dodged for cover behind a pile of rubbish.

"Damn it, it's an ambush."

He heard an odd, ominous, familiar rumble and the wall above his head exploded in a shower of stone that fell painfully over his shoulders and back.

"Deuced hell, it's one of those wretched beam weapons!"

"That's right, *Agent*. Now it's your turn to surrender, or we'll blast you to pieces!"

"Not damn likely!" Fred popped up from his cover, firing his pistol, before dropping to relative safety again. He counted four more men, besides the two he had chased into the alley. He was quite outnumbered.

The noise of their infernal gun sounded again and Fred barely evaded the deadly beam, as well as the bullets that ricocheted off the wall behind him. He returned fire, hitting one of the henchmen.

"You'll have to do better than that chaps, if you want to kill me!" Gunfire answered his shout; happily, the shots went wide of their intended mark.

"It's a blessed thing you fellows have such bad aim, or I would be dead by now."

Another blast from the beam weapon answered him, and scorched the wall to his right. He flinched involuntarily before he shot back with his pistol, wounding another one of his opponents, who went down with a scream.

Two more shots echoed, but surprisingly, not in Fred's direction. He snuck a peek, to see a third henchman fall to the ground. Fred smiled. His partner had arrived.

About confounded time, too.

He reloaded his pistol and sped, shooting from concealment, joining the power of his weapon to his partner's. Caught in crossfire, the remaining adversaries went down with a minimum of fuss. Then Fred's lovely partner, Mary, stepped out of the shadows and wisps of gun smoke to view the aftermath.

She holstered her weapon, raising the hem of her skirts and stepping lightly around the dead bodies. "I almost didn't find you this time. Luckily, I arrived at the waterfront to see you duck down the street in a pursuit. I ran into trouble of my own following your lead, or I would have arrived sooner." Something caught her attention. "Is that one of Muggins' focused-beam weapons?"

Fred walked over to the device. "Yes, indeed. Not much to look at, is it?"

Mary ran her hand over the three-foot-high metal contraption, lightly stroking its long cylinder and crank. "No, it's all tubes and wires and gears. How can anything this cumbersome be so dangerous? It's difficult to believe."

"Most of Muggins' inventions defy belief. The man might be wicked to his core, but he is a mechanical genius without peer."

"That he is, unfortunately for us." Mary took a step forward and leaned against him. She whispered, "I'm glad you are not hurt," and lightly kissed his cheek. Then she flashed him a bright smile, causing him to grin back, marvelling at her adorable dimples.

But then, he marvelled at everything about her, from her kissable mouth to the liveliest pair of eyes in which he oft had the pleasure to drown. Sometimes Fred found it difficult to believe that such a delicate and beautiful creature excelled as a skilled government agent for the Clockwork Department. He counted himself a lucky man indeed to have fallen in love with such a woman and have her return his feelings. He reached out and took her hand.

"Not the source of information we were hoping for, my dear, but this ambush they set for me proves we are making Muggins and his gang nervous."

Mary gave his hand a little squeeze. "True, but unfortunately, that may not be enough to satisfy our superiors at the Foreign Office. Mr. Griffith will not be pleased with our lack of progress."

Fred grimaced at the thought of giving his report to his director, Edgar Griffith. The man would give him a dressing down to be certain.

"And we still have to clean up this muddle." Mary swept her hand through the air over the dead bodies littering the alley.

"Right you are. We should send in a signal to summon a cleanup crew."

"Already done." Mary held up her wrist, waggling the intricate homing bracelet she wore.

"Excellent. And if we can keep the Peelers off our backs until we've taken care of everything, we might just make it out of this scrape without more misfortune."

After leaving the cleaning crew—and Mary—to deal with the disposal of the evidence, Fred entered the offices of the Clockwork Department, secreted deep in the bowels of the Foreign Office of London. He went to his immediate superior, Edgar Griffith, to make his report, and found a scowl and angry words to greet him.

"Muggins is running us in circles! This morning's debacle has us no closer to finding the villain! We don't have his whereabouts or any credible information on what he is planning! He has the run of the city, and we have nothing! The man is making us look like fools!"

"True, sir, the skirmish this morning went to Muggins, but we have yet to assess any evidence found at the scene and we did capture another one of his beam guns."

Griffith glared. "Yes, you did, but only after a very public battle. What were you thinking? Exchanging gunfire in the street like common thugs! And with a beam weapon, no less! Great Scott, man! Are you *trying* to bring unwanted exposure to this department? You can be thankful it was such an early hour and that most decent people were still abed!"

He sighed heavily. "You can't keep having these very showy encounters with our foes, Fred, old boy. It's all this office can do sometimes to keep these exchanges out of the papers. If word got out about these fantastic devices we keep under wraps, there'd be inquiries, a call for an accounting of our department, and that would never do."

Fred took a deep breath. "Yes, sir. Next time I'll do better."

Yes, next ambush, I'll just let them kill me.

"See that you do. Now get back out there and find Muggins." Griffith waved his hand in dismissal and Fred left his presence.

A weary and thoroughly rebuked Fred left the Foreign Office with one task left to accomplish. He made his way through the late afternoon streets of London to the counting house of Scrooge and Marley. His adventure with Mary reminded him that he had happy news to impart to his Uncle Ebenezer, though he doubted the old man would wish him well.

Upon arrival, he found his uncle temporarily gone from the place, so he settled in to wait, leaning against the dividing doorframe so he might chat with Bob Cratchit, his uncle's clerk.

Fred gave him a friendly smile, in hopes that he might brighten the mood of the clerk's dismal workplace. "How goes it with you, sir? Is your family well?"

Cratchit put down his pen and looked up from his copying.

"'Tis fine with me, Master Fred, and I thank you for asking. The family's fine as well." A slight frown marred his face. "Although, my youngest, Tim, has been feeling poorly of late. No doubt it will pass, and he'll be right as rain again."

"No doubt. Children are a resilient lot." A noise from the adjoining room brought his attention away from the idle chitchat, and a gruff voice rang out.

"Who's there? Who's in with my clerk?"

"It sounds as if my uncle has returned." Fred gave Cratchit a grin. "It is only I, Uncle, your nephew, Fred." With a wave, Fred took his leave of the clerk and went to see his uncle, who was hanging up his shabby greatcoat.

"By what displeasure have you come to see me today, nephew?" Scrooge, now divested of his coat, shuffled to his desk and sat in his creaky, well-worn chair. "If you are looking for a handout, you will be sorely disappointed. I'm in the business of making money, not providing charity."

"No need to fret, Uncle, I am not here for money, simply to impart some happy news. I am engaged to be married."

"What! What nonsense is this? You barely have two pennies to scrape together and you want to burden yourself with a wife? Rid yourself of such youthful folly at once, is my advice."

"I shall do no such thing, Uncle. Mary and I are in love, and plan to be wed."

"Love? Bah, useless twaddle. No good for anything, and certainly not a reason to marry. Why you come to bother me with this tripe, I can't imagine. Be off with you. I have work to finish."

"As you wish, Uncle, but be warned, you shall be receiving an invitation to my wedding."

"Bah! Be off with you I say, and take your silly notions of marriage with you."

"Good-bye, Uncle, and despite everything, I do hope you attend the wedding."

Fred slipped out the door and went on his way. The visit to his uncle went as he expected. Ebenezer Scrooge was not one for sentiment. With spirits in disarray, Fred walked back to his rooms to settle in for the night and put the difficult day behind him.

The next morning, as he sipped his tea and munched on buttered toast, a loud knocking sounded at his door. With a sigh, he left his breakfast and answered it. Mary burst into his rooms, flush with excitement, and waving a longish, much folded wad of paper.

"Yesterday may not have been the disaster we feared! Plans, Fred! We found plans hidden in the lining of one of their coats." She waved the paper under his nose, causing him to step back and clutch closed his dressing gown.

"Calm down, Mary. Let me dress and we can discuss this development over breakfast."

Mary blushed, realising he stood before her in his night clothes, and sat down without another word. Fred left the room and came back more properly attired, wearing a smart suit, pressed shirt, and cravat. He found Mary had removed her pelisse and hat and made herself more at home in a plush armchair by the fire. The sight made him grin.

"Well, now, let's see those plans."

Mary rose and they both moved to the dining table, where she spread the paper across the surface, pushing aside the remains of Fred's interrupted breakfast. Fred retrieved his repast and poured her a cup of tea as he looked at the unfolded document covering his table.

"Is that some sort of a design?" He frowned, taking a closer look. "It's a mechanical diagram, for a—good heavens! A mechanical rat? What in the world could Muggins want with a design for a two-foot clockwork rodent?" Flabbergasted, Fred sputtered his words.

"I have no idea, but if the notations in the corner are any indication, we may find out at four o'clock today."

Mary pointed at handwritten scribbling on the plans.

Fred peered at the writing, reading aloud. "*Initial testing. Hyde Park. Four o'clock.* And with today's date. That does sound rather ominous, and that is definitely where we want to be this afternoon. We should pay a visit to Topper before we go."

Mary smiled. "I already sent word. He's expecting us." She deftly folded up the plans and tucked them under her arm. "Shall we go, then?"

"After you, my dear."

۞

Fred and Mary soon found themselves threading through winding corridors deep beneath the Foreign Office, on their way to Topper's laboratory. While both a friend and a colleague, Topper was also the agency's resident inventor.

As they entered his sanctum, Topper greeted them, "Hello to you both," and waved them forward.

As was his customary habit while in the lab, Topper presented quite the image, wearing his frayed and stained white coat, tarnished brass goggles, and shockingly unkempt head of hair. A dark smudge of unknown filth on his youthful, ruddy cheek completed the odd picture to perfection.

"I hear you have a bit of an adventure planned this afternoon. I have quite a few new gadgets that may aid in your quest." He grinned. "Come, follow me." He beckoned them like a schoolboy as he pranced across the floor.

"How's that cantankerous uncle of yours, Fred? I heard you paid him a visit yesterday."

"How did you—never mind. He's as bad-tempered as ever."

"He is a character, that one." Topper turned his attention to Mary. "How are your lovely sisters?"

"They're well. Matilda asked after you the other day."

"Did she now? Excellent."

Topper led them to a table, covered in all manner of mechanical wonders. Dozens of strange looking items littered the surface: spheres, cylinders, weapons, small automatons, enhanced spectacles, and a jumble of assorted tools, wires, tubes, gears, nuts, bolts, and other metal parts.

"I see you've been busy," Fred remarked.

"Oh, yes. I've made notable progress. Unfortunately, I'm still working on that portable, smaller version of Muggins' beam gun. It would come in handy, I know, but no such luck today."

He reached down and picked up a diminutive orb, made of brassy metal, gears, and fittings. "But this, now . . . this is quite the useful weapon. Simply turn the top half here,"—he mimed swiveling the ball's top—"and you arm the device and start the countdown machinery. When the mechanism rotates back into position, it releases sleeping gas. And here,"—Topper pointed to what appeared to be a clock apparatus—"you can set the clockwork to different rates of rotation. You can release the gas after a few seconds, a minute, two minutes, five minutes, and so on, up to an hour."

"Oh, that is very useful." Mary picked up another contraption from the table. "What does this do?"

Topper beamed in pride. "That's my navigation contrivance. Completely wearable—on your wrist—it is a miniature sundial, compass, and sextant. Excellent for wilderness or sea adventures, but not truly necessary for London jaunts." Mary put it down in disappointment.

Topper picked up a metal wrist cuff, decorated with an array of small cylinders. "This—this is a much better choice. Each tube has a poison dart and can be rotated and fired by air compression. Also, it is easily concealed under the sleeve of a dress or jacket, or displayed as a fancy bracelet, if you prefer."

Fred laid a hand on Topper's shoulder. "Quite impressive,

but do you have anything with a bit more firepower? Say, something that would stop a mechanical rodent in its tracks?"

"I have just the thing. Wait here." Topper ran off to a back room and returned moments later carrying a leather case. He made room for it on a corner of the table and opened it to show the contents. Three parts of an odd-looking gun rested inside.

Fred snorted, unimpressed. "How do pieces of a weapon help us?"

"They don't. However, when you assemble them . . ." Topper took the parts from the case one by one and rapidly built a fully formed, albeit strange-looking, weapon. He held it out for Fred and Mary to inspect.

"It's a prototype. I've been working on it since you had your encounter with that signal-controlled automaton man at Oxford. I call it my scrambler gun." A broad smile formed across his face. "You can see here,"—he pointed at some of the workings—"I've enhanced it with a clockwork operating panel, and it has been calibrated to fire an emission beam that will disorientate any automated command function in the subject you are aiming at. I noticed when examining the plans for the rat, that it had a component that used sound waves to direct movement and intent."

"That's brilliant, Topper. So this thing will disable whatever Muggins has invented?"

"Theoretically, yes. It should confuse it long enough for you to destroy it. But be warned, this gun has a limited range. Not more than a foot in diameter, and only a few feet in distance. So you will have to be rather close to fire it. And it has no effect on humans. It is also a bit unwieldy for toting around London. Hence, my brilliant idea of disassembly and portability."

"Oh, how perfectly marvellous." Mary laughed with delight.

Fred hefted the gun, getting the feel of it. "My word, I'll say, it's marvellous. Deuced marvellous. This should deal with Muggins and his mechanical monstrosity. Good job, Topper."

An early winter wind blew crisp in Hyde Park, and the people strolling about did so rather briskly. Fred and Mary sat on a bench, partially concealed by trees, the leather case placed between them.

Mary absently tapped her foot. "This is a bit nerve-wracking, waiting to see what will happen. I think I prefer being in the thick of it."

Fred chuckled. "That's what I love about you: a real go-getter of a girl."

Mary gave him a teasing punch on the arm and a pout. "Don't make fun. I know all too well how much *you* like the action."

"True, but I'll be happy with any course that takes down Muggins. And a little waiting never—"

"Shh. Do you hear that noise? It sounds like it's coming from the water over there." Mary rose abruptly and pointed. "Look!"

Fred grabbed for the case as the water in the nearby lake bubbled uncontrollably. His hand fell on the handle as Mary shrieked and the water erupted into the air. From out of the lake burst dozens and dozens of mechanical rats that scurried and swarmed into the park.

Women screamed and men shouted as the rats attacked, biting and clawing at anything that moved. The air filled with the awful sound of their chittering cries and the clang of metal as people tried to defend themselves.

Mary drew her pistol and Fred did likewise while desperately attempting to assemble the scrambler, as hordes of rats advanced on them.

"Try and hold them off, Mary. We need the gun!"

Mary ran forward, firing at the rats, her bullets hitting their metal with echoing pings, but barely slowing their hideous advance. She stopped to reload.

"Hurry, Fred! I can't stop them!"

She fired again, before screaming as rats overran her position. She felt them pulling at her skirts, crawling around her feet, and she fired her last bullets into the horde. She kicked out and swung her pistol like a club, ever fearing she would lose her footing and be lost under a surge of vicious rodents.

Then a buzzing blare rang out, and another. She turned to see Fred atop the bench with the gun. Around her, rodents staggered and ran in wobbly circles. He cleared a path for her retreat and she joined him in relative safety. She reloaded her gun and snatched up Fred's pistol. Three weapons were soon firing upon the invasion of Hyde Park.

"We'll never be able to destroy them all, I—"

A piercing loud whistle interrupted Fred, his words silenced as every rat suddenly froze. He stared across the park and locked his gaze on a lanky man standing serenely in the middle of a mass of now still rats. He held an elaborate walking stick in one hand and, with the other, he brushed at his dark, stylish suit. When he saw Fred gawking, he tipped his hat.

"Muggins!" Fred dropped the scrambler and let out a roar. He leaped off the bench and ran toward his foe, unthinking. As he ran, Fred saw Muggins twist the top of his cane and another high-pitched whistle sounded, penetrating the air. At once, the rats surged forward, racing from the park, Muggins fleeing with them.

"Fred, wait!"

Fred heard Mary call to him and, from the corner of his eye, he saw her running to catch him, but he didn't stop. He sprinted to reach the villain, Mary close at hand, sporadically firing their pistols, but they were both impeded by the stampeding rodents snarling around their feet. Even as he laboured forward, extricating himself from the pack, grinding his teeth in frustration, Fred watched Muggins stay beyond his reach.

Then he remembered. "Hell, the orb." Still fighting off rats, he reached into his pocket, pulled out one of Topper's sleeping spheres, set the timer for several seconds, armed it, and let it fly at Muggins. It hit the ground in front of him and discharged a flurry of pale yellow smoke. Fred watched Muggins disappear into the cloud of gas, a hand pressed over his nose and mouth.

"Where did he go?" Fred battled onward, following the sound of his enemy's coughing, until he glimpsed Muggins still moving at a stumbling run, leaving the park.

"After him, Mary! He's getting away!"

"It's no use. The rats won't let us catch him. Blast! I should have brought Topper's dart cuff. It has more range than a pistol."

Reduced to fighting off rats to advance, they lost Muggins in the crowded London streets upon exiting the park. The rats then fled, a metal mass of unthinking beasts teeming through London.

"Follow those rats! They may lead us back to Muggins!"

Fred bolted after the escaping creatures, Mary quick at his heels. They chased them all the way to the Thames, only to watch in amazement as the entire throng of mechanical rats dove into the river and disappeared under the water.

"What in the world was it all about?" Griffith paced his office, red-faced and shouting in the general direction of Fred and Mary.

"Clockwork rats! Attacking people in Hyde Park! And you two," he whirled to face down the pair, "a blasted shootout, bullets everywhere! This is England, not the Wild West! What were you thinking?"

"That it might be best to defend ourselves," Fred replied.

"Did I ask you? Did I say you could speak?" Griffith harrumphed, puffed a breath, and resumed his pacing. "The whole fiasco could have been a department catastrophe. We could have been exposed, shut down! Luckily, we were able to explain the calamity as a science experiment gone awry. Not to mention, we had to retrieve that experimental gun you carelessly left behind."

He glared at Fred, who had the decency to look sheepish and cast a gaze to the floor.

Griffith snorted and threw up his hands. "I know Muggins is a madman, but he's always had a plan, a scheme before. This ... this was just anarchy."

"Sir," Mary spoke softly, hesitant to arouse his ire, "it may have been a trial run—for something bigger."

"What? What's this? Speak up, girl! What's in that mind of yours?"

"The plans we recovered mentioned a test, and you're right. This attack makes no sense on its own. But if it were a trial run, a test of the rats to see how they worked, responded, well, that makes sense. It would explain the whistle and why they ran off. It must have been a signal, a sound to retreat."

Fred smiled to himself.

Oh, you clever girl.

Griffith paused and stared hard at Mary. "You may have the right of it, and it bodes very ill indeed. If he means to unleash more of these beasts on London, I dare say he has a sinister purpose." Griffith turned to Fred. "Has that egghead, Topper, come up with a way to stop these nasty rats, yet?"

"Not yet, sir, but he hasn't been at it long, and the specimens he examined were damaged by bullets."

"Well, he'd best hurry his efforts. We'll need a better defense than that gun you used. It came in handy this time, but it isn't effective or practical as a weapon against an invasion of those things. Is there anything else to report?"

"We are investigating a possible supplier of the mechanisms. Some fresh scuttlebutt came in today about a new shop in a small lane off Oxford Street that may be dealing in illicit mechanisms and clockwork. It's possible they might know something. The underground network for that type of thing is rather small and close-knit. They tend to know the players."

Griffith cleared his throat. "Well, what are you two waiting for then? Get out there and find Muggins."

He waved his hand in dismissal and Mary and Fred left his office. They headed out at once towards Oxford Street and the supposed shop dealing in black-market goods.

From bustling Oxford Street, they took a twist here, a turn there, and found themselves walking down a narrow cobblestone lane. Rows of one-storey houses and shops, most with peeling paint and chipped brick, lined the street which was remarkably clean of filth and garbage.

The district had an off-center feel to it and a strange atmosphere, for tucked into doorways, perched in the windows, rested odd bits of mechanical contraptions. To the right, a clockwork bird sung a tinny tune and an automaton monkey danced for pennies. To the left spun a miniature, mechanical windmill, puffing steam. Even the street lamps were decked out in anomalous devices and embellishments.

As they walked, it seemed almost every building had some similar contrivance as decoration, adorning the street in a cacophony of clangs, bangs, and whirs. The street's surroundings danced with steam and smoke, the scent of oil and grease its perfume.

"I believe we've found the right place," Fred whispered.

"Yes." Mary tugged his sleeve. "Look at that."

Fred turned his head to see a man in a leather apron and goggles tinkering with a mechanical arm—his own!

"Excuse me, sir," Mary rushed over to speak to the man before Fred could object. "I couldn't help but notice your unusual appendage. Where might one obtain such a wonder?"

"Shop down the street. Where I got mine. Godsend it is, that shop." He stopped tinkering and gave Mary a stern glare. "You ain't looking to give the owner a hard time, now? People 'round here wouldn't like that, now."

Mary smiled her sweetest, most disarming grin. "Oh, heavens, no. I'm merely interested in purchasing one such curiosity. A mechanical marvel is just the thing I need for the sitting room."

The man grunted, the sound mixed with a slight cackle. "You toffs, with your peculiar ideas. Shop's down the street like I said. Called The Gear and Far."

"Thank you, sir, for your kindness and trouble."

The man grunted again and turned his attention back to his work. Mary returned to Fred.

"The place we want is called the Gear and Far and it's further down the street."

They found the structure well enough, a small, dingy building, the storefront all grime and soot and peeling paint. A faded sign with the name painted in crooked red letters hung slightly askew above the door. A tiny bell rang as they entered and a gruff voice called out from the rear of the shop.

"I'll be there in a minute."

Fred gazed around the cramped interior, its recesses crowded with shelves and stacks of metal jumbles, iron scraps, gears, pistons, gadgets, and other junk and odd apparatus.

"Look at these things." Fred whispered. "He's a dealer in clockwork and mechanicals for certain."

"But we don't know to whom he sells, Fred. We don't have any evidence of illegal commerce."

"Not yet, we don't."

A noise from the back room interrupted their discussion, and a young man, smallish in stature, shuffled out past the dividing curtain. He wore brass goggles that he pushed to his forehead, and wiped his grimy hands on his apron. As he approached them, he lifted a corner of his mouth in the semblance of a smile and held out his hand in greeting.

"Hello to you both. I'm Crocker. I run this fine establishment. Might I be helping you with something today?"

Fred grasped his proffered extremity in a firm handshake. "I think you can aid us. We've been told you are quite the maker of strange and unusual clockwork mechanisms."

"Yeah, I've been known to dabble. You looking for something specific or you wanting a custom order?"

"Actually we're looking for *someone* specific—someone who may have done business with you for parts or gadgets. A tall, thin man who goes by the name of Rupert Muggins."

Crocker scowled. "Who are you two? Government types or scoundrels? Up to no good, one way or the other, asking after the likes of Muggins. Besides, I don't ask questions of my customers. They pay their money owed and I leave it at that."

"To answer your question, we are not scoundrels, and we can make your life very unpleasant if you don't tell us what we want to know. I don't think you want the Peelers coming around your shop on a daily basis, now, do you?"

"You foul crushers, thinking you can control everyone. One of these days you'll get yours." He spat on the floor. "I ain't no snitch."

Fred seized the man by the shirt front and yanked him forward. "You can be a snitch or I can beat the information out of you."

Crocker turned pale and squirmed in Fred's grip. "Typical law. I hate you lot. Bullies, the lot of you. But you win. I don't like it, but I don't want your kind of trouble, neither. I might be able to help, but you didn't learn nothing from me, if anyone asks. Can't have it getting around I squealed to the likes of you. Agreed?"

Fred nodded and let the man go.

"Good. I hear rumours sometimes. In this business you do. Word is, something is going down soon, by a group of nefarious types who like the mechanicals. Something at the Tower, you understand. And word is, it's coming from underground." He laughed. "That's all you'll get out of me."

A pensive look blossomed over Fred's face and he mumbled, "I wonder if he's found the tunnel?"

"What are you blathering about? Wait, I don't want to know, just get out of me shop."

Fred took hold of Mary's arm and rushed them out of the building.

"Fred, what is it? Do you know something?"

"I'm not sure. But I think we'd best investigate the situation at the Tower of London immediately."

⋞⋟

"How did you know about this underground entrance and tunnel, Fred?" Mary asked the question as she stepped gingerly through what she hoped was mud and tried to avoid the steady drips of water from overhead.

Fred shone his wrist torch into the darkness ahead. He gave its clockwork another crank for good measure, to ensure it didn't fail and leave them in the dark. They were far underneath the Tower grounds, looking for any signs of recent passage.

"One of the old agency warhorses told me about it. Claimed it was built as a secret passageway around the time of Henry VIII. He said it ran directly under the castle, and it used to connect to other tunnels with entrances leading into the White Tower and the Martin Tower. He also claimed some thief tried to steal the Crown Jewels this way, in decades past, and that the other doors and tunnels were sealed off after the attempted theft."

"Do you really think Muggins knows of the existence of these tunnels? And he plans to reopen them to steal the Crown Jewels? It seems a bit of a stretch in deduction. Even if he could gain entrance to the proper tower, he'd still have to access the Jewel House. It's practically impossible. We're most likely on another fruitless search." Mary wrinkled her nose in distaste at the foul smell which wafted up from where she stepped.

"Perhaps, but we can't ignore the possibility. It is just the type of outlandish thing he would attempt. And if Muggins is after the Crown Jewels, we have to stop him."

"True, I suppose, but I don't fancy the idea of encountering our foes down here. It's a perfect place for an ambush."

"Well, there's a horrid idea: falling into another trap. I've had enough of being shot at this week. Of course," Fred grinned wickedly, "that may not be the only thing we have to worry about. There may be a few ghosts down here as well." His hand shot out and grabbed Mary's shoulder. She started and let out a faint squeal of alarm.

"Stop that." Mary swatted her hand at him in irritation and frowned disapprovingly. "Stop teasing. If we're not careful, we may be the ones who end up as ghosts."

As they travelled onward, they began to see signs of recent use, a few bits of metal, and odd tracks on the muddy floor of the tunnel.

"Perhaps your theory isn't so far-fetched after all," Mary whispered. "My apologies, Fred."

They pulled out their pistols and peered into the dimly lit gloom for the slightest signs of trouble. Their footsteps grew quieter now, and their voices stilled as they stalked any potential enemies. They stopped in unison as noises sounded from far ahead in the tunnel.

"Careful, now," Fred murmured. "We don't know what lies before us."

Fred and Mary crept forward, straining their eyes as they peered into the gloom. Slowly they saw shapes moving in the dark and the noises got louder.

"Fred," Mary whispered, "That sounds like—"

"It is. It's the rats."

"What are we going—"

A great, deafening explosion shook the tunnel, sending them backward off their feet, bits of stonework debris raining around them.

Fred landed on his back, choking on dirt and dust, the stench of smoke in his nose, his ears buzzing and his head reeling. He could hear Mary to his right, moaning softly.

"Mary!" He croaked her name, coughing, sloughing off grime and small chunks of stone as he struggled to sit. "Mary, are you hurt?" He groped about until he managed to find her hand. He gripped it tight for a moment, squeezing.

"I think I'm fine. I don't think anything's broken. I'm just dazed, I think." Her frail voice floated from the surrounding blackness. Fred's torch had gone out. He fumbled about, checking his pockets, before rummaging out a match and lighting it. In the faint, flickering light, he found Mary, and then the match sputtered out.

"Can you stand?" Fred asked, as he lit another match.

"Yes, I think so." He watched her rise on shaky limbs, as he found his own unsteady feet. His match died again. "Does your torch work?"

In the darkness, he heard her fussing with the wrist device as he cranked his own. No comforting glow came from either and Fred sighed.

"It's no good, Fred. It's broken."

"Mine, too. We'll have to use the matches to move forward."

"Are you sure we should—no, we have to investigate." Fred felt her fumble and then grasp his hand. "Lead the way."

Fred lit another match. "Try to keep to the wall and watch out for loose stones and debris."

They stumbled and groped through the murky tunnel, their way illuminated only by the slight flame of match after match. Fred guided the advance, Mary clutching to his arm, her pistol ready.

"Stop. I think I see light further on." Fred dropped the already sputtering match he held and peered ahead. A steady gleam of light illuminated the passage, showing a spectacle of strewn stony rubble.

Fred and Mary inched forward slowly, struggling through the scene of destruction, clambering over the rocks and debris littering the floor of the tunnel. As they grew closer to the apex of the damage, they saw a gaping hole exposed in the wall, where the light filtered out.

"They've breached the sealed entrance. We must follow them." Fred rushed his advance, hastening over more wreckage, Mary scrambling to keep pace.

"Fred, be careful. We still don't know what we're facing."

Fred glanced back. "It doesn't matter what we face. We must stop this attack." He dashed through the hole and into the unknown.

"Just watch out for those rats!"

They found a crude stairway and raced up the steps, taking two at a time, as noises and shouts from above them became audible. They emerged from the stairwell into the confines of the Martin Tower, and a scene of havoc and chaos.

Around them darted mechanical rats: dozens of scuttling, scampering rodents, attacking the Tower guards; a complete infestation. Fred and Mary stared at one another and simultaneously said, "The Jewel House!"

The pair raced as one, fending off biting, snapping rats as they ran. They arrived at the Tower Jewel House in time to behold a dazzling display of mechanized rats bedecked in the splendid finery of crowns and tiaras, bracelets and rings, carrying sceptres and orbs, spoons and swords, fleeing the site. The mad metal league of thieves led a parade of guards on a merry chase, with Mary and Fred joining the melee, all in a wild dash to the courtyard. They emerged into dappled sunlight and a surprise attack.

"Take cover!" Bullets greeted Fred's shouts as a gang of armed men filling the courtyard opened fire on them all. They had rushed straight into a gunfight. "Try to retreat to the Tower!"

He and Mary dodged bullets, making their way to safety, firing back with their own pistols, as did many of the Tower guards. The rats had disappeared into the crowd of foes, taking the Crown Jewels with them.

Fred glanced back at Mary who seemed to be rubbing her wrist. "Are you hurt?"

"I'm fine, now pay attention. We're being shot at, Fred."

"I know that—"

His words were cut short by the sound of high pitched laughter ringing out above the sound of gunfire.

"Great Scott! Is that . . . ?" Fred scanned the courtyard and saw him: a gangly gentleman in a stylish black suit, standing out in a sea of men.

"Muggins." Fred spat the word and ground his teeth.

"What! He's here? Oh my, Fred! Look up!"

Fred raised his gaze to where Mary pointed.

"What the blazes!" Above his head flew a fantastic airship, a mechanical marvel of gears, propellers, and an inflatable balloon. "It's a two-pronged attack."

"And now he's escaping. He's getting away, Fred."

Fred saw Muggins rising in the air, clinging to a suspended, ascending basket. "And, no doubt, he has the Crown Jewels with him." Fred watched Muggins trade shots with guards as they tried to hold his basket to the earth.

"We're never going to explain this one to Griffith."

"We can if we catch Muggins. Come on, Mary."

Fred leaped forward into the path of the enemy gunmen, dodging bullets and the still-attacking rats on an insane sprint for Muggins, who yet struggled to escape the clutch of defending guards. He heard Mary behind him, shooting, as he too, fired through the enemy; their guns and bravado somehow cleared a path. Fred jumped as the basket began to ascend again, and caught the edge. He hauled himself in and greeted Muggins with a punch on the nose.

Muggins staggered back, then raised his pistol and fired. The hammer clicked on an empty chamber. With a cry of rage, Muggins leaped at Fred, and the pair fought in the precariously swinging basket.

Muggins landed two blows to Fred's stomach that doubled him over in pain. A vicious kick to the shins sent Fred to his knees. Desperate, Fred lashed out with an uppercut to Muggins' jaw. Muggins staggered back a step and Fred rushed forward, tackling him. The pair hit the side of the basket. The wicker contraption swung violently and the frail connecting ropes creaked under the strain of their brutal brawl.

Fred slammed three punches into Muggins' face while Muggins countered by smashing a fist into Fred's gut. Fred wrenched away and both men stood apart, gasping for breath. An ominous lurch shook the basket. They both looked upwards.

Immediately, they grasped the awful danger. Helpless, they stared in horror as fast-unravelling strands of rope fiber gave way with a snap, and the left side of their lifeline released into the sky.

Time seemed suspended before Fred and Muggins crashed against the side of the basket, their weight upending it. Fred grabbed at the edge to break his fall, clinging on frantically. He watched a shower of jewels and crowns tumble to the ground and land in the midst of men and rats.

He dangled precariously from the rim of the basket. Below him, an angry, shrieking Muggins clung to a remaining piece of frayed rope. Shouts came from above and Fred saw henchmen lower a rope ladder to his enemy. He glimpsed another man slicing at the remaining line holding the basket aloft.

Unable to stop it, Fred shouted in frustration as Muggins ascended to safety. Then the final threads of the fraying rope broke and Fred plummeted to the ground. As he collided back to earth and lost consciousness, Fred witnessed Muggins climb into the airship.

When Fred regained his senses, the first thing he realised was that he rested on something soft, certainly not a tangle of men and mechanicals. He opened his eyes. Mary's face filled his vision. She sat beside him, on a narrow bed.

"Finally decided to wake up, did you, sleepy head? You missed the last bit of the fun."

"What happened? Where am I?" Fred tried to sit up and immediately changed his mind, staying supine, where a piercing pain did not invade his head.

"You're in hospital. You came out of it all with a few bruises and scrapes, one or two broken ribs, and a bump on the head. You're quite lucky."

"I don't feel lucky." Fred sighed. "The last thing I remember is Muggins getting away."

"Yes. That dastardly villain slipped through our grasp again. But at least he did not abscond with the Crown Jewels. You managed to dump the whole lot with you when you fell."

"Entirely by accident I assure you, but at least they were

recovered." Fred frowned. "Why were they recovered? I fell in the midst of Muggins' henchmen. Surely even some of them had the sense to try and make off with the loot?"

"Oh, no doubt they would have tried, had the agents I signalled not arrived in the nick of time. They rounded up the lot and the jewels. It was just like something from the Penny Dreadfuls." Mary giggled. "Good thing this device wasn't damaged in the tunnel explosion." She waggled her wrist signalling apparatus under his nose.

"What on earth?! When did you have time to signal for more agents?"

"After we burst into the courtyard. I thought it a prudent idea, faced with all those armed men. And the rats. And Muggins."

"Crikey, I never even thought to signal."

"Of course not. You were too busy running headlong through gunfire without a plan. You know, you really have to stop that tendency. We're both damned lucky we're not dead."

"Mary! Watch your language. Ladies don't swear."

"Please. I think I'm entitled to a little swearing. And you'll be hearing a lot more when you finally get to meet with Griffith."

"Oh, heavens. I forgot about Griffith. He must be pulling out his hair."

Mary nodded. "He's livid. Although, mostly at Muggins." Mary absently smoothed back an errant lock of his hair. "About the only one who has taken any joy in this escapade is Topper. He has dozens of rat specimens to tinker with now, both destroyed and still functional." Mary reached around him and fluffed his pillow. "Just relax and rest. You have to get better."

Fred closed his eyes, ready to drift off to the sound of Mary's voice.

"Stand down, nurse, and get out of my way!" A familiar bellow echoed in from the corridor.

Fred's eyes flew open. "Deuced hell," he exclaimed as Griffith stormed into the room.

Mary giggled. "I guess there's no rest for the likes of us, Fred, my dear. Time to go back to work."

Styled after A Christmas Carol by Charles Dickens

Lavenza, or the Modern Galatea

ALYSON GRAUER

My name is Elizabeth Lavenza, and I am dreaming the same dream that has haunted me since I was a child.

I am lying on my back in my bed, and my skin is hot with fever. There is a sound like metal clicking, and a gentle voice is humming some unidentifiable, soothing tune. I open my eyes slowly, the room around me blurry and swimming with too-vibrant colors. My body is heavy as lead, my limbs limp against the mattress as someone peels back the sheets from my prone form. Gentle, firm hands cradle my head and prop me up against a pillow, and I can see before me.

My mother, beautiful and serene, is there beside me, her touch loving and careful. She is the source of the humming, the melody some foreign lullaby that calms me despite my inability to move my body. She pulls a pair of goggles down over her eyes, and there are gloves on her slender hands. She pushes aside more cloth, and my vision blurs again, the room spinning.

She has a set of small, strange tools on a tray beside her, and she is using them on me, somehow, in a way that I cannot quite make out from this angle. My heartbeat is loud as a metal drum, and there is a whirring of gears and clacking of cogs.

I am suddenly afraid, for I do not understand what I see with my own eyes, but then the fever takes me into blackness once more.

Then I awake, and I am whole and well, with no trace of fever, no sign of any surgery upon my form, and my mind is full of questions.

I have had this recurring dream since I was a child, but it is not the first thing I remember. If I am to tell this tale, I ought to start from the beginning of my life.

I was once an orphan, brought to be the ward of a well-off couple when my poor Italian foster family could no longer afford to keep me. This fine couple, whose name was Frankenstein, told me that I was the daughter of a German lady and a Milanese nobleman, an illegitimate child and the cause of my mother's death.

For as long as I could remember, my new parents determined that I would one day wed my foster brother, whom I have called 'cousin' all my life. He and I were playmates as children, the best of friends, and it did not seem unusual that we should one day be man and wife.

Despite my rise from destitution to comfort, from abandoned

to loved, I had always understood my own existence to be average in every way. I was comfortable and happy, and there was nothing strange or out of the ordinary about me or my adopted family.

Oh, the lies we tell to protect the ones we love!

After my adoption by the Frankensteins, my childhood was very much a warm and happy one. My dear cousin Victor was a deeply inquisitive, quiet, intelligent soul. We were constant companions, and I often found my own curiosity piqued by his. He revealed unto me endless wonders of the world and its habits, and we explored the way children do: fearlessly and often, without stopping to rest. We spoke of stars and mountains, rivers and caverns, of flame and electricity, of steam and iron.

Victor was fascinated by the progress of invention, and I found myself often peering over his shoulder at things he studied, curious in ways of my own. More than anything, however, I loved his passion, the gleam in his eyes that spoke of rushing, fathomless thoughts too quick for even his own tongue to keep up.

I suppose I always knew he would be a scientist of some sort; a scholar, definitely. His father wished for a doctor, or lawyer, and indeed, my Victor could have achieved all this and more. But, Victor wanted the thrill of discovery, the sleepless nights of research and experimentation. He wanted a more difficult path.

Victor always got what he wanted.

When we were still quite young, I contracted an illness, that which went by the name of scarlet fever. I was quarantined in my chambers upon diagnosis, to suffer it through or be taken to the arms of God, and my adoptive mother was barred from caring for me as she so wished, on the chance she might contract the fever too.

I remember little of this time spent in dim firelight, rolling in the sheets in a haze of heat and weakness and worry. And then I woke to find my mother there, feeding me soup and giving me water to drink, and dampening my brow with a cool cloth.

"But Mother," said I, fearful, "the doctor said you could catch my fever!"

"Better to catch your fever, my angel, than let you suffer alone," said she, then continued to care for me as bravely as any soldier on the front lines of a war.

Again, I dipped into dreamless, fuzzy sleep, and was lost for a time in darkness and warmth. Once, I thought I opened my eyes and saw my mother there, bent over my abdomen with gloves and spectacles on, using a tiny set of metal tools to fix something, like a surgeon. I slept again in confusion.

When I woke again, my mother was there, looking weak and tired herself. I felt somewhat better. The little tools and gloves and spectacles of magnification were nowhere to be seen. I wished to ask her why I had seen these things, but had not the courage to do so, lest I be seen as mad.

"You will get well now, my Elizabeth," said my mother, smiling distantly. "Your fever has broken and you will mend."

"Are you well? Have you had the fever, Mother?" My voice was filled with dread, but she only smiled.

"I am still here, am I not? We have so much to do together," she added. Then, she drifted off to sleep in her chair.

But my mother did catch the fever from me, and though my strength and appetites quickly returned to me, a healthy pink to my cheeks, she grew pale and weak and warm to the touch. When she was confined to bed, I could not bear to leave the room, for fear of losing her, as she had nearly lost me.

When she was at her weakest, she held my hands in hers and lay on her side in bed, smiling at me. I felt full of emotion and fear and worry, but she calmed me as she always had with her steady eyes and gentle hands.

"I have lost one mother," I said. "I do not want to lose another. Please get well again." She squeezed my hands. "Illness is unfair, but you should rejoice, Elizabeth, for you will never be ill again and all will be well."

"How can you know this?" I wondered, perplexed by her words.

My mother's reply was one I did not expect or quite understand, at first. She told me that she had given of herself to make me whole, and ensured that I would never fall prey to sickness again, and that it had, by some turn of events, made her ill, too.

"But I need you," I protested. "I cannot let you die this way for saving me."

"But death for a loved one is not a death wasted," my mother said, gently. "And Victor needs you. Without you, he will be lost. Always remember that, Elizabeth."

When Victor was summoned to join us, that our mother

might say her goodbyes, he was anxious and pale as any son who fears for his mother. She held our hands in hers and smiled bravely.

"It is my wish and that of your father, that when you two come of age you should be wed. You are meant for each other. Keep each other safe and happy, that's all I ask, and your father will be comforted."

When she died, our father mourned deeply, as did we all, for she was beloved in our household and our town. Victor and I sat in the garden in our mourning clothes, watching the wind in the grass and the clouds passing quickly overhead; a storm was doubtless on its way.

"She went peacefully," I said gently. "She wasn't angry or upset. That's good isn't it?"

Victor said nothing for a while, but I could see the familiar gleam in his eyes, full of thought and pressing need.

"We shall miss her," he said. His chin quivered a moment, then was still.

"Yes, but we have each other. We shall always have each other, Victor. I shall always be here for you."

"I know you will. But you will stay here, and I shall be going away to school." When he spoke, his voice had lost its childlike bounce and fervor, and now withheld a tremble of determination, unusual in a child our age.

"Will you study medicine or law?"

"Both, I should think. And science. There are so many questions, Elizabeth, and I must answer them all."

"You will be brilliant at whatever you do. And you will come back to me, and all will be well."

From our mother's death, I had no wishes but to serve and help the family. I acted as mother and sister and daughter. I was a well-mannered young woman as I grew older, selfless and as kind as I could be to anyone and everyone I crossed paths with. I took over much of the house management, and was well used to the care and keeping of our rooms.

When Victor went off to school, we said a hopeful, but teary, goodbye. When his coach disappeared down the road, I felt a peculiar pang in my chest. For the first time, I wished I was going with him, and learning all the things he would learn. But it was not my place, and so I continued to exist in the small world of our home, waiting for his return, and writing him letters from time to time.

I never thought about the fever dream of my mother with the tools again—not until I found the letters. I was airing out the cupboards in her private rooms which had been locked by the house staff since her death.

My mother's room felt like just another room in the house, for years had passed, and I was older. I missed her daily, but taking on her responsibilities had helped me to see my place as I grew into adulthood.

This day was different from my usual cleaning routine. Something caught the toe of my shoe while I crossed the room, and I stumbled. On investigation, I discovered that the offending object was the corner of a loose board in the floor. Without hesitation, I knelt and began to pry it out, curious to see what had caused it to come loose.

In the hole beneath the board was a cloth packet, tied with string.

I reached down and pulled it free, and after a moment, decided to unwrap it. The old, stiff cloth peeled away heavily to reveal a leather journal and a stack of letters in envelopes. Most were sealed, many unaddressed. Two were addressed to me, but the second of these had the heading "On Your Wedding Day."

I opened the first.

My dear angel Elizabeth,

If you are reading this, then I am gone, and I must yield unto you a part of my deepest self, and reveal several things which may come as rather a shock to you. You must not reveal any of this information to your Victor or to my husband, your father. If you cannot promise me these things, you must hereby burn these letters and bury the journal in the soil. There is no shame in this, my dear one, but if you choose to read on, you must be strong, for all our sakes. Flesh of my flesh and bone of my bone you are, Elizabeth, and from your state and mine shall never be parted, bliss or woe, no matter what happens.

I paused in my reading. This was most unprecedented. But even as I pondered the meaning of this, the vision of my fever dream, my mother in spectacles and accoutered like a surgeon over my prone form, sprang before my eyes.

There was no way about it but to read on, know the unknown, and keep my mother's secrets.

When my mother was a young girl, she wrote in her careful, sweeping hand, she and her family, called Beaufort, encountered a small company of gypsies on the road to Paris. The gypsies had broken a wagon wheel, and it was such that my mother's mother longed to hurry by without stopping.

But my mother's father was a kind gentleman, and he ordered the coachman to slow warily and ask if the little ragged family was well or if they required assistance. Mrs. Beaufort insisted that this was a certain invitation for trouble and robbery, but Mr. Beaufort refused to hear her.

It was such that the gypsies were not of ungrateful stock. The patriarch of their patchwork family doffed his cap and thanked the gentleman kindly for his offer.

"Our wheel has broken, monsieur," announced the gypsy man, "and we can go no further. We are too far from town and my wife is with child. We cannot walk."

He gestured to the woman, seated on the slanted wagon, her belly round and full. She had a sad, knowing look about her, and when Mrs. Beaufort peered out the coach window to see with her own eyes, the gypsy woman sat up straighter.

"Your own daughter, madame," pleaded the gypsy woman suddenly, reaching out to her. "She is your life's light, your only joy. You would do anything to see her comfortable and happy."

Mrs. Beaufort was doubtful, for she feared that there would be dishonesty behind the sentiment, but the pregnant woman seemed gentle and true, despite her destitution.

"If your servant assists us," said the gypsy man, "I will offer a few coins to spare, although it isn't much to the likes of you. But my wife, she tells fortunes."

There was then an obligatory squabble between my mother's parents regarding the legitimacy of the offer. Mr. Beaufort, in his infinite kindness, agreed to let one of their servants step down from the coach and assist the attachment of a new wheel to the gypsies' wagon. When the deed was done, Mrs. Beaufort held out her hand from the window, saying, "Very well, read my palm."

The gypsy woman slowly came alongside the coach, and squinted at the palm proffered to her. "You will have your heart's desires," she said, "but it is not your fortune I am meant to tell, madame. It is hers."

"Whose?" demanded Mrs. Beaufort.

"Your daughter's."

At this point, my mother, a polite girl of eight, stood up inside the coach and peered out the window at the gypsy with curiosity. The gypsy woman smiled at the little girl.

"Your mind exceeds your heritage, child," said the woman kindly, "and your accomplishments will be grand and extraordinary, though few will credit them to you. Do not be disheartened by this, for your own son someday will be an extraordinary mind, too. His dreams will see fruition, but it will be at a terrible price which cannot be avoided."

"This is foolishness," said Mrs. Beaufort, upset. "Caroline is but a child!" Mr. Beaufort shushed her. The gypsy had more to say.

"There is one thing that may redeem your son: your daughter. When you have a daughter, she will be an angel from heaven, if you have the means to save her. Do not let your own brilliant mind be wasted in preparing for your children's future." The gypsy turned away, leaning on her husband for support, and the husband thanked the couple for their generosity again.

"What does that mean?" demanded Mrs. Beaufort, but the fortune was told and done.

For years, my mother toiled over what the prophetic words could mean. As she grew older, she read a great many books and was considered 'unhealthily educated' by her mother. Thinking perhaps the gypsy meant there would be something wrong with her daughter when the girl was born that would require fixing or even prevention, she read all she could about surgery and medicine.

She studied anatomy and engineering and sciences to further her understanding of life, the mechanics of the human body, and the untapped potential therein. The words regarding her son were full of praise and success, linked inexorably to the fate of her daughter. If she could save her future daughter, her son would also be saved.

When her father died, my teenaged mother was taken into the care of her father's friend, a man called Frankenstein. A romance bloomed there, and ultimately, they were married. She bore him a son, Victor, so-called for his predestined victory in whatever field or profession he should chose. The next child to be born was also a son, whom they named Ernest. My father would have been quite settled with these two healthy boys, but my mother was determined that a daughter should be born.

"Then, my dearest Elizabeth, the unthinkable happened," wrote my mother. "I was, at last, with child again, but tragedy struck me, and the infant was lost. The doctor revealed to me after the incident that it had been a female child, and I lost much of my health and ability to carry on, thinking very much that I had failed my prophecy. The doctor advised your father to take me to Italy for warmer, more temperate climes, and so we went. It was there, my dearest girl, my true angel, that we found you."

I realized that I had been holding my breath for a little too long. I sat back and breathed, closing my eyes for a moment to clear my head. The rest of this letter was professions of faith and love, and reassurances that I would be well all the days of my life if I entrusted myself to Victor faithfully, and cared for him in deepest love and honesty.

I studied the second fat envelope, marked "On Your Wedding Day." This first letter was the hitherto untold story of my mother's journey up to her most generous adoption of myself. What else could possibly lie unsaid? Curiosity spread through my veins like poison, and I ran my fingers over the paper. I wanted very badly to open it and read it, though it was not my wedding day. With Victor away at his studies, I had no idea when that day would come, I realized with a sad twist in my gut.

I shook my head to clear it of confusion. My mother hid these things knowing—or at least hoping—that I would find them someday, and I must trust her to know when the truths would be most rightly revealed.

I hid the journal and letters back in the floorboards, replacing it and carefully dusting everything with a rag, so as not to betray any one place that had more or less dust than the hiding spot. I would wait. I had to wait. I would continue to do her proud by caring for the family, and loving Victor, even in his absence, and waiting for the day of our marriage.

The time passed like hazy, fitful dreaming. My nights were haunted by memories of my mother, both merry and sad ones. Most prominent of all these visions was the fever dream that I tried so hard to understand, and it pained me to have no one to turn to for advice or soothing words. Although Victor visited with us at home from time to time, he was never the same as he had once been as a boy.

Where in youth he had been lively and eager and curious, he entered adulthood with pallor and exhaustion in his eyes, like a man starving for rest and food but unable to afford the time to stop and feed his body. When asked of his studies and research, Victor's replies were often cryptic and very terse, even defensive and cold at times.

Our father was a little worried, but in his aging years and ongoing grief in the absence of his wife, he had little of his previous energy to bestow upon worrying endlessly over the matter; this task, then, fell to me.

As often as Victor was home, I did the best I could to try to divine the nature of his scientific inquiries. I sought his journals and notes, but whenever I caught a glimpse of anything important, it was either indecipherable to my eyes or snatched away by Victor himself. He did not seem to suspect me of anything, however obvious some of these instances became. Victor's world was contained mostly within his own mind, and little else penetrated his keen focus. It was as though he saw things beyond the normal range of sight, and his mind was constantly working to interpret them.

I had no doubt of Victor's brilliance. But I yearned for the days of our childhood when his inquisitive nature was shared with me fully, and our adventures were of equal footing. His newly detached, distant nature put me ill at ease and made me worry, especially knowing what the gypsy had told my mother.

To distract myself from my concerns about my betrothed, I snuck into my mother's old rooms anytime I was able, and studied the open letters in the packet under the floorboards. Many were of a strangely poetic nature; some of my mother's correspondences were with a Frenchman, a doctor of some kind, whose name on the pages had been rather obscured by time and smudging.

It took three or four letters for me to consider that they may be mostly in code, that being a possible excuse for my confusion at the importance of seemingly vague literary drivel. If my mother was so desperate as to hide these correspondences beneath the wooden boards of her bedroom floor, it wasn't too great a stretch to consider the possibility of encoding the messages.

I puzzled over it all, wondering helplessly what on earth could be so important as to force my mother to this level of secrecy?

Then I found the sketches.

These were not a lady's idle dalliances into the realm of art and portraiture. These were serious, detailed illustrations and diagrams of myriad unknown apparatuses, some which looked like carriages, some like weaponry of varying kinds; some resembled exaggerated and unique versions of ordinary items, like tea kettles, stovetops, bookshelves. Mixed into the pile were several diagrams of certain organs in the human body, including a heart, lungs, and stomach, yet which in every apparent way were devised of materials other than the organic tissue which comprises our forms. The annotations of these sketches were as blurry and ill-written as some of the letters, the handwriting hurried and sharply slanted, as though scrawled in excitement.

The connections between all these seemingly informational sketches were utterly lost on me, no matter how long I studied them, no matter how I tried to decipher the writing. I longed for understanding, but without my mother to interpret, and no one to consult on the matter, I was alone with my questions, these thoughts which haunted my dreams and waking hours both with even and equal ardor.

Victor was away again when the unthinkable happened.

My two younger brothers, my father, and I had gone for an evening stroll in the warmth of the May twilight. The teenaged Ernest was very fond of the young, round-faced William, who had been born just a year before our mother's death, and it was comfort to Father to watch them play together. Ernest reminded me so much of our father, and little William recalled Victor in looks, but they both shared the loving temperament of our mother.

It was exceptional weather that day, and the ground was not too soggy, and so we allowed ourselves to stray a little farther out into nature than usual, to enjoy the evening to its fullest. Ernest and William, in a burst of boyish sport, had broken off from the main path to play at hiding and seeking, while my father and I walked on and circled back again from the wood toward home once more.

I paused and looked at my father. "You go on ahead. I shall linger a moment for my brothers, and we will overcome you on the path home anon."

My father did not argue, for the light of sunset was still good and warm with orange and crimson hues, and he trod on slowly.

"Boys," cried I, clapping my hands for their attention. "Come away now, toward the house. Father shall not wait for you in this footrace!" I was, of course, only teasing, but I heard nothing but birds in the trees and the wind in the leaves.

A flock of birds startled out of a tree some ways away, within view but not quite walking distance, and I watched them go.

I felt my eyes drawn rather strangely to a gap in the tree-line, as though some unknown beacon called to my attention. After a few moments, I indeed saw something most peculiar: there came a great, hulking thing, shaped like a man, half-running, half-limping through the wood.

This creature was somewhat obscured by evening shadows, its skin appearing mottled and patchwork in color and texture. Its gait was powerful as that of a mighty animal, perhaps some jungle hunter, but it was of an awkward frame and seemed unevenly formed, and thus it appeared to lope along with great strength behind an uneven stride.

At that first moment, I was struck by the profoundly unusual sight this man-creature made. It was majestic, even though not in the same way that other wild animals in their natural habitats appear to be; but it was, above all, very strange to see. I wondered if it were some hairless bear come down from the wilderness of the mountains. It was not; I was fooling myself. I determined that it must be some remote, forest-dwelling man with a giant's birth deformity to account for his size and shape.

By the time I had reached this conclusion, the thing had passed into the cover of trees once more, and I was quite as alone as I had been before. Nonetheless, a shiver ran down my spine after it had vanished from view, and I wondered about the sense of foreboding in my stomach. I called out to my brothers again, hoping they were nearby.

"Ernest! William! It is time to go up to the house. Come along immediately!"

There was no answer but my own faint echo and the rustling of trees. My heart pounded as I began to wonder where my brothers were. In my rising concern, my mind began to fill with possibilities grim and distressing, and I could not stop seeing the strange man-thing in my head.

I tried to slow my breathing, advising myself that calm was the only way to proceed. I then moved about, in search of a higher vantage point where I might better see the lay of the land, and determine if my young brothers were sneaking about and hiding to give me a scare, perhaps. As I was still young and strong, and there was no one to declare me unladylike for doing so, I opted to climb a nearby boulder that would boost my height sufficiently to see beyond the trees.

Visibility was slightly better from on high, I found, though the shadows of dusk were filling the empty spaces of the world around me with rapid succession, and I knew that, before long, I should not be able to see much else, and the only light would be that of our house down the way.

It was then, in the dying rays of sunset, that I saw the shape of the huge thing I had seen mere minutes before upon the hillside, making its way down the shore of the lake, and just a little ways beyond its steady strides was a much smaller shape, digging in the sand, which I knew then in my heart to be my dear little brother, William.

My breath stuck in my throat as I watched from my perch. I wanted to scream, or climb down and run to them, to protect my William, to save him from what could only be some kind of attack . . . But as I watched, the giant of a man made no aggressive movements. He approached slowly, like a curious dog, and William seemed unbothered by the thing's presence. Perhaps I was wrong, and William was not in danger. Perhaps it would be all right . . .

The strange-skinned giant paused some distance away from little William, and I saw my younger brother start to turn to look back and stop suddenly, the man-creature having spoken something sharply, with one wild hand outstretched in a halting gesture. I saw William give a kind of shudder that could only be attributed to fear, and my heart leapt in my chest.

There was no doubt in my mind that William was very afraid, and the strange creature did not mean him well. I instantly set in motion to run down to the shore and *do* something to stop the stranger from harming my brother.

These thoughts came blindly and too quickly to be individualized in my mind; one moment I was stock-still upon the rock in terror, and the next, I had dropped onto the ground, running before I had even registered what I had done. Excitement and urgency rushed through my veins, my breath deepening as I ran through the woods over the uneven ground. I ran, for my brother was very probably in danger, and I could not afford to stop and think.

I soon emerged from the trees onto the rocky shoreline of the lake and found myself quite alone.

The giant stranger had vanished, but so had my little brother. My stomach lurched, and I stood still, listening for any sign of which way they had gone. Hearing nothing but the gentle breeze moving over the water, I could not bear to be still. I moved quickly to the nearest sturdy tree and, without hesitation, I began to climb.

Even with my skirts about my legs, I had climbed trees during many games and adventures over the years. I was glad that Father had gone ahead, for he'd never have allowed it, but I did not care. I knotted my dress to one side and hitched it up a little, to better access the branches at my disposal with all four of my limbs.

Thus, I carefully hoisted myself up into the branches of the tree, with only mild difficulty and discomfort due to my apparel. As quickly as I dared, I raised myself up through the tree's boughs to peer out through the smaller branches. I pulled myself higher and higher, no time to be wasted, and then, rather suddenly, a voice pierced the otherwise quiet evening air.

"Elizabeth! Elizabeth! Father! Someone!"

It was Ernest's voice. I was filled with sudden relief at hearing him so nearby, but he took me by complete surprise. Thus startled, I twisted too quickly and lost my footing. Before I could catch myself, I fell from the tree to the hard ground below with a sick thud.

I landed mostly on my back, the wind utterly knocked out of me, and knew without a doubt, looking back up at the tree, that it must have been a drop equivalent to that of falling from the balcony on the second story of our home. I had scrambled quite high into the branches in my desperation to get a better view of where William could be. Losing my grip had been a dire misfortune.

My head rang with a momentary loss of hearing from the shock of the impact, and I fought to regain my breath, my amazement at having survived such a fall causing my heart to beat rather wildly in my chest. First, I leap from high rocks to go running off into the woods without pause, and then I climb two stories into a tree, only to fall and undoubtedly break my back? What had gotten into me? And where had poor William gone?

I gasped for breath and tried to bring myself to an upright position, and a thought occurred to me. I rather ought to be in a great deal of pain. Perhaps it was shock that kept me from truly feeling the fall, but then, I wondered why I had not fainted. I managed to sit up with some stiffness, but no real pain, whereupon I began silently to thank God for His protection.

I stopped praying abruptly when I found that my right shoulder had dislocated entirely. My right arm was bent at a sick angle, like that of a china doll after having been flung across the room by a child in a tantrum, and yet I felt no real pain, just a kind of dull strain or throbbing in my fingertips.

I stared at it in newfound disbelief, and without thinking, I took hold of it and rotated it back into place in one slow, smooth twist. I felt the elbow joint click into place, and noted some resistance still at my shoulder. With a bizarre sense of calm, I gave a sharp tug at my upper arm, and felt it reconnect with a soft pop.

I was quite sure that as a child I must have suffered injuries before. I had never experienced this sort of . . . anatomical phenomenon.

When Ernest emerged from the trees some yards away, I was

sitting on the ground, staring at my lightly skinned hands, which had scraped on the tree bark no doubt, and there was dirt all over my skirts.

"Elizabeth! Are you well?" Ernest rushed to my side and helped me up carefully, as though I had the same fragile bones as a songbird.

"I am well," I assured him, dusting myself off with only a slight tremor of nerves in my voice. "I simply lost my balance on the uneven ground. I have been waiting for you, and Father went on ahead to the house. Where is William?"

Ernest looked pale. "I have lost him somewhere, I fear. We were playing at hiding and seeking, and I had him a few times, but then he hid so well I could not find him again. I sat and called for him, 'til I thought I might go hoarse, but he never came. When it got darker, I thought I better find you and Father. Oh, Elizabeth, what will we do?"

I embraced my brother. "We must stay calm." I thought about what I had seen, the man-creature and the unmistakable shape of little William.

"I hope he was not so stupid as to stray into the lake," added Ernest breathlessly.

"William is an excellent swimmer," I managed to say, turning this way and that to ensure that the giant was not lurking nearby.

"What should we do?" Ernest's fear was beginning to amplify, and thus I knew I must play the calm one.

"Perhaps he has already returned to the house," I suggested, anxiously. "Let us go there and if he is not home, Father will send a search party. We will find him, Ernest. We will find him because we must."

We hurried back the way we had come, and were nearly in the safety of the grounds of our home when the front door was flung wide and a parade of servants and neighbors spilled out onto the lawn.

"Thank Heavens you found Ernest," my Father cried, embracing us both. "But tell me, was there any sign at all of our William?"

I felt the anxiety and guilt of having seen William, but not having told of it, bubble up into my chest and throat, and I felt tears begin to form in my eyes. This was apparently answer enough, for soon the searching party was on its way, torches and lamps lighting their way in a macabre procession towards the woods. Ernest and I were ushered inside by the servants, there to be wrapped in blankets against the chill of the outdoors and drink hot tea to soothe our nerves.

My tears, I will confess, were not solely for the yet unknown fate of our William, nor were they for the unidentified giant whose appearance I kept hidden from the search party. They were tears shed for both of these and yet one more: the strange occurrence whereupon I had fallen from the tree without a scratch, and had certainly fixed my own broken arm without hesitation or pain. I felt lost and conflicted, and wished more than anything that Mother was alive to calm me from my panic.

When the search party returned nearly at dawn, I raced

downstairs to hear what there was to know, but the tears and sour faces were verdict enough. My father bade me go to my rooms lest I fall down in hysterics at the sight of my poor brother's body, but I was determined to lay eyes upon William once more. They laid him out on a table, pale as fog and adorned with bruises about his neck and face. He was quite dead.

Why, I thought, had I been able to fall from a tree and be unbroken, when my poor baby brother was doomed to helplessness against an unknown assailant?

No, not entirely unknown. I thought of the long-limbed giant of a thing I had seen, and knew precisely what had transpired. No doubt William had spoken to it in a friendly way—for the boy had never feared anything but his father's disapproval, and God—and then surely these markings on poor William's thin neck were proof of the vile creature's unreasonable wrath. It must have been like a wild animal striking out in defense, reasons for murder otherwise unknown and unknowable.

My heart ached for William, so suddenly taken away, and I felt a gnawing pain for thinking I could have done something to prevent it. If I had survived the fall from the tree, I may have been strong enough to stop the giant stranger from attacking my baby brother.

I was numb with grief, tears spilling down my cheeks. "This is my fault, all my fault. I have killed my darling boy!"

"No, how could it be?" cried Ernest.

My father embraced me and bade me not take the blame for so foolish an idea. He said that he would write immediately to

Victor and demand his return to the family home for the imminent burial of poor William. What I heard him say to Ernest as I went up the stair would have startled and excited me any other day, but it merely rolled off of me as rain from a leaf: "We must marry Elizabeth and Victor immediately. As soon as he returns. Our family cannot take any more losses; we must heal these wounds with a wedding."

With the sudden death of my youngest brother, my wedding day was in view, and with it, the unfolding of my mother's prophetic dreams for me, and the opening of her final letter.

Upon Victor's return to the house, we were able to rejoin our ragged family together in mourning the loss of William. But even the air of grief that pervaded our home could not disguise that Victor was very much changed since his last visit, and grief was only a fraction of his transformation. Father noted instantly the loss of weight and pale, hollow expression Victor wore. He was deeply troubled, and insisted it was the loss of William that dogged his steps, but Father and I knew that there must be more.

Every day that passed, Victor kept to himself, locking his doors and shutting himself away to work on whatever it was he had brought home with him. Rarely did he eat or sleep, or even change his clothes. He was unkempt and unaware of his surroundings, and it was painfully clear that something had happened during his studies abroad that had changed him deeply, and not for the better.

I waited and waited, even sleeping with the final letter from my mother under my pillow. My anxiety toward the discoveries yet to be made was keeping me very much awake at night. I had pored over the other notes and diagrams, and even considered bringing them before Victor. It would break my silent oath to my mother, but at least it would get Victor's attention, if not some answers regarding the scientific and utterly mysterious nature of the pages.

The day, at last, dawned, and it was with the eagerness of a child upon Christmas morning that I rose and pulled the envelope from under my pillow, the anticipation too much to bear any longer. With trembling fingers, I opened the envelope and unfolded carefully the letter contained within, which was comprised of two pages. The first began thusly:

My dear child Elizabeth,

I am more proud of you than ever I could begin communicate to you, and I can only pray that you know and feel this truth deep in your heart. Like Galatea, the perfect woman sculpted by Pygmalion and brought to life by the gods, you have always been the perfect daughter, and you will make the perfect woman in your own right as you continue your life married to Victor. You have always been my angel, and with loving thoughts, I here endow you with my blessings upon this, your wedding day.

I am pleased past reckoning that you will be joined eternally to Victor on this day, although I know your reading this letter is a sign that I have passed and am not there to weep joyfully for your beauty in person. I truly hope your father is present to witness the junction of your soul with Victor's, and thus the realization of the dream he and I shared since your very early childhood.

It is not only the dream of your parents, my sweet Elizabeth, but it is the hope of others whom you know not. Others who have invested both time and money into the formation of our family and the lineage which you may yet see to fruition once you are wed.

My good-hearted, loving girl! Oh, how I wish I could explain this all in person. But the Fates had other plans for me, my angel, and took me away before these truths could be explored. Be not frightened, my daughter, for you have the strength within you to prevail through any circumstance, large or small.

By now, I wonder what little things have happened to you along the way. As a child you were bold but not careless, and only rarely did you bleed from injury in playtime. You never scraped your knees or cut your little fingers. I wonder if you have had any injuries since? I wonder if, since your fever, you have even been remotely ill at all?

I wonder, of course, but I may hazard to guess that you have not been ill, and any injuries you may have sustained were minor—including the ones which could have been major. I dare not dream what may or may not have happened to you, but I do trust you are whole and in one piece and still ticking, as it were. You have always been strong, my darling, but perhaps until recently you did not truly know how strong.

The other pages in these packets must have baffled you so, the diagrams and notes and correspondences. I trust you kept it all whole and safe, having shown it to no one. Now that it is your wedding day and your life to be changed henceforth forever, I must ask you to burn everything, including this letter, when you are done reading it.

The truth is that the gypsy's fortune foretold of my daughter being an incredible force for good. I was determined to fulfill this prophesy, and thus made my studies in anatomy and physiology, as well as medicine, hoping the studying would lead me to answers as to how my girl child would be born in the first place, and then from that to encourage her to be ready for her chosen path.

When I miscarried my firstborn daughter, I was truly devastated, and thought I would never recover from the grief, but my doctor at the time had another suggestion, and through the miracles of science, found a way to use my biological matter and create you, my angel. For you see, although you did not come directly from my womb, your blood is the same as my own, and you are truly my daughter.

But science is not perfect, my angel, and though your creation was successful, you were very sickly as an infant, and my good friend Doctor Moreau was forced to take drastic measures to ensure your survival, to assure me that you would not break or grow ill in your youth, that by the time I was able to rescue you from your poor foster family, you would still be alive and well.

You must forgive me my somewhat peculiar methods, Elizabeth, for I love you, and did all that I did out of selfless love for you. I know your previous interests in scientific theory and literature, and thus I know that while rather fantastic, all this is indeed possible, and you know it, deep in your steel-infused bones.

I know this must all be quite a shock, my child, but remember always and above all that you are my angel, and your destiny lies with Victor. That is why you could not know until your wedding day. Victor must not know what you truly are. If his scientific mind begins to suspect that you are more than a sweet and loving human being, I cannot tell what he may do. If you love and obey him, all will be well, but never forget that you are destined to protect him, even if that means you are protecting him from himself.

Now, you must prepare for your married life, and think no more upon the things I have told you. Know that I am proud of you and will always love you, my angel, my daughter, Elizabeth.

Yours in eternity,

Your mother, Caroline

I found that I was weeping in silence. I felt my hands shaking as I read and re-read the letter a thousand times in those few minutes. How could any of this be true? And yet the strangeness of it rang with familiarity. The fever dream of my mother with the tools bending over my prone form flashed into my mind, and I saw it clearly; it was an act of what theorists and surgeons would call vivisection, and my mother was carefully mending my inner parts with her own two hands, transferring her own blood and providing the broken pieces of my organs with matter of her own.

I flipped the letter to the next page, and saw a full diagram of myself, with skeleton and major organs showing, with notes in my mother's hand which described the changes that she and her Dr. Moreau had made over time. It was true that I was strong and exceedingly healthy, but it was also true that I was not simply human: my bones were lined with steel, some of my organs replaced with industrial clockwork.

The scarlet fever of my youth had been a ruse to excuse the necessary surgery my mother had performed to fix the inner cogs of my cardiovascular system. She had managed it successfully, but at the cost of her own health, for, to provide me with immunity from disease, she was forced to take from her own organs. It seemed impossible . . . and yet, there I was: in many ways, I was not and had never been fully human.

This revelation was the most unusual wedding gift I could ever have imagined.

The arrival of the servants to rouse me and help me dress for the wedding interrupted my thoughts. Immediately, I threw the letters onto the fire, so that they might not be found and their content discovered by the wrong persons. I admit it was then something of a struggle to convince those attending me that I was not ill. I assured them I was simply overcome with the emotions of the day to come. In a daze, I was prepared and dressed and sent to church.

At the ceremony, I gazed at Victor, who seemed as agitated as I was that the wedding was finally taking place, and I wondered what it was that had changed him so markedly from the clever, loving boy I had grown up alongside. Had it been the death of our mother? Had it been some cruel professor he had encountered in school? Had some other milestone taken place, one that I knew not?

During our vows, it occurred to me that perhaps Victor had discovered my secret; perhaps it was out of shame, disgust, and even revulsion that he had lost all interest in me and had postponed the wedding for so long. If he already knew, then I could not be held responsible for my mother's wish that I keep the truth from Victor. I resolved to get Victor alone as soon as I could after the ceremony, to try to sound him out and see what he knew.

I did not have to work very hard at separating my husband—how new and strange the word!—from the rest of the party, for after the meal, Victor steered me by the arm to our wedding chambers and closed the door behind us.

"My love," said I, suddenly nervous and choosing to make a light joke, "are we not meant to wait until after all the guests have gone home to consummate our vows?"

Victor, pale and cold-eyed, gave me what would have been called a withering glance. "Do not be so lewd, Elizabeth. It does not suit you." He moved about the room quickly, checking the latches on the windows and doors and investigating all the nooks and crannies of the chambers.

"Victor, you have barely spoken to me all day; indeed, barely spoken to me these last several years. We were once the most loving of childhood companions. What has happened to you, and why aren't you happy on the day that Mother longed so much to see for herself?"

Victor turned to look at me, the pain in his eyes evident. He looked as though he had not slept in weeks. "This is not about you, Elizabeth." His voice trembled, and I was sure then that it was with fear.

I pressed on. "What is it, then, which has broken you? What is it that you have kept secret from Father, from Ernest, from me? I am your wife now, and I must know what brings such horror to my husband's eyes."

He paused long, then, and crossed the room in a few great strides to stare into my face, searching, demanding.

"I have done what others failed to do," he intoned, a creeping note of ecstatic pride in his voice like the tendril of a curling, growing vine. "The secrets of Nature are mine, now, and I hold the spark of Life in my hands."

I was surprised. It was certainly not what I had expected him to say. "What do you mean by this?"

"You will not understand," he hissed scornfully.

"Then explain it to me," I demanded. "What do you mean by the secrets of Nature being yours?"

Victor's voice dropped to a whisper. "I have become God. I have brought the mystery of Life to matter that was dead. And my creation lives, now seeking his wrathful vengeance upon me and those I hold dear. He is coming tonight and I must end his miserable—"

I felt an anxious laugh bubble up from my chest. "What are you saying? Victor, what do you mean? The mystery of life? Dead matter? This is insane," I heard myself say, despite the pounding in my chest that reminded me my heart was made with metal. Insanity was not too far from reality, I thought, recalling my mother's words.

Victor's gaze was full of fire. "I have created new life from old, from death, and he is angry, and he took William, and he vowed to be with me upon my wedding night, and I refuse to allow him to win—"

"Oh, Victor!" I exclaimed, the memory flashing before my eyes, causing my breath to run short and my knees to tremble. "What have you done?"

The image of the ungainly giant whose hands had no doubt been the source of William's untimely demise was burned onto my vision. The sudden revelation that Victor was claiming responsibility for the existence of the creature was almost too much. That Victor had spent his time searching for the spark of Life only to bestow it upon a dead thing, just to prove that he could do it . . . I could practically hear my mother's voice in my head: *'Your destiny lies with Victor, to love and obey and protect him, even if from himself.'*

I was numb as Victor declared that he must lock me in our chambers for safety until the thing was dispatched, and watched him go in shocked silence. I had reached the culmination of my young life, having married my intended and uncovered the incredible truth about myself through my mother's letters, but I felt utterly empty, and did not know which way to turn.

Victor may once have loved me, I was fairly sure, but there was no longer love, for his life had been overrun by fear and guilt and ego. He had tampered with the very seams of the world, the very magical ties that keep the universe together. Having stumbled across some kind of answer, he thought himself a god, and intended to banish his creation into the cold blackness of death once more, as God banished Lucifer to Hell.

I changed into my nightgown and brushed out my hair in slow, trembling motions. There was no question in my mind that the giant creature I had seen was the product of my husband, the ill-begotten creation of Victor's scientific toils and research. I understood that Victor meant to kill it, partly in revenge of William's death, and partly for his own terror, but I felt that Victor did not discount the possibility of his own death in the process. And I? I was meant to wait in silence, something that seemed impossible, knowing my own hidden strength. I knew it was my duty to obey my husband, but it was also my duty to protect him. What would Mother say if she could see Victor, and know what sins he had committed?

There was stirring in the corridor, a sound like floorboards creaking. I rose from my little chair to listen at the door, which was locked from the outside as Victor had planned. There was silence again, and so I turned back to my vanity table.

I stopped reaching for the hairbrush when I realized that there was another presence in the room.

The creature stood quite tall, towering over me, uneven shoulders falling into unusually long arms. Its head was tilted, its eyes full of lightning and ferocity despite the calm expression of its face. It appeared, for all intents and purposes, male, just as it had that day on the hillside, but I could not conceive that it was still a true man, after death and unnatural rebirth in this way. It reminded me again of a huge animal in the jungle, perhaps, wild even in its stillness, and haunting in its silhouette.

It stared at me, across the room in which I was locked, and I stared back at it.

"Hello," I said. I was surprised by how soft and calm my voice sounded in the dark room. "I suppose you have come to kill Victor."

The Creature tilted its head the other way, and there was such a silence that for a moment, I wondered if it could speak at all. Then I recalled that Victor had said it promised him aloud to be with him on his wedding night. And it had kept its promise indeed.

"Will you not speak to me a few moments?" I asked as gently as I could, trying not to be angry with it for having killed William. I could not tell whether or not it had ended William's short life in true consciousness of its actions, or if it had been merely an accidental feat of strength.

"He . . . lied to me." The Creature's voice wrought me with

323

tension, yet gave me hope that perhaps reason could be found within its mind. "He promised me a companion, a female, and he lied . . . oh, he lied most grievously . . .."

"What do you mean, he lied?" I thought about moving to the vanity, but remained calm, standing still, lest the thing be frightened.

"I am . . . so *lonely*," it moaned. "I only wanted another to share . . . to stay with me, always, and I swore I would leave him alone forever. But he could not give me what I asked—no! He *would* not give me what I asked."

"I see."

I did see. This was not what I had expected, not at all. I found myself strangely calm in the moment, and breathed slowly. "You did not ask to be brought to life, did you?"

The Creature did not respond, but it made a low sound of pain, of anguish, and stared at me most piteously.

"And since Victor will not give you a wife, you are utterly alone in the world, but for your creator. Is that why you killed William?"

"He lied," said the Creature, suddenly, harshly.

"William never lied a day in his young life," I replied as evenly as I could, fighting the urge to snap. The pain of losing William swelled within me as freshly as the day he'd died.

"Little boy said that he knew where Frankenstein was," the Creature growled, taking a step towards me, "but he would never tell, never, never tell me where. And then when I grabbed him . . . he cried out that he was Frankenstein's brother. And so I killed him, so that Frankenstein would know I was coming. That I meant to keep my promises."

"What other promises have you made?" I demanded.

The Creature's strange, mismatched eyes gleamed in the dim light of my wedding chamber. "He took the one thing I wanted to love, so I shall take *all* that he loves."

It lunged for me, but I found myself darting forwards and sideways to evade its long arms. For as fast as this giant creature was, I was somehow faster. It stumbled and swung at me; I stepped back again and reached for its incoming fist, which I grasped in both hands and twisted hard back the other way. It cried out in an animal cry, and swung with its other hand, which connected with my gut. I barely felt the impact.

In this manner, we fought for several minutes, my heart pounding in my ears, and then, the Creature gained the upper hand. Its arm was tight around my neck, my hands grappling to peel it away and free myself. My knees were bent somewhat and I was pressing my back against my attacker, seeking some kind of leverage to twist out and away, but it was determined to keep me pinned.

"I must punish him," the Creature growled in barking, disjointed tones. "He killed my wife, so I must kill his!"

"Then we are at an impasse," I said, gritting my teeth, "for you killed my brother William. Must I not then kill you?"

We struggled against one another, and the monster began to drag me about the room, bashing me against wall and table, closet and bed, in hopes of knocking me unconscious, no doubt.

I fought as best I could, but knew that it was mostly show, for I felt only the pressure of his grip, and no pain, thus far.

We made a pass by the vanity once again, and I grabbed for the letter opener I kept on the tabletop. I would have missed it if the monster had not stumbled over the hem of my nightgown. The blade landed in my hand and I shifted it neatly, reaching back and up and slashing at the thing's face. I must have struck it, for it yowled and fell back, releasing me from the headlock. I spun and stabbed at it again, landing blows to its shoulder and chest several times while it clutched at its face, the noise it was making being most terrible and nightmarish.

It was then that I realized I did not wish to kill the Creature; it was really most pitiful. Yes, it had killed William, but it acted as it did seemingly only out of rejection and desire to be loved. Had Victor not been so entranced by his own sin, perhaps he would have understood that . . .

My thoughts on forgiveness were interrupted brutally as the Creature lunged at me again, and my little knife made a vain sweep through the air as it fell upon me, its hands at my throat and face. I heard the letter opener clatter to the floor in the dark, and stared up in blank amazement at the monster, who snapped my neck sharply to one side.

My breath caught in my throat and I crumpled immediately to the floor. I heard my heart stop, my lungs cease to fill, my internal mechanisms as loud as timpani drums at the opera in the sudden absence of my breath and pulse. The monster stood over me in silence as I lay on the ground, unmoving, listening to my insides wind down.

Ah, I thought to myself, *so the gears are wound continually by the breath. This is most ingenious of my architect, to create a system wherein I am constantly winding myself, so as never to run down, save in an event such as this one.*

I wondered then how long it would take the monster to realize I was not dead, but merely immobile. Instead, the Creature made a sad, angry sound low in its throat, and it lumbered away, disappearing out of the window into the night.

A little while later, Victor arrived with our father and found me lying on the floor, staring without blinking, utterly motionless in every way. There was a great deal of emotional outbursts, and then, when they had calmed down a little, the servants placed my body on the bed and covered me with a sheet.

I was at once both amused and quite put out to no longer be able to see the comings and goings of the room; but then, how was anyone to know that I was still apparent within my broken body? I could hear and see and sense as well as any living thing, though my casing was bent the wrong way and I could feel my cogs and springs slowing their internal motions more and more by the second.

I was rather amazed, and admittedly, quite pleased that I was not dead. I wondered if this meant that I was to live forever, or if it meant that once my springs stopped unwinding that I should be as good as dead rather permanently. It was a confusing sort of limbo to find oneself in. I drifted off into a sort of sleep, my ruminations on this new development fading into a kind of trance of my own subconscious formation.

And then something of a little miracle happened.

When the coroner, or whoever it was, came along to prepare me for burial, they realigned my neck with my spinal column, and when the bones clicked back into place, I felt the jolt of mechanisms within my body begin to click and whir and hum once more. They had closed my eyes at one point or another, so I kept them closed, but proceeded to allow my internal clockworks to start up again. Once I was alone in the room—which, as it turns out, was not the same room I had died in—I opened my eyes and sat up.

I was rather well dressed, indeed, and my hair had been brushed and plaited. Of course, it had been their intention to bury me this way, and I was certain that they would have rather a shock when I vanished, but it was of no question to me what I must next do.

My husband Victor was pursuing a monster, which in turn pursued him. One was bound to kill the other, but it was more likely that they would both die in the endeavor. I knew that there was no way I could return to Ernest and my father and the house. I would have to excuse myself from the burial process and take my leave of the town. Then, I would be free to search for Victor and his creation wherever they may have gone, and try my best to facilitate the justice which each deserved in their own way.

As a child, my mother told me that angels were God's messengers, sent to Earth to bring glad tidings to mortals, protect them from harm, and share the love of Heaven. I had always been called my mother's little angel, and as children, Victor had shared that sentiment towards me.

I saw that it was time to do what my destiny had always been, and that by the determination of my mother and some other unknown geniuses who had taken part in my creation, I had the means and the strength to take hold of my duty and my fate.

Victor had taken his fire from the gods and brought it down to the level of common men, and had sinned in doing so. I found myself ready to set things right, both for the poor damned Creature, and for my husband, the modern Prometheus.

For, like the statue built by Pygmalion to be the perfect woman, I had been given new life and purpose, and my will was my own. Although my heart ticked as steadily as any grandfather clock, I thought of myself not as a machine, but as a Galatea, created not by God, but by human hands, and free to fulfill the destiny my mother had wrought for me.

 relax ❀ relax

Styled after Frankenstein, or the Modern Prometheus
by Mary W. Shelley

About the Authors

AARON AND BELINDA SIKES

Aaron Sikes began his adult life wearing a soldier's Kevlar® helmet. He's worn several hats since, including the toque of an apprentice pastry chef. Now, he's a full-time dad, and writes science-fiction as A. J. Sikes. His stories lean towards the weird side of the shelf, and tend to be located in his favorite American city: Chicago. If he's not writing, he's probably tinkering with something in the woodshop. Or doing laundry. Aaron tweets @SikesAaron, follow at www.facebook.com/SikesAaron.

Belinda Sikes wrote her first story at age five and her first novel at age twelve. She writes historical and fantasy romances, but since earning her Doctorate in Plant Pathology, has detoured into the life of a science writer.

ALYSON GRAUER

Originally from Milwaukee, WI, Alyson Grauer is an actor and writer currently living, working, and performing in Chicago, IL. She is a staff writer for You Know You Love Fashion (www.youknowyoulovefashion.com) as well as for Doctor Fantastique's Show of Wonders (www.doctorfantastiques.com), and co-writes a nerdy blog at Comma-Chameleon.com. Alyson has previously contributed to the ongoing Tales from the Archives podcast/ebook anthology through the Ministry of Peculiar Occurrences by Pip Ballantine and Tee Morris, and has published non-fiction in the Journal of Perinatal Education for Lamaze International . She plays the ukulele and can be found on Twitter @dreamstobecome.

ANIKA ARRINGTON

Anika Arrington is a devoted wife and mother of five. She has been reading and writing stories since she was four years old. She has lived in Arizona since the age of three, and feels quite at home in the desert, despite dreams of greener landscapes. She spends most of her time chasing toddlers, trying out new recipes, and chipping away at the novels that will make her famous someday. She is a monthly contributor at mommyauthors.blogspot.com and transiently maintains her own blog www.necessarynurture.wordpress.com.

A. F. STEWART

A. F. Stewart was born and raised in Nova Scotia, Canada, and still calls it home. The youngest in a family of seven children, she has always had an overly creative mind and an active imagination. She is fond of good books (especially science fiction/fantasy), action movies, sword collecting, and oil painting.

Ms. Stewart is an indie author with several published novellas and story collections in the dark fantasy and horror genres, with a few side trips into poetry and non-fiction. She has a great interest in history and mythology, often working those themes into her books and stories. Twitter: @scribe77.

DAVID W. WILKIN

A graduate in History from UCLA, David Wilkin has written in various genres for thirty years. Extensive study of pre-modern civilizations, including years re-enacting Medieval, Renaissance and Regency times, has given Mr. Wilkin insight into such antiquated cultures. He studied Micawber and Copperfield's period of Victorian Colonialism under John Semple Galbraith.

With a proficiency in historical conventions, his fantasy and historical work encompasses mores beyond hero quests, and adds depth to his created worlds. Mr. Wilkin regularly posts about Regency history on his blog thethingsthatcatchmyeye. wordpress.com, and as a member of English Historical Fiction Authors (englishhistoryauthors.blogspot.com). Mr. Wilkin is the author of several Regency romances; his most recent, a sequel to the epic Pride and Prejudice by Jane Austen, called Colonel Fitzwilliam's Correspondence. Twitter: @DWWilkin

M.K. WISEMAN

A Wisconsin gal with a Southwest soul, M. K. Wiseman can generally be found wandering happily amongst the pages of the largest book she can get her hands on. She came upon writing rather accidentally, finding that, sometimes, there are stories that simply must be told.

A techie with a penchant for typewriters, she is a magnet for misadventure, though her own story has yet to unfold. Harboring such dreams as someday possessing a library complete with hidden bookcase doors, piloting a hot air balloon, and running away in a sailboat, she currently subsists contentedly between worlds in the company of her hypoallergenic fish.

She tweets @FaublesFables. Connect on Facebook at www.facebook.com/faublesfables.

NEVE TALBOT

As a child, Neve Talbot, developed the habit of lulling herself to sleep by dreaming up continuations of her favorite books too soon ended. She never left off the habit, and eventually gained confidence in worlds of her own creation. She first cracked open a spiral binder in high school, and has spent the past decade dutifully penning her prerequisite one million words of bad writing before getting to the good stuff.

Now author and journalist, Neve currently lives with her husband in a quasi-reality filled with fantasy, sci-fi, historical fiction, Regency romance, the classics, and history books, suspended between the piney woods and sprawling metropolis of southeast Texas. She plans on exploring the world when she grows up.

SCOTT WILLIAM TAYLOR

Scott William Taylor lives and writes in Utah. He grew up living on the side of a mountain and lives on that same mountain today, with his family and a dog that loves cheese. Scott is married, with four children. He received his undergraduate degree in Communications from the University of Utah and a Masters in English from Weber State University. Scott is the creator and producer of A Page or Two Podcast. He also wrote the award-winning short film, Wrinkles. When not writing and working, Scott enjoys participating in community theater productions with his children.

Follow Scott on Twitter @Hyggeman..

About Xchyler Publishing

X chyler Publishing prides itself in discovery and promotion of talented authors. Our anthology project will produce four books a year in our specific areas of focus: fantasy, Steampunk, suspense/thriller, and paranormal. We proudly present Mechanized Masterpieces: a Steampunk Anthology as the second installment of this endeavor. Authors include Aaron and Belinda Sikes, Alyson Grauer, Anika Arrington, A. F. Stewart, David W. Wilkin, M. K. Wiseman, Neve Talbot, and Scott William Taylor; edited by Penny Freeman.

ALSO FROM XCHYLER PUBLISHING:

Vivatera by Candace J. Thomas, April, 2013

Vanguard Legacy: Foretold by Joanne Kershaw, April 2013

Grenshall Manor Chronicles: Oblivion Storm by R.A. Smith, December 2012

Forged in Flame: A Dragon Anthology, by Samuel Mayo, Brian Collier, Eric White, Jana Boskey, Caitlin McColl, and D. Robert Pease, edited by Penny Freeman, October 2012

LOOK FOR MORE EXCITING TITLES FROM
XCHYLER PUBLISHING IN 2013, INCLUDING:

The Phoenix Conspiracy, a fast-paced suspense/thriller by seasoned author Kim Dahlen, July 2013.

Shadow of the Last Men, a dark dystopian fantasy, the first installment of The Next Man series by J.M. Salyards, summer 2013.

Mr. Gunn and Dr. Bohemia, a Steampunk action/adventure by Pete Ford, summer 2013.

Primal Storm, Book II of the urban fantasy series The Grenshall Manor Chronicles by R. A. Smith, October 2013; sequel to *Oblivion Storm*.

Held quarterly, our short-story competitions result in published anthologies from which the authors receive royalties. Additional 2013 themes include: **Mind Games** (psychological thrillers, summer),**Extreme Makeovers** (paranormal, fall), **Back to the Future** (fantasy, winter), and **Around the World in Eighty Days** (Steampunk, spring 2014).

To learn more, visit www.xchylerpublishing.com.